# Flawbulous

# Flawbulous

*Shana Burton*

**www.urbanchristianonline.com**

Urban Books, LLC
97 N18th Street
Wyandanch, NY 11798

ISBN 13: 978-1-60162-674-5
ISBN 10: 1-60162-674-6

First Trade Paperback Printing October 2014
Printed in the United States of America

10 9 8 7 6 5 4 3 2 1

Distributed by Kensington Corp.
Submit Wholesale Orders to:
Kensington Publishing Corp.
C/O Penguin Group (USA) Inc.
Attention: Order Processing
405 Murray Hill Parkway
East Rutherford, NJ 07073-2316
Phone: 1-800-526-0275
Fax: 1-800-227-9604

# Flawbulous

by

*Shana Burton*

# Dedication

This book is dedicated to Deirdre Neeley and Theresa Tarver, the messiest, craziest, most loyal, most fabulous, and best friends I could ever ask for.


It is also dedicated to "Double A."

*My heart's dictionary defines you as*
*love and happiness . . .*

# Acknowledgments

As always, I give honor to God first and foremost. He could've given this gift to anybody, but He chose me. I'm eternally thankful and owe any success I have to Him. All I have is a notebook and a laptop. He is the one who breathes life into my thoughts and words. Without God, I'm nothing.

I would like to thank my family for always having my back. Myrtice C. Johnson, Shannon Johnson, Shelman Burton III, Myrja Fuller, James L. Johnson, Jr., and James L. Johnson, Sr., your love and support sustain me. I wouldn't be who I am if you weren't who you are. I love you all tremendously!

Thank you to my friends Deirdre, Lola, Aaliyah, Rashada, Dwan, Tammie, Stephanie, Melissa, Shameka, Tralia, Tanisha, and Theresa for being the definition of true friends. I can call on you anytime, tell you anything, and drag you everywhere with me, and you always come through without hesitation. You are my sisters, and I love you so much!

Thank you, Crystal, Latravius, and Traci, for your support and encouragement, and for being my writing coaches. You ladies rock!

Thank you to all my supporters. I know you're out there, and I'm so grateful that you're a part of my life. I can't name all of you or possibly thank you enough. Please know that I love you, and I'm praying for you.

Okay, enough about me! Enjoy and happy reading!

# Chapter 1

"Any couple who can go through hell and back like you have and still come out feeling something that resembles love deserves to be together!"

*– Lawson Kerry Banks*

Lawson Kerry Banks scanned the anxious crowd gathered inside the fellowship dining hall at Mount Zion Ministries in Savannah, Georgia, on a dreary Tuesday evening in October. Whether by choice or coercion, they were all there to celebrate First Lady Sullivan Webb's thirty-fourth birthday. Forty-five minutes into the party, the guest of honor was still a no-show.

Exasperated, Lawson looked down at her watch for the third time. "Is it physically impossible for that woman to be on time for anything?"

Her close friend, Angel King, laughed and tossed back her chestnut ringlets. "Charles called Sullivan again a little while ago. She said she's on her way. Plus, it's a surprise party. Technically, Sullivan doesn't know she's late."

"Not to mention those fifty extra pregnancy pounds she's lugging around!" added Kina Battle, joining them, trying to balance a plate of vegetables and a cup of punch. "Having a human being occupying your uterus slows down even the best of 'em. I do wish she had let one of us pick her up though."

As she sifted through the remnants of food left on her plate, Lawson overheard someone complaining about Sullivan's tardiness. "Sully needs to forgo the grand entrance and hurry up. The natives are getting restless! You know our girl isn't exactly the church's favorite person. It was like pulling teeth to get this many to show up. I practically had to bribe half of them to come and had to guilt the rest into being here."

Angel defended their wayward friend. "I think the congregation has started to warm up to Sully, thanks to that gut full of baby bump she's carrying and the DNA proof that Charity is the pastor's child, not Vaughn's. Those kids have been the best PR Sullivan could've asked for. Besides, her affair with Vaughn and all that drama was years ago. Nobody is holding that against her anymore. I doubt if most of the folks here even remember it."

Lawson rolled her eyes. "Girl, please! Who do you think can forget something as messy as the first lady getting chopped down by the church's mechanic? Not church folks! We can give elephants a run for their money when it comes to remembering acts of foolishness. Don't get me started on all the fallout that came afterward."

Kina scoffed. "Don't look at me! Charles was bound to find out about the possibility of Charity not being his daughter whether I told him or not. Anyway, she turned out to be his baby, and there's no doubt that soon-to-be born baby Christian is his child. All's well that ends well."

Lawson plucked a carrot stick from Kina's plate. "Actually, Kina, I wasn't even thinking about you. I was talking about Charles's failed campaign for commissioner and the impact the affair had on their marriage, but thank you for reminding everybody how loudly hit dogs do holler!"

"Be careful what you say to Kina," cautioned Angel. "You don't want to end up scandalized in your cousin's new book."

Lawson cut her eyes toward Kina. "Yeah, I forgot. My sister had to learn the hard way how shady Kina can be for the right price."

Kina balked. "I neglected to check my calendar this morning. Is this National Beat Up on Kina Day?"

"Oh, don't try to whip out your victim card now." Lawson set down her plate of food. "You lost that privilege when you decided that family loyalty came second to fame and your so-called reality show."

"A reality show that never even got picked up," Kina reminded them. "I don't know why you all are still giving me flack about exposing Reggie. Aside from a handful of my social media followers, who even saw that video of her in all her naked glory at the strip club?"

"Um, her fiancé, for one!" answered Angel. "Your little exposé almost tore them apart."

Kina raised her index finger. "Instead, it was the catalyst for Reggie getting off the stripper pole for good and going back to college. Now she and Mark are off on a romantic gambling weekend in Biloxi, and their relationship is stronger than ever. Honestly, Lawson, you should be thanking me for saving your sister, not raking me over the coals."

"I'm sure that's the Hollywood spin you'll put on it in this tell-all book," predicted Lawson.

"It's not a tell-all book about my friends. It's about my journey from being an abused widow to a weight-loss starlet to, apparently, a condemned woman." Kina sighed. "Unfortunately, no matter how I spin it, my editor still won't like it. She hates me. The only thing she hates more than me is anything I submit to her in writing. I'm absolutely dreading my upcoming meeting with her."

Angel patted Kina on the back. "Kina, I'm sure she doesn't hate you. She probably jus—"

"*Hates me!*" blurted out Kina. "She's rejected every single thing I've written, and she's made it very clear that the only reason she's even giving me this book deal is because she wants to capitalize on whatever fleeting fame I have left from being the winning contestant on *Lose Big*."

"Well, you did get a pretty nice book advance, Kina," noted Angel. "It's no surprise that your publishing company is expecting a return on their investment."

Kina grimaced. "Twenty thousand dollars is nice, but it's not like I can retire on that. Anyhow, I'm a secretary, not a writer!"

"Perhaps you should've revealed that to your publisher before cashing that big check," deduced Lawson.

Angel tried to reassure Kina. "You'll be fine. Just do what we always do. Put it in God's hands and let the pieces fall into place."

Lawson checked the time again. "Somebody needs to put Sullivan's sense of punctuality in God's hands too. We've been waiting over an hour now."

"Yeah, this is a little beyond fashionably late," conceded Angel. "I can't stay much longer. Duke is leaving for LA in a couple of days, and I want to spend as much time with him as I can."

"He left you for eight years while he was immersed in marital bliss with his late wife, Theresa. Does it really matter if y'all miss a few more minutes?" joked Kina.

Angel frowned. "Very funny. All things work together for the good of those who love the Lord, including husbands who cheat and abandon their starter wives for a few years. Obviously, all that time apart showed Duke and me that we want to be separated as little as possible."

Kina smirked. "Tell that to his *replacement* wife—God rest her soul!"

Lawson tried to muffle her laughter. "Don't listen to her, Angel. You and Duke have survived affairs, dead wives, addictions, and bratty step-kids. Any couple who can go through hell and back like you have and still come out feeling something that resembles love deserves to be together. You're soul mates. It's just took you a while to figure that out."

"Thank you, Lawson. You and Garrett have been through the fire too," said Angel. "I don't smell any smoke on you, either."

"Oh, it's there. It's just covered with a lot of perfume," replied Lawson. "But we're definitely in a much better place than we were a year ago. My husband's mistress-slash-baby mama still works my nerves, but Simon has become an important member of our family, especially now that Namon is in school in Atlanta."

"I still can't believe he's in college! It seems like only yesterday that you were waddling around campus, trying to hide Mark's illegitimate seed growing inside your belly," said Kina. "Now he's all grown up."

Lawson nodded. "Thank God everything turned out as well as it has. Five years ago, when Mark reentered my life and discovered that Namon was our love child, I never would've predicted that Mark and I would end up as great friends, or that Namon and Mark would grow as close as they have. Now Namon is at Georgia State on a full academic scholarship, Mark and I have found a way to co-parent, he and Garrett are somewhat getting along, and Reggie is great at playing the roles of both aunt and stepmother-to-be to Namon. It's one big happily dysfunctional family!"

"Just wait until Reggie and Mark start procreating, and Namon has a bunch of 'brother cousins' running around," interjected Angel.

"Admittedly, it's a little unconventional," granted Lawson.

"Unconventional? Try incestuous! I could never get involved with someone my relatives had been with." Kina sneered. "It seems so . . . icky."

Angel gave Kina the side eye. "You didn't think it was so icky when you had the hots for Sullivan's husband."

Kina's olive skin reddened from embarrassment. "Sullivan's a friend, not a relative. You all know I was confused at the time. I wasn't thinking straight."

"You certainly weren't thinking *straight* when you dove into the lady pond with Joan, but I digress," Lawson added snidely.

Kina groaned. "Can we change the subject?"

"Gladly." Lawson checked her watch again. "My goodness, where is that girl? This is late, even by Sullivan's 'anything under an hour isn't late' standard."

"I'm getting kind of worried now," admitted Angel. She turned her back to make a phone call.

"Yeah, people are starting to leave," said Kina. They looked up in time to see Charles and his assistants bolt toward the door. "I wonder what that's about."

"I don't know, but I'm not getting a good feeling about this." Lawson dug her phone out of her purse. "I'm gonna try to call Sully again."

"Don't bother." Angel hung up her phone. "I just tried. It's going straight to voice mail."

"That's not good. Sullivan always has her phone on." Lawson put her phone away. "You two stay here. I'm going to look for the pastor and find out what happened."

Kina and Angel stayed behind while Lawson darted off to find Charles.

Kina rubbed her arms, finding herself here chilly and nervous. "You don't think something's seriously wrong with Sullivan, do you?"

Angel let out a deep breath. "I don't know. I'd feel much better if we prayed about it, though."

As Angel and Kina joined hands to pray, Lawson returned, frantic. "We've got to leave right now!" announced Lawson, grabbing her purse and jacket. "Sullivan was in an accident."

Angel gasped. "Is she okay?"

"The car flipped over, and she was thrown through the windshield." Lawson looked her friends in the eyes. "It doesn't look good."

# Chapter 2

"I know what the doctor said and what his medical charts say, but God is still in charge."

*—Angel King*

After three days of no change in Sullivan's condition, Lawson and Angel petitioned the Lord in prayer and didn't care who in the hospital saw or heard Lawson interceding on their friend's behalf

"God, we come right now, acknowledging and proclaiming you as our strength and our healer. We praise you, and we thank you for letting both Sullivan and her baby see another day. Lord, our friend has suffered trauma to her brain and hasn't opened her eyes in three days, but we walk by faith, not by sight. We know that one touch from you will heal and deliver Sullivan and her son, little Christian. God, we profess that you heal the brokenhearted and bind up our wounds. We know that your son, Jesus, bore our sins in His body, and by His wounds we have been healed. So we put our faith in the Word more than the doctor's diagnosis. We thank you for a full recovery for Sullivan and Christian and declare it done!"

"Yes," whispered Angel, squeezing Lawson's hand with one hand and wiping tears as they dripped down her cheek with the other.

"God, we ask that you watch over Charles and Charity. Strengthen them during this difficult time. Lord, we pray that they remember that you are our comforter. You are strongest when we are at our weakest. Keep them covered, Lord," pleaded Lawson. "Let the church continue to function in our pastor's absence as it does in his presence. Lord, it's hard right now, but we know that you never allow us to go through anything we can't bear. We pray that we all come out of this with a testimony and that you will receive the glory and that others may be healed and helped through this ordeal."

Lawson went on. "God, we love you, and we believe we receive everything we ask for according to your Word. We thank and praise you in advance. It's in the name of Jesus we pray. Amen."

Angel nodded and sniffed, smearing the last of her tears away. "Amen."

Angel and Lawson huddled together outside of Sullivan's hospital room, staring at her through a small crack in the door as doctors examined her. Sullivan's husband, Charles, looked on. The stress of watching his wife's life hang in the balance weighed on his face, causing him to look older than his fifty-two years.

"She looks so small and . . . helpless," remarked Lawson in a hushed tone, not accustomed to seeing her childhood friend so defeated.

"All those machines hooked up to her makes it look worse than it really is," Angel assured her.

Lawson walked away from the door and out into the waiting area, not wanting Charles to overhear them. "Angel, she's been in a coma for three days! The longer she's like this, the harder her recovery will be."

"Maybe, but she's alive. That alone is a lot to be thankful for. Charles showed me pictures of the car after the accident." Angel shook her head. "It's a miracle that she made it out at all. Sullivan is healthy and strong. She'll pull through this."

Lawson exhaled and flopped down onto a love seat. "I, on the other hand, feel completely powerless right now. There's literally nothing we can do to help her or baby Christian."

Angel joined her. "You're never powerless when you serve a God with all power in His hands. We get our strength through prayer."

"I've been praying since they brought her in."

"And we'll *keep* praying until she wakes up and until that precious baby is out of the neonatal intensive care unit," asserted Angel. "The prayers of the righteous availeth much."

Lawson hesitated before asking her, "Do you honestly think he's going to make it?"

"Yes, Lawson. I know what the doctor said and what his medical charts say, but God is still in charge. We have to have faith. Sullivan is our sister, and she wouldn't want us giving up on her baby."

Lawson faced Angel head-on. "Angel, you're a nurse. Christian was barely two pounds at birth, and he's in an incubator, on breathing machines. Speaking as a medical professional, do you think that baby is going to survive?"

"A lot of preemies live and go on to have normal lives," replied Angel, hoping to keep Lawson encouraged.

"What about ones delivered three months early, like Christian? What's the likelihood that he'll survive or live to see his first birthday?"

Angel lowered her head. "I won't lie. The odds aren't in his favor. We just have to pray that the Lord's will is done and that His will is that both that baby and Sullivan will be okay."

"Sullivan would lose her mind if anything happened to that baby." Lawson sighed. "If only they could've kept him inside of her a little longer . . ."

"Every day—every hour, really—that he stayed in utero would've helped him, but it would've been detrimental to Sully. Charles didn't want to take that kind of chance with her life. I don't blame him for telling the doctors to deliver the baby in order to save Sullivan."

"It's such an awful position for Charles to be in. Can you imagine having to choose between saving your child and saving your wife?"

"I think he made the right decision."

"I hope Sully sees it that way. I think we all know that she isn't the most selfless person in the world, but she does love her kids. I think if it was up to her, she'd risk her life to give her son the best chance at survival. Any mother would. I know I'd give up my life in a heartbeat to save Namon."

"I'm not a mother, so I'm probably not to the best authority on this, but I think that's different," replied Angel. "Namon is here. He's a living, breathing person. You've loved him and taken care of him for eighteen years. I'd expect you to feel that way, but Christian is practically a fetus. Sullivan hasn't had time to form the same kind of attachment to her son that you have to yours."

Lawson shook her head. "It doesn't matter. From the moment a woman finds out she's pregnant, she's a mother to that baby, and she'll do anything to protect her child."

"Hopefully, knowing how much her baby needs her will give Sully the will to keep fighting. I think once Sully wakes up and sees Charity and Christian, she'll be fine."

Lawson turned solemn again. "You mean *if* she wakes up, don't you?"

Angel was riled up and bolted from her seat. "No, I don't! Sully will make it through this, Lawson." She took in a breath and sat back down. "She has to."

Lawson squeezed her friend's hand. "You're right. She will."

Angel nodded in agreement. "Christian will too."

Lawson was less hopeful about his chances. "I pray he does. If he dies, I'm scared a big part of Sully will go right to the grave with him. We both know how destructive Sullivan can be when she's hurt or desperate. Charles could end up losing both of them."

"He won't let Sullivan self-destruct again."

"How can he stop her?" Lawson stood up and walked toward the glass panel on Sullivan's door. She peered into the room and saw Charles kiss Sullivan on the forehead. "He'll probably be the one she lashes out at the most. I know her."

"So then we'll keep praying. Sullivan can't lose that baby, and she certainly can't lose her husband and the only real family she's ever known."

"And we can't lose our friend." Lawson turned to Angel. "Angel, Sullivan's been my best friend since we were nine years old. What in the world am I supposed to do without her?"

# Chapter 3

"I don't care how old he is. He's still my baby."

*–Lawson Kerry Banks*

Lawson dragged herself into the house and found Garrett loading plates into the dishwasher.

"Any change?" asked Garrett, but one look at his wife's downcast eyes confirmed that there was no change in Sullivan's condition.

Lawson set her purse and keys down on the breakfast bar. "She's just lying there, you know? It's weird because Sullivan has always been so full of life and zeal. Now she's . . ." Lawson pursed her trembling lips together, and her eyes began to water.

Garrett pulled Lawson into his broad and comforting arms. "I know it's hard seeing her like that, but Sullivan's a trooper. She'll get through this."

Lawson nodded and wiped her eyes. "That's what I'm believing God for."

"Then that's what will happen." Garrett slowly released her. "I think I have something that will put a smile back on that gorgeous face."

Lawson composed herself and smiled. "Is he here?"

Garrett chuckled. "Namon just called. He'll be here in about twenty minutes."

Lawson squealed, her mood lifted. "My baby is coming home! I know it's been only a couple of months, but it feels like we haven't seen him in forever!"

"I know you miss him. We all do."

Lawson quickly snapped into Mommy mode. "We've got to make sure his room is fixed up." She glanced over at the clock. "I wonder if I have time to run to the store and get those caramel apple cookies he likes so much. I've been so swamped with work and Sullivan that I completely forgot about them. What about that portable speaker thing he's been talking about? Were you able to pick it up? Oh, and his favorite cereal. We need to get that too."

Garrett grabbed his wife by the waist. "Whoa! Calm down, woman! I know you want to baby him, but Namon's a college man now. He doesn't want his mama making a big fuss."

"I don't care how old he is. He's still my baby."

"Well, he's Shari's baby too now," Garrett teased her. "Don't be surprised if he's a little more interested in spending the weekend with his girlfriend instead of his mother."

Lawson wrinkled her nose at the mention of Namon's lady-love. "Little Miss Shari will have to get in line and wait her turn. I don't remember seeing any tuition checks for him coming in or going out with her name signed on them."

Garrett laughed. "Babe, Namon is in love. Shari has her name signed on his heart and probably a few other places too!"

"Don't joke like that." She shoved him playfully. "In my eyes, Namon will always be my sweet, innocent little boy."

"I'm sure he will. All I'm saying is that I remember what I was doing at that age. Shoot, you know what *you* were doing at that age!"

"Yes, I do. I was changing his diapers! That's why I'm hoping he has enough sense to keep it in his pants or at least wrap it up."

"Don't worry. Namon has the good sense and morals you gave him. If that fails, he has the box of condoms that I gave him. He'll be fine."

Lawson's brow furrowed. "It's not just about sex, though. I don't like him spending so much time with her."

"Shari seems like a pretty good kid to me."

"Under the circumstances, she is. It's a wonder she even made it to college, with that jailbird daddy of hers and cracked-out mother, who is usually either getting high or coming down off of something. Shari's siblings haven't fared much better. She's the only one in the family who's trying to be something, and that's probably due to Namon's influence."

"You've got to give the girl credit for trying, Lawson."

"I applaud her efforts. I do. But she's not going to be able to shake that lifestyle. I don't want her bringing down Namon in the process."

"Namon is too smart to get caught up in all that. You raised him right."

Lawson smiled up at her husband. "We both did."

Lawson looked out the kitchen window when she heard the sound of hip-hop music booming from the driveway. "He's here!" she shrieked. Lawson's face dropped when she saw Shari step out of the passenger side of Namon's truck.

Garrett sidled up next to her at the window. "It looks like he brought home more than just his laundry." He wrapped his arms around his wife. "Now, don't trip. He probably brought her over to say hello before taking her home."

Namon unlocked the door and walked in with Shari at his side. "Hey, Mama. What's up, G?"

"*Namon!*" Though Namon stood more than six feet tall and towered over his pint-size mother, Lawson still managed to pull him into a bear hug. "Oh, I've missed you so much!" She stood back and beheld him. "Look at you, all grown up! You look bigger. Have you been working out?"

Namon blushed. "Yeah, I've been doing a little something."

Lawson stood on tiptoe to squeeze his jaw. "And what's all this? Where did this hair come from? You left here with a little peach fuzz. Now you've come back looking like Santa."

"I'm trying to grow it out a little."

"Looks good, man." Garrett hugged Namon. "So I'm just G now?"

Namon laughed. "I was messing with you, ole man!"

Garrett was taken aback. "*Ole man?* I think I prefer G."

Namon ushered his shy, pretty, but gangly girlfriend, Shari, in front of him. "Y'all remember my girl, Shari, don't you?"

"How are you, Mr. and Mrs. Banks?" asked Shari with a timid smile.

"We're fine, especially now that this guy's here." Lawson forced a smile. "How are you, Shari? Classes going okay?"

Shari nodded. "I was having a little trouble in my math class, but Nay's a great tutor. I got a B on my last exam."

"So the two of you have been burning the midnight oil, studying and whatnot," observed Lawson. "Hopefully, you're doing more *studying* than *whatnot*."

Namon diverted the conversation. "How's Sullivan? Is she getting better?"

"No change, but you should still go by and see her while you're home this weekend. Maybe you can go after dinner. I'm making all your favorites. Shari, you're welcome to stay for dinner if you want," offered Lawson.

"Actually, we can't hang around here too long," Namon informed them. "We've got to go to Shari's place and see her folks."

Lawson was peeved. "Sweetheart, you haven't been home five minutes. You and Shari have all day, every day, to see each other at school. This weekend is for your family. The two of you can go without each other for two days."

Namon and Shari exchanged glances. "It's more than that. We've got to talk to her mom and you too. We just decided to come here first," Namon explained.

Lawson fastened her hand to her hip. "Talk about what? Boy, don't tell me the two of you are thinking about marriage!"

"Not yet . . . maybe moving in together," admitted Namon.

Lawson's mouth fell to the floor. "*What?* Did the two of you have a big ole bag of crazy on the way over here?" She raised her voice. "We sent you to that school to get an education! You can play house after you graduate. Furthermore, just who do you think is about to finance this love shack? 'Not I,' said the cat!"

Namon tried to get a word in. "Will you hear us out before rushing to judgment?"

Lawson pointed at Namon. "You see that, Garrett? This boy has been gone two months and is already coming back, smelling himself!"

"What brought this on?" Garrett asked in a calm voice as Lawson seethed at his side. "I know that you're in love, and it feels like you want to spend every waking moment together, but I don't think either of you is ready for all that. You're just eighteen—"

Lawson cut in, moving her hands wildly as she continued ranting. "Namon, I don't care how old or how infatuated you are, you're going to stay your behind right there in that dorm room! Ain't nobody paying for some nest for the two of you to be holed up in. The answer is no! Shari, take it from me. Don't even waste your parents' time having this discussion with them. They're going to tell you the same thing I did!"

Namon groaned. "We don't want to move in together to be doing it for no reason, Ma."

Lawson shook her head. "I'm sure that to you being in love is a very good reason, but you can be in love without cohabitating."

"What's going on, Namon?" asked Garrett. "What's the rush?"

Shari spoke up. "We think it may be the best thing to do for our situation right now."

Lawson rolled her eyes. "Why now? What *situation?*"

Namon looked down.

Shari nudged him. "Just tell 'em, Namon."

Garrett crossed his arms in front of his chest. "Tell us what?"

Namon took a deep breath. "Ma . . . Dad . . ." He paused and reached for his girlfriend's hand. "Shari's pregnant."

# Chapter 4

"Sister or no sister, I won't hesitate to throw some blows
if that's what it takes. . . ."

*—Reginell Vinson*

Mark Vinson crept up behind Reginell as she reached
for a roll of paper towels on top of Mark's refrigerator. "I
see London. I see France. I see Reggie's . . ." Mark playfully lifted the oversized T-shirt Reginell was wearing and
squinted his eyes. "Wait a minute. Why aren't you wearing underpants?"

Reginell giggled and swatted Mark away. "Stop looking
up under there!"

"Why should I do that?" He picked Reginell up, sat her
on the counter, and kissed her. "You're mine now, Mrs.
Vinson."

"Yeah, but no one else knows that. They all think we
spent last weekend in Biloxi, gambling, not in Montego
Bay, getting married."

"Well, I guess technically, it's not legal until we have it
cleared in the United States, but as far as I'm concerned,
you were my wife last week, today, tomorrow, and forever." He kissed her again. "Now, if I'm not mistaken, Mrs.
Vinson, I do believe this shirt belongs to me. I think I
want it back."

Mark started lifting up her shirt, but Reginell stopped
him and pulled the shirt back down. "No time for all that,

baby. Did you forget that your son will be here any minute?"

Mark reluctantly pulled away from her. "I didn't forget. I was just hoping you'd be down for a quickie."

Reginell laughed. "So what do you want to tell Namon when he gets here?"

"I'd like to tell him and his sister that we're married before we announce it to anyone else, but we don't have to say anything right away if you're not ready to."

Reginell wrapped her arms around his neck. "Good, because I like having it be our little secret. I want to enjoy being here and being newlyweds without all the well-intentioned interference."

"Are you positive you don't want to at least tell Lawson?"

"Telling Lawson is the same as telling all of them. Baby, the last thing we need is my sister and her friends nagging and asking a bunch of questions."

"Don't you think they'd be happy for us?"

"Their happiness comes with a lot baggage—trust me! Plus, everyone should be focused on Sullivan and everything going on with her and the baby."

"How is she, anyway?"

Reginell sighed. "Still in a coma. Lawson went by to see her today. It's hitting her pretty hard. She thinks of Sullivan like a sister."

"You do too, don't you?"

Reginell chuckled a little. "More like an evil stepsister. Sully and I don't exactly have the best track record with each other, but I have to admit that life wouldn't be the same without her. Nobody can give a good read quite like Sullivan. Sometimes it's fun having people like that around."

"Maybe the reason you two butt heads so much is that you're so much alike. You're both feisty and tough, and it's no secret that you both know how to drive men wild!"

"Correction— used to drive men wild! I drive only one man wild these days."

"And you do that very well, I must say."

Reginell winced and clutched her stomach.

Mark was alarmed. "What's wrong, baby? Is your stomach still giving you trouble?"

She shrugged and brushed it off. "I'm cramping a little, that's all."

"Your stomach has been bothering you for a few weeks now, and you said your period has been a little off. Maybe . . ." He flashed her a mischievous grin.

"The pregnancy test came back negative, remember?"

"That was a week ago. It could've just been too soon to tell. I think we need to make an appointment with your doctor to be sure one way or the other. And if you're not pregnant, we need to find out why you've been in so much pain lately."

Mark's phone rang before Reginell could respond. He answered and found a hysterical Lawson on the other end of the line.

"Mark, I need you to come over right now!" demanded Lawson.

"What's going on? Where's our son?"

"He's here. I can't get into this with you on the phone. Just come and hurry up."

Mark stared at the phone for a few seconds after Lawson abruptly hung up on him. "That was your sister."

Reginell hopped off of the countertop. "What does she want?"

"I don't know, but it sounds serious. I think it has something to do with Namon." Mark searched for his car keys. "She wants me to come over."

"Okay, let me grab my shoes." She looked down at her bare legs. "And some pants. And some panties."

"The panties are optional." Mark kissed her on the cheek. "Babe, you don't have to come if you don't want to."

"Mark, I'm your wife now. Your problems are my problems too. Plus, Namon is my nephew and stepson, and Lawson is my sister. We're family. If something is going on, I want to know about it."

"I'm sure it's nothing and Lawson is overreacting, as usual."

"Then, in that case, she'd needs a stern lecture from me for interrupting our honeymoon." Reginell slipped into the pair of jeans lying across the sofa. "I'm serious, Mark. Now that we're married, she can't be calling here all hours of the night, expecting you to rush over and deal with some crisis she's manufactured for attention."

"Reggie, she's my son's mother. I can't ignore her."

"I didn't say you had to do that. I'm just saying give her boundaries. You already work together every day. How much of this handsome face does she need to see?"

"Don't be jealous," Mark playfully admonished his wife. "And don't read more into it than it is. Lawson and I have been over a long time."

"Yes, *we* know that, but I think sometimes she forgets." Reginell followed Mark to the door. "Sister or no sister, I won't hesitate to throw some blows if that's what it takes to remind her!"

# Chapter 5

"No one can tell my story the way I can."

*–Kina Battle*

Kina's no-nonsense editor shook her head and drew a big red mark through Kina's manuscript. "No, no, no!" declared Terrilyn Smiley. "This won't do at all, Kina!"

"Are you serious?" asked Kina, seated across from Terrilyn's desk in her Atlanta office, which was as cold and uninviting as Terrilyn herself. "This is the third draft I've submitted to you!"

"And it's the third draft I've hated!" Terrilyn thrust the manuscript at Kina. "This is just a collection of flowery little anecdotes about your kid and your friends, with a few scriptures thrown in here and there. Where's the heart of your story? Where's the red meat?"

"You said it should be uplifting and encouraging to others," Kina reminded her.

"No, I told you to write a cautionary tale about the price of fame and fortune. You were supposed to write about how you went from being a victim to a victor and how you lost it all—friends, the money, your scruples—in one fell swoop because you got greedy and selfish and didn't care who you had to trample over to get what you wanted. This book is supposed to be your comeback, Kina! It's your chance to tell your side of the story. The public knows your son shot and killed his father. What they want to know now is why and how you dealt with it. They know you claim to be this devout Christian, yet you got caught up in a scandalous affair with another woman and attempted to seduce your best friend's preacher husband."

Kina corrected her. "I never had an affair with Charles."

"But you wanted to, and you betrayed your friends and family once you got fame. Here's your opportunity to tell the world why."

Kina offered up a few pages of the manuscript. "I thought I did that."

Terrilyn shook her head. "The fact that you think this piece of crap did that is one of the many reasons why I'm bringing in a ghost writer." Terrilyn buzzed her assistant. "Lola, will you send Desdemona in please?"

"Why are you bringing in a ghost writer?" questioned Kina. "*I* should be the one writing my book. No one can tell my story the way I can."

"I need someone who can tell your story *better* than you can, which I why I'm bringing in Desdemona." Terrilyn broke her stern scowl when she saw Desdemona standing in the doorway. "Come on in, Des. I want you to meet Kina. Kina, this is author extraordinaire Desdemona Price."

Desdemona walked in and extended her hand to Kina. "It's great to finally meet you. I am a huge fan of *Lose Big* and was one of your biggest supporters."

Kina's first thought was, *How in the world is this frumpy specimen in Bohemian rags, wearing glass jars where her eyes should be, going to be the best person to write about me?* Instead of asking the question aloud, Kina simply shook Desdemona's hand.

"Des is a fantastic writer," bragged Terrilyn. "She's one of the best in the business. You'd be surprised by how many celebrities she's ghostwritten for. You should feel honored that she agreed to work with you on this book, Kina."

Kina smiled politely. "No offense to you, Desdemona. I'm sure you're an excellent writer, but I don't really think I need any assistance in telling my story."

Desdemona adjusted her glasses, confused. "Oh . . . I was under the impression that you needed my help."

"She does!" answered Terrilyn. "And she will get it whether she likes it or not!"

Kina huffed. "Don't I have any say in this?"

"Your say-so with this book has been redirected to the circular file, along with this latest round of garbage you've written."

"I don't think you're being fair," insisted Kina.

Terrilyn stood up and stared Kina down. "You want to talk about fair? Kina, I went out on a limb for you! I pitched this book as a salacious tell-all and garnered you a nice five-figure advance. Not only is it your butt on the line if this book flops, but it's mine too, which I don't think is *fair*. Nor is it *fair* to me to let some sexually confused, fake Christian wannabe reality starlet screw up ten years of solid sales and a stellar reputation at this publishing company!"

"She didn't mean it like that," said Desdemona, embarrassed for Kina.

"No, that's exactly how I meant it! Kina, you're on your fourteenth minute of fame. You have only a small window left to remain relevant in the public eye. The new season of *Lose Big* is already well under way. In a few weeks, they'll crown a new fatty, and you'll be last year's news. The only way to capitalize on the little bit of notoriety that you have left is to go big and go hard. I don't have the luxury of time to coddle you through this process. Desdemona is going to write the book, and that's all there is to it!"

"I'm not writing it alone," Desdemona assured her. "Kina, you'll have lots of input. It's still very much your story. All I'm doing is bringing your words to life and putting your story down on paper in a way that the company can market and sell it. This is a partnership. You're as important to the equation as I am, and my only objective is for us to put out the best book possible."

Terrilyn sat back down at her desk. "I'm sending Desdemona back to Savannah with you."

Kina's eyes bulged. "What?"

"You heard me." Terrilyn turned to her computer. "She's going to follow you. She's going to interview your friends. She'll even administer your next Pap smear if she has to! That's how well she will get to know you over the next couple of months."

Desdemona shook her head. "Don't worry, Kina. I'll give you plenty of space. I'm renting a loft downtown, so you won't have to look at me twenty-four-seven. However, we will be spending a lot time together getting to know one another."

Kina was flustered. "Does anyone even care what I have to say about this or how I feel?" she asked.

"No!" Terrilyn printed out a contract and handed it to Kina to sign. "Slap your John Hancock right here, and we'll be ready to get down to business."

Kina skimmed over the first page. "What is this?"

"It is an agreement to let Des write the book. The contract is pretty cut and dry. It basically says everything Des and I told you."

"Are you expecting me to pay her?"

"The publishing company pays her. You, of course, will pay us back in the form of future book sales."

"What if it doesn't sell?"

"It will—trust me. Between Des's writing and the marketing push we're going to put behind it, it'll be a bestseller," Terrilyn promised.

"That's all the more reason why I don't want people thinking she wrote this book instead of me," argued Kina. "It'll hurt my brand."

"You have to have a brand in order for it to be hurt," barked Terrilyn.

"There's a confidentiality clause." Desdemona pointed it out in the contract to Kina. "No one has to know I wrote it if you don't want them to."

Kina copped an attitude. "What if I refuse to sign this?"

Terrilyn passed her a pen. "Then you can give back the twenty thousand we advanced you and get the you know what out of my office. Now sign it."

"I know you have misgivings, but I promise you that nothing will go in this book that you didn't sanction, Kina," swore Desdemona. "You have my word that this will be a book you can be proud of and a powerful legacy to leave behind for those who love you. You still have fans out there who rooted for you while you were on the show. They're vested. They believe in you and want to know everything there is to know about you. Let's work together and write this book for them."

"Sign," commanded Terrilyn.

Kina was still hesitant. At the very least she wanted time to pray and to have a lawyer look over the contract, but Terrilyn was breathing down her neck, signaling that time was of the essence. Seeing as how she'd already blown through a good percentage of the advance money, Kina tucked her tail between her legs and signed.

# Chapter 6

"Don't be fooled for a second by those big brown doe eyes. I've seen the way she looks at you!"

*—Angel King*

"I wish I didn't have to go. I hate that I have to leave with you feeling this way," lamented Duke, zipping his suitcase as he and Angel prepared to part ways at the Thomas Square Streetcar Historic District home he once shared with his late wife and hoped to share again with Angel.

"I know I've been a little down since the accident, but I'm fine. I'm not giving up on Sullivan," vowed Angel.

"It's not too late for me to cancel, you know. You, Miley, and Morgan are my priorities. If you need me here to help you get through this, say the word."

"No, don't do that. You've already booked the flight and hotel, and you have people at work depending on you to make this deal happen. It's only two days," said Angel with a smile. "I should be able to survive that long without you."

Duke kissed her forehead. "You always take other people's feelings into consideration. It's one of a thousand things I love about you. Thanks again for volunteering to come over and look after the girls. They love having you here."

"Duke, neither Miley nor Morgan has my blood coursing through their veins, but you know those girls are as much mine as they are yours. You never have to thank me for loving them, or you, for that matter."

"I hope you know how much you're appreciated. Not only for watching the girls, but also for the way you stepped up to help out after Reese died. You have so much going on in your own life, but I don't think there's ever been a time when you weren't here for us."

"Nor will there be! We're a family."

Duke nodded. "Indeed, which is why I've been trying for months to get that ring back on your finger and make it official! You keep blowing me off."

"You know nothing could be further from the truth, babe. I just want to be sure this time, you know? We've broken up so many times before."

"But we always find our way back to each other, Angel. All those issues we had with infidelity and trust—that's over now. I'd never hurt you that way again. You believe that, don't you?"

Angel exhaled. "I'm getting there. At Sullivan's party, Lawson said any couple who has been through everything we have and still wants to be together must be soul mates. I'm starting to believe her."

"Well, I've known that since seeing you that day in the library at Howard," recalled Duke. "I knew at that moment, you were going to be the woman I was going to marry."

"Did you know I was going to be the woman you divorced too?" Angel replied, ribbing him.

"What can I say? I was young and selfish when we got married the first time. Not to undercut anything I felt for Reese, because I loved her until the day she died, but my heart never strayed too far from you."

The painful memories of their split came flooding back to Angel. "Maybe not, but the rest of you did."

"I won't make the same mistakes twice, though. Angel, having you in my life is the reason I know God is real. I know I don't deserve those girls or you, but God looked past all my faults and sins and led me back to you. I'd die before I'd do anything to screw it up again." He planted a tender kiss on her lips. "I love you, baby."

"Aww," gushed Angel, moved. "When you say things like that, you make it almost impossible for me not to be crazy in love with you!"

"Do you want me to stop?"

"Yes, unless you want me to rip up this plane ticket so you can't go anywhere," quipped Angel. "Actually, I don't mind you going to LA as much as I hate that you're going with your starry-eyed assistant."

Duke laughed. "Mya is harmless, trust me!"

"About as harmless as a rattlesnake!" exclaimed Angel. "Don't be fooled for a second by those big brown doe eyes. I've seen the way she looks at you!"

"Mya's a kid. She's what? Twenty? I like my women grown and seasoned like you." He leaned down to kiss her. "Honestly, she's a good girl. She has never crossed the line and is always professional. She's there trying to fulfill her internship requirements, that's all."

"If you say so," said a doubtful Angel. "A woman knows these things, Duke."

"There is nothing that girl can do for me. She's practically Miley's age. However, I know exactly what you can do for me. . . ."

She pulled away from him. "Now, now . . . we agreed to wait, remember?"

Duke released his sexual frustration in a heavy sigh. "That's a lesson I've learned the hard way, pun intended."

Angel giggled. "I know, but I want us to get it right this time, which means no shacking up, no sleeping over, and no sex until we get married . . . again."

"I guess we're working our way backward. We got married first, divorced, then shacked up, and now we're waiting to have sex."

"It'll all work itself out in the end. In the meantime, you better get out of here. I don't want you to miss your plane."

"You're right. I'm just going to run upstairs and kiss the girls good-bye one last time. Then I'm coming back to kiss my other girl one last time too." Duke winked at Angel before heading upstairs.

Duke's phone vibrated, signaling that a text message had just come through. Angel's curiosity got the best of her, and she picked up the phone and read it. Looking forward to a great time in LA. Mya.

Angel placed the phone back where Duke had left it, trying to convince herself that the text was innocent and that she had nothing to worry about. She smiled, remembering both Lawson's and Duke's words about their relationship. For a moment, she wholly believed that Duke could go with Mya and keep everything platonic and professional while they were in Los Angeles.

Then she eyed his plane ticket and remembered her mother's harsh warning to her the first time she took Duke back after he cheated on her. A *leopard never changes his spots. He changes only his location.*

# Chapter 7

"You know the saying . . . *Mama's baby,
Daddy's maybe.*"

*—Lawson Banks*

Sitting on Lawson's living room sofa, Mark lowered his head into his hands as the news sank in. "*Pregnant?* You all are just kids yourself."

"Yeah, kids who've been playing grown folks' games!" retorted Reginell and poked Namon. "Boy, what happened to all those condoms I gave you?"

"You too?" murmured Garrett.

Lawson eyeballed Shari with suspicion. "And you're positive that Namon is the only one who could be this child's father?"

Shari nodded. "He's the only one I've been with."

Namon was offended. "It's my baby, Ma, so stop asking her that."

Lawson sucked her teeth. "You know the saying . . . *Mama's baby, Daddy's maybe,*" she grumbled.

"Lawson, don't make it worse," cautioned Garrett. "Namon says it's his child, so let it go."

Mark sat up. "Well, look, what's done is done. Now we've got to figure out how to make the best of this situation." He turned to Shari. "Do your parents know?"

Shari shook her head. "Not yet. I'm going to tell my mama when we leave here. I'll write my dad and tell him sometime next week."

Mark was confused. "Write him?"

"He's in jail," said Lawson, filling in the blanks. "He'll make a fine grandfather, won't he?"

Namon groaned. "Mama . . ."

Lawson threw up her hands and walked away from him.

"What are y'all going to do about school? Living arrangements?" questioned Mark. "How are you going to take care of this baby?"

Namon stepped forward and spoke up. "I was thinking maybe Shari and me could find a place together, maybe even get married in a year or two—"

"One mistake is gracious plenty!" interjected Lawson, returning to the fold. "We don't need the two of you making another one."

"Lawson, this baby isn't a mistake," announced Reginell. "Just a surprise."

"I wasn't talking about the baby. I meant the situation," explained Lawson. "At the same time, we're not going to stand here and sugarcoat this disaster, either! Neither one of them is in any kind of position to take care of a baby!"

"I can get a job," volunteered Namon.

Lawson rolled her eyes. "Doing what? Flipping burgers or waiting tables somewhere? I hope you realize that's all that's out there for an eighteen-year-old with no education, no experience, and no connections."

"She ain't lying!" added Reginell, recalling her own odd jobs waitressing, which soon blossomed into exotic dancing to make ends meet. "Why do you think I'm back in school?"

"And what happens to school?" Lawson asked her son. "Are you simply gonna drop out?"

Namon gulped. "If I have to, I can leave school for a little while or go online."

Lawson tried to reason with him. "Namon, I don't think you're being realistic. Everybody can't excel in on-line classes, and if you drop out, chances are that you're not going back. I've seen it too many times."

"You didn't go to college right off, but you made it, and you were younger than me," asserted Namon. "If you did it, we can do it too."

Lawson shook her head. "It wasn't easy, son, by any stretch of the imagination. You don't remember this, but there were plenty of winter days when we were somewhere cold because I couldn't afford to pay for heat, and more than one night that we had to eat sleep for dinner. It was a daily struggle for years. You think I want that for you and Shari or this baby?"

"We're not stupid, Ma. We know it'll be hard at first, but we can do it."

Lawson was confounded. "How, Namon?"

Namon shrugged his shoulders. "I don't know, but Shari and I will figure it out."

"'We'll figure it out' is not a plan! When that child is hungry or needs a doctor or day care, 'we'll figure it out' can't be your response."

"We plan to give this baby all the love he needs," said Shari. "That counts for something, doesn't it?"

Lawson dismissed her comment. "You can't feed and clothe a baby on love, Shari. That takes one of the many things you all don't have, which is finances. I bet you don't have the cost of a package of diapers between the two of you!"

"Lawson, they're scared enough without you being so negative," chimed in Reginell.

"I'm trying to get them to see reality, Reggie. This baby started costing money the second it was conceived, and they don't even know it. You kids are living in a fantasy world. You have no idea what you're about to face. Everything costs money—*everything!* The only thing free these days is salvation. You can't even bring this child into the world without paying off the doctors and the hospital. Who's paying for that and prenatal care? Have you gone to the doctor yet, Shari?"

"I had a pregnancy test at the free clinic on campus, but I can get on Medicaid," Shari answered in a quiet voice.

Lawson sighed. "It's not the government's responsibility to take care of you or this child." Lawson turned to Namon. "You don't even have the money to pay for the vitamins the baby needs to come out healthy."

"Well, we were kinda thinking our families could help us out too," admitted Namon.

"Oh, really?" Lawson laughed. "You see that, Mark! They're already planning to pawn this responsibility off of us! I don't think so."

"Lawson, you're not being reasonable," said Mark. "We can't act like we don't know what it's like to be in their position." He placed a hand on Namon's shoulder as a sign of support. "Of course we'll help you, son."

Lawson fired back. "No, Mark, you mean *you* don't know what it's like to be in their position. I know exactly how it is. I was going through it alone, while you were living your carefree life in college!"

"And we both know why that is, don't we?" Mark's temper flared, as evidenced by his throbbing veins. "Nobody told you to keep my son from me! That was your choice!"

"Mark, you wouldn't have stepped up to the plate, and you know it!" ranted Lawson. "You were in no better position to take care of our son than Namon is to take care of his child."

Mark frowned. "You don't know that. And if you hadn't been so selfish—"

"*Selfish?*" Lawson interrupted and charged toward Mark, ready for a full-on verbal attack. "First of all, if you hadn't brought your li'l nasty self to the party—"

"Wait a minute," protested Reginell, stepping to her sister. "You ain't gon' be gettin' up in my man's face like that, Lawson!"

Garrett cut in and pulled his wife away. "You know what? I think we need a time-out. Let Reggie and me take the kids in the kitchen and talk with them, and we'll let the two of you hash this out and try not to kill each other."

Lawson rolled her eyes and exhaled heavily.

"Babe, you okay?" asked Garrett.

"I'm fine," huffed Lawson, before deep breathing to allow her anger to subside. "You're right. Mark and I need to discuss this alone, rationally and calmly."

"I know that's asking a lot of you," grumbled Mark. Lawson and Reginell both pierced him with stinging glares. "Sorry. We'll discuss it calmly and rationally, like you said."

Garrett led Namon and Shari into the kitchen.

Reginell kissed Mark on the cheek. "Be good," she warned him and followed behind Shari.

"You know we can't let this happen, don't you?" asked Lawson once they were all out of earshot.

"Lawson, he's eighteen. He's an adult. All we can do at this point is support his decisions."

"Are you kidding me? Being eighteen makes him an adult by law, but we both know that Namon lacks the wisdom to make adult decisions. This is the same kid who, just six months ago, couldn't decide between Pop-Tarts or Toaster Strudels! We're talking his future, Mark. This could affect Namon for the rest of his life. We can't let him decide all willy-nilly without having some input."

"Okay, we'll tell him where we stand, but the rest is up to him. I know you don't like it, but those are the facts."

"And where *do* you stand, Mark?" Lawson demanded to know.

"I agree with you. I think they're in way over their heads, but I'm going to support whatever they decide to do."

"Including keeping the baby?"

"Of course," he replied flippantly. "Why wouldn't I?"

"Mark, you know they have no business having a baby."

"Well, I think that's a moot point now. Shari's pregnant."

Lawson looked up at him. "Being pregnant isn't the same thing as having a baby."

"I'm no doctor, but isn't that what usually happens at the end of a pregnancy?"

Lawson began slowly pacing the floor. "Usually . . . not always."

Mark watched her with misgivings. "What are you getting at, Lawson?"

She stopped. "All I'm saying is that there are options."

"Yes, but those are options for Shari and Namon to ponder, not us."

"But he listens to you, Mark," beseeched Lawson, clinging to his arm. "If you told him that an abortion was the best thing—"

Mark eased her aside. "Do you hear yourself, Lawson? I'm not going to tell our son to make Shari abort their baby!"

"You don't have to put it in those terms. Just help him to see that it's the best thing."

Mark shook his head in disbelief. "You're a piece of work, you know that?"

"Call me what you want, but I'm trying to protect my son."

"From what? Accepting responsibility?"

"From taking on more responsibility than he can handle!"

"I think you underestimate him, Lawson. He's smart and resourceful. Besides, Namon hasn't done anything we didn't do at his age."

"And you see how well that worked out! Namon and I struggled, living off welfare and food stamps in poverty for the first fourteen years of his life."

"That's because I didn't know he existed. I would've provided for you and Namon. You know that."

"I know you would like to think that, but, honestly, how much different would it have been if you had known, huh? You probably would've had to drop out of school to work, forfeiting your football scholarship and your chance to play professionally overseas. You would've ended up resenting him. Even though you were able to thrive professionally, look how much your relationship with him suffered. It was months before Namon could even stand to be in the same room with you."

"Yeah, but we got through it. He will too."

"Mark, Shari's home life is a mess. Her dad's a career criminal. Her mother is in and out of rehab when she isn't strung out on God knows what. Her sister already has three bastard babies, and she's only twenty-one. Her gangster brothers are following in their dad's footsteps to the nearest prison, to boot."

"Yet despite all that, Shari finished high school with honors, got into college, and rose above her circumstances. From what I can see, she seems to have a good head on her shoulders."

"Really? She got pregnant less than two months after being in college! Where was that *good head* then? I guess we know the answer to that one."

"I believe our son played a big role in that conception too."

"I'm not saying that Shari's a hood rat or anything like that, but she does come with a lot of baggage. Do you really want to introduce all that drama into our family?"

"We're not exactly a picture-perfect family, either. I have slept with you and your sister and have two baby mamas. Your husband fathered another child during your marriage. Reggie was a stripper. You were a teen parent. We're a far cry from the Huxtables!"

"We have morals and God in our lives," Lawson stated, reasoning with him.

"Yet you're asking me to tell our son to kill his unborn child. How does that fit into your morals and spirituality?"

Lawson was silent.

"I shouldn't have said that," admitted Mark. "I'm sorry."

"It's fine. I know I won't earn any crowns in heaven for feeling this way, but, Mark, we're both educators. We see firsthand every day what happens to kids born to parents who aren't prepared to raise them. We see the cycle of poverty perpetuated generation after generation. We don't have to guess how this'll turn out, because we already know. I don't want that for my son or my grandchild. Namon isn't ready to be a father. You know he isn't ready. Nor is Shari ready to be anybody's mama."

"It's not our call, Lawson. Believe me, I don't like it any more than you do. I wanted more for Namon, but actions have consequences. We had to learn that the hard way. Because he didn't listen, now he does too."

Lawson couldn't hold back the tears any longer. "I wanted better for him. I didn't want him to repeat the same mistakes we made," wailed Lawson. "He's my baby, Mark."

Mark pulled her into an embrace. "I understand. He's my baby too."

Lawson sobbed softly in Mark's arms.

Reginell returned to the living room unnoticed and was unsettled by the sight of her sister wrapped in her new husband's arms. "Oh, am I interrupting something?"

Mark quickly released Lawson. "No, it's fine. Lawson was feeling a little emotional."

Reginell glared at them both. "I can tell."

Lawson dried her eyes. "Were you and Garrett able to talk some sense into them?"

"Garrett talked to Namon. I mostly helped Shari think of some cute baby names," revealed Reginell. "What do you think about Amari if it's a girl? Isn't that adorable? Amari and Shari."

Lawson was stumped. "Reggie, that is not . . ." She flung her hands, frustrated. "Forget it."

Reginell stood next to Mark. "Lawson, this baby is coming whether you like it or not. You might as well get excited about it."

Mark draped his arm around his wife's shoulders. "Babe, I think *acceptance* is probably more realistic than excitement at this point."

Lawson sighed. "You're right. Shari is pregnant, and there's nothing we can do about it. All we can do is help them make the best decisions going forward."

"That's the right attitude, and cheer up!" Mark pinched her playfully. "We're about to be grandparents!"

Lawson forced herself to smile. On the surface, she conceded, but in the back of her mind, she vowed that there was no way this child would ever see the light of day.

# Chapter 8

"When it's a true sisterhood bond like this one, nothing or nobody can tear it apart."

*—Angel King*

Lawson, Reginell, and Angel gathered at Kina's newly purchased town house a few days later to break bread and meet Kina's ghostwriter.

"That was Desdemona on the phone," Kina informed them. "She got held up, but she's on the way. She said we can start dinner without her."

Reginell rubbed her stomach. "Good, because I'm beyond hungry! My appetite has crossed over into famished."

"Kina, everything looks so . . . healthy!" remarked Angel, surprised, surveying the health-conscious dinner spread following the grace. "There's not a piece of lard or fatback in sight!"

"And there won't be!" Kina assured her, setting a spinach salad on the table. "My porker days are behind me. Mostly salads and grilled fish from here on out."

"Well, that certainly beats bottles and bibs from here on out," Lawson deadpanned, helping herself to a serving of sautéed vegetables.

"I still can't believe Namon is going to be a daddy!" exclaimed Angel. "He's still that kid riding around with training wheels to me. It's hard to picture him with a child of his own."

"I *can't* picture it!" retorted Lawson. "Plus, he has no idea how they're going to take care of this child. All he does is insist that he and Shari love each other and that everything is going to somehow magically work out."

"And it will. Lawson, I told you that you worry too much," asserted Reginell.

"Spoken like someone who's never had children to worry about!" replied Lawson. "Until you do, you can't possibly understand what it's like to watch your child make a mess of his life and opportunities."

"Namon having a child is not the absolute worst thing in the world, Lawson," said Kina. "You and I both had our kids young, and we survived. Yeah, it's disappointing that it's happening this way, but think of the blessing in all this."

"Oh, yeah?" Lawson gave her the side eye. "And what is that?"

"You'll have a new person to control," said Reginell. "And Mark and I will have a new grandbaby to spoil rotten, at least till we have our own baby."

"Try making it down the aisle first," cautioned Lawson.

Reginell smiled smugly, knowing she already had.

"However, the bottles and bibs I was referring to are Simon's, not Namon's. As if there's not enough going on right now, Simone called last night with a little surprise of her own," hedged Lawson.

Angel made a wry face. "Oh, no! She's not pregnant again, is she?"

Lawson shook her head. "No, nothing like that, at least not by my husband again! Apparently, she landed some big interior design contract for a swanky new hotel in New York."

Angel stacked her plate with vegetables. "Is she moving and taking Simon with her?"

"The move is temporary, a few months, tops," Lawson informed them. "She wanted to take Simon with her, but you know Garrett. He can't be away from his son that long, and he wasn't comfortable with the idea of Simon being in a strange place with new caretakers. So guess who'll be a full-time stepmom for the foreseeable future?"

Kina filled everyone's glass with tea. "I don't think it'll be that bad, Lawson."

"No, I'm actually looking forward to it. Simon is a good baby, especially now that he's walking and is potty training. It's nice having him around now that Garrett and I are empty nesters."

"See? You didn't think you'd be able to accept Garrett's on-a-break baby, but you did. It can be that way with your grandchild," pointed out Angel.

"Even more so because your husband didn't have to bang another woman to get that baby!" added Reginell.

Lawson pricked Reginell with an icy gaze. "Thanks for bringing that up, Reggie."

Angel giggled. "That kind of shade throwing is usually reserved for Sullivan."

"It would be nice to have Sully around to get her take on all this," said Lawson wistfully. "She doesn't dish out the soundest advice, but it's always amusing. Lord knows I could use her sense of humor right now. I'd give about anything to see her strutting in thirty minutes late."

"Sullivan is going to pull through this," upheld Angel. "And she'll be as crazy and as feisty and as fashionably late as ever!"

Lawson nodded. "From your lips to God's ear."

"Was there any change when you visited her at the hospital yesterday?" asked Kina.

Lawson shook her head. "She's still just lying there."

"I talk to her. I keep telling her how much we love her and how much Charles and the children need her. A lot of patients who were comatose say they could hear. Hearing is actually the last sense to go when a person is dying." Angel caught herself. "Not that I'm suggesting she's dying. I'm positive she's going to come back to us . . . she has to."

Reginell sighed. "I know I'm not Sully's biggest fan, but I wouldn't wish what she's going through on anyone. Mark and I have earnestly been praying for her full recovery. Her baby's too."

"Thanks, Reggie. That's sweet. You and Sully fight like rival gangs, but I know deep down—like, two thousand leagues under the sea deep—the two of you really love each other." Lawson patted her sister's hand. "If I live to see the day that the two of you stop cutting each other down, I'll know that miracles can truly happen every day."

Angel laughed. "That would be almost as big a miracle as the one-hundred-eighty-degree turn Vera has made. Can you believe Sullivan's mother has been acting so— dare I say it?—civilized and concerned?"

Lawson nodded. "Despite their combative history, I think Vera loves Sullivan. As much as she has the capacity to love, anyway."

"I don't know if you can call allowing men to molest your daughter love, but she's been here helping Charles with Charity. Charles won't allow Vera to take Charity home, of course, but she's still been here with her granddaughter every day," noted Angel.

"I'm glad Vera is making herself useful," said Kina.

Reginell switched gears. "Kina, what's up with this writer you wanted us to meet today?"

Angel looked around the room. "And where is she? What kind of guest of honor is late for her own celebration?"

"You mean the author my editor has saddled me with!" Kina snarled. "But I have to admit, she's not as bad as I thought she'd be. She has been open to my suggestions about the book and has been good about running her ideas by me before typing anything up. She hangs around but doesn't crowd me. She's definitely a breath of fresh air compared to my editor, I'll tell you that!"

Angel swallowed her food. "Sounds like a winner. I can't wait to meet her."

"Assuming she ever gets here . . ." muttered Reginell.

There was a knock at Kina's door.

"That must be Des." Kina stood up to let her in. "She's as sweet as pie. You all are gonna love her!"

Kina exited and then shortly thereafter returned to the dining room with her ghostwriter in tow. "Everybody, I want you all to meet Desdemona Price, also known as one of the best in the publishing biz!"

Desdemona waved. "Hello. I've heard so much about all of you that I feel like we already know each other."

Angel thought for a moment. "Desdemona . . . that's an interesting name. That's the wife's name in *Othello*, right?"

"Yeah, my mom has a thing for Shakespearean tragedies. I guess that's why I'm attracted to the darkside of things."

"You're in the right profession." Lawson pulled out the chair next to hers. "Please have a seat. Welcome."

"Thank you." Desdemona sat down. "You must be . . ."

Lawson extended her hand. "Lawson Kerry Banks. Kina's favorite cousin."

"Favorite after me, that is!" interjected Reginell.

"You must be Reginell, Lawson's sister," said Desdemona.

Reginell nodded. "I'm the fun sister. She's . . . *not*."

Desdemona giggled. "I think it's best I stay out of that."

Angel, who was sitting across from Desdemona, extended her hand. "Hi. I'm Angel King."

Desdemona warmly received her hand. "The nurse, right?"

Angel nodded. "Yes, and Kina's old boss."

Desdemona was impressed. "And the two of you are still friends? You must've been a great boss!"

"She was the best!" replied Kina and sat down next to Desdemona. "All these ladies are awesome."

"I can tell," said Desdemona. "I'm looking forward to spending time with all of you. I don't know if Kina mentioned this or not, but I will need to set up some interviews with everyone."

"For what?" asked Reginell, immediately wary.

Desdemona explained. "All of you play such significant roles in Kina's life. In order to get a complete sense of who she is, I think it's important to talk to all of you since you're the ones who know her best."

"Yep, we know where all the secrets and bodies are buried," teased Lawson.

Kina passed Desdemona the platter of grilled chicken breasts. "Go on. Help yourself."

"It looks delicious, and this is such a beautiful table and place setting," remarked Desdemona, admiring Kina's Wedgwood dinnerware. "In fact, I love the way your whole home is decorated, Kina."

"Thanks, but I can't really take all the credit. The china was a splurge after I won *Lose Big,* but the furniture was all of them." Kina gestured with her hand toward her friends. "Mostly Sullivan."

"We all pitched in and got Kina new furniture for her birthday after her husband passed," reported Angel.

"I bought the punch bowl," crowed Reginell.

"We didn't have much money between the three of us, so Sullivan bought the bulk of it," confessed Lawson. "Or at least her husband's account did."

"That was sweet," replied Desdemona. "Kina told me that she was in a bad car accident a few days ago. How is she?"

Angel smiled. "According to the Word and our faith, she's healed."

"Just from talking to Kina and from the vibe I get from all of you, I can tell that religion is very important to you all," remarked Desdemona.

Lawson shook her head. "Not religion. I don't think any of us subscribe to the notion of legalism and fixed religion in the traditional sense, but we all have a strong relationship with God. That's the root of everything we are and everything we do."

The concept fascinated Desdemona. "Wow. So I guess that's the secret to how you manage to do what's a struggle for so many people."

"God and these girls," said Kina. "They've been my rock. I don't know what I'd do without them."

"That goes for all of us," affirmed Angel. "Through all the drama and madness, they've been there."

Kina went on. "Yeah, some of us go back almost to the womb together! Lawson and I are cousins, we were born two weeks apart, we lived in the same neighborhood, and we went to the same school. You name it, we did it together!"

"Sullivan moved to the neighborhood when we were in elementary school, and the three of us were inseparable and have been ever since," added Lawson.

"Well, the *two* of you, anyway," Kina said, correcting her. "Sully and I are still working past our issues, but things have gotten much better."

"What issues?" asked Desdemona.

The ladies all exchanged glances.

Kina patted Desdemona on the hand. "We'll discuss it off-line."

Desdemona faced the group. "Kina has been filling me in about all of you. Obviously, I know that Kina is an aspiring author and television personality. Lawson is a high school social studies teacher, I think . . ."

Lawson nodded. "Working toward administrator."

Desdemona pointed at Angel. "Angel, you're a nurse, and Sullivan is a stay-at-home mom. I'm not really sure what you do, Reginell."

"I'm a retired stripper," answered Reginell.

Desdemona blinked back. "Oh . . . you really *are* the fun sister, huh?"

"Honey, I'm many things!" boasted Reginell. "These days, though, I dance exclusively for my man when I'm not in school."

"Incidentally, her *man* is also my son's father," expounded Lawson. "It's a long story."

"And no doubt an interesting one. I can't wait to hear all about it." Desdemona looked around at all the women seated around the table. "It's so refreshing to see women, especially sistas, supporting each other. Reality TV and movies will have you thinking it's impossible, but you're the exception. You ladies have it all."

Lawson became sullen. "That's debatable. Right now, we don't have the one thing we all want most, and that's our sister Sullivan."

"I have to agree with that, and I don't even like her!" Reginell conceded, then winced in pain.

"What's wrong?" asked Angel.

"Nothing . . . I got a cramp in my lower back. I've been getting them lately."

"You haven't told me anything about that!" admonished Lawson. "How long has this been going on?"

"Lawson, I don't tell you lots of things, but it's no big deal. Besides, I promised Mark that I'd have it checked out, and I will."

"When?" Lawson and Angel asked at the same time.

Reginell let out a breath and massaged her back. "Soon."

"See? You all support each other without even thinking about it. That's beautiful," observed Desdemona.

"Don't you have friends back in Atlanta like that?" asked Lawson.

Desdemona shook her head. "Not really. Work keeps me pretty busy. Even when it doesn't, I've found that females don't really get along that well for an extended period of time. Somebody gets jealous or someone betrays someone else or someone takes someone else's man. There's always some kind of drama. It's easier to have one or two girlfriends I can hang out with sometimes and to keep to myself the rest of the time."

"Don't get me wrong. We have our moments," Lawson said, clarifying the situation. "We argue and fight just like sisters, but we always find our way back."

"We're family," affirmed Kina, looking at her friends. "All of us."

Desdemona was in awe. "That's amazing. Quite frankly, it's miraculous that your friendship has survived this long. My mother used to always say that if you have more than one best friend, you're setting yourself up to get hurt. I guess you ladies are the exception."

"Absolutely!" affirmed Angel. "When it's a true sisterhood bond like this one, nothing or nobody can tear it apart."

Desdemona nodded, then turned her head in the direction of a ringing phone.

"Oh, that's me," Lawson said and looked down at her phone. "It's a text from Charles."

Kina held her breath. "What did he say?"

"He said to come to the hospital as quick as we can," reported Lawson.

Reginell gulped. "You don't think they're calling the family in, do you?"

"We can't assume the worst," cautioned Angel. "I witness medical miracles all the time. Maybe she woke up."

"Don't you think Charles would've put that in the text, though?" asked Kina.

"I don't know." Lawson pushed her plate away. "Let's just go and see, okay?"

"Do you think we should pray first?" asked Angel.

"We should pray in the car." Lawson nervously bit her lip. "I don't know how much time we have."

The ladies mechanically rose from their chairs, collecting their cell phones and purses. They didn't speak on the way to the hospital and forgot to pray. They were too preoccupied, not knowing if they were about to witness a miracle or were going to the hospital to tell Sullivan good-bye.

# Chapter 9

"Wonders never cease!"

*—Angel King*

"Well, wonders never cease!" exclaimed Angel as she entered Sullivan's hospital room, flanked by Kina, Reginell, Lawson, and Desdemona.

"Praise be to God! I've always believed in miracles, but there's nothing like seeing one to reaffirm my belief!" attested Lawson. She was nearly brought to tears at the sight of Sullivan sitting up in her hospital bed, awake and alert. She rushed to Sullivan's side and enfolded her in a zealous embrace. "You don't know how happy I am to see these gray contacts!"

"Dang, Lawson," croaked Sullivan. "I just came back to life. Don't try to kill me!"

Lawson pulled back. "I'm sorry. I can't help it. I'm so thrilled to see my best friend again."

Charles chuckled, bouncing toddler Charity on his knee. "Don't feel bad. I had the same reaction. I can't tell you how good it felt to see my baby open her eyes. I think I scared half the hospital when I shouted up and down the corridor!"

"The people in this hospital may not understand your shouting, but we sure do! How long has she been awake?" asked Angel.

"A few hours," answered Charles. "I would've called you sooner, but the doctors had to run some tests and examine her. I didn't want to call until we knew she was all right."

Lawson held Sullivan's hand. "How are you feeling, sweetie? Are you in any pain?"

Sullivan stretched out on the bed. "If I am, I can't tell. The drugs here are fabulous! Angel, I can see why you got addicted."

"Looks like the sadistic witch of Savannah is back!" announced Reginell. "I wouldn't have it any other way!"

"Yeah, I love you too, Reggie," Sullivan replied sarcastically. "And thank you for keeping my broomstick warm while I was sleeping."

Lawson laughed. "Yep, she's definitely back!"

"Well, she's still not at one hundred percent, but she'll get there," proclaimed Charles. "The Lord wouldn't have it any other way."

"You had us worried for a minute there," said Kina. "But we never gave up hope, and we never stopped praying for you."

"Thank you, Kina." Sullivan looked over at Charity and Charles. "I had a lot of motivation right here and in that NICU to come back."

Angel cooed. "Have you seen Christian?"

Sullivan beamed with pride. "Yes. He's teeny, but he's perfect."

"It must've been wonderful seeing him for the first time," said Kina.

Sullivan nodded. "When I woke up to a flat stomach, I almost had a heart attack. I didn't know what had happened to my baby. The doctors wanted me to wait before going to see him. They thought seeing him with tubes and on that breathing machine would freak me out, but I made such a fuss that they soon figured out that *not* seeing him was making me freak out even more! I think they know now not to mess with me when it comes to my kids."

Angel tried to mask her concern about Christian's undeveloped immune and respiratory systems. "How is he? Is the breathing machine working for him okay?"

"I don't know, but God is," attested Charles. "We put our faith in Him, not some machine."

"Amen," said Lawson.

Sullivan spotted Desdemona hanging back in the corner. "Wow. I'm down a few days, and y'all have already replaced me?"

Kina snickered. "Not a chance. This is Desdemona. She's helping me with my book."

Desdemona stepped forward. "I hope it's okay that I'm here. I was with Kina when they got the call. She said it would be okay if I tagged along."

"No, it's fine," said Sullivan.

"I'm glad you're awake. They've all been worried sick about you," Desdemona told her.

"It'll take a lot more than a teenager texting while driving to take me out!" professed Sullivan.

"You're a tough cookie," joked Desdemona. "Believe me, it takes one to know one! And if you ladies will excuse me, I have a few errands to run. I get lost after the sun goes down, so I better head out while there's still daylight."

Charles shook her hand. "Thanks for coming, and nice meeting you."

"I'll be right back," Kina said before walking Desdemona out.

"So Kina has a new entourage now?" teased Sullivan.

"She's harmless, and I'll take Desdemona over Kina's cameramen any day. Remember how creepy they were, filming and following her around everywhere?" Lawson glanced over at Reginell, who appeared to be in pain again. "Reggie, are you all right?"

Reginell nodded, gritting her teeth and gripping the arm of a chair.

Angel's nursing instincts took over. "Reggie, I can look at you and tell you're in agony. Let me take a look at you."

"I'm fine," Reginell replied breathlessly. "Excuse me." She gathered the bit of strength she had left and dashed out of the room.

Lawson rose. "I'm going after her."

"No, stay here with Sully," instructed Angel. "I'm the nurse. This is my territory."

Angel made a quick exit and found Reginell doubled over in pain right outside Sullivan's door, with Kina tending to her.

"Call Mark," groaned Reginell, holding her stomach and struggling to breathe.

"Forget Mark." Angel looked at Kina. "We need to call a doctor."

# Chapter 10

"There's really not a lot of space on my plate to
add *jealousy* at this moment."

*–Lawson Kerry Banks*

Mark charged down the hospital corridor, frantically
searching for Reginell. He found Lawson, Angel, and
Kina instead. "Where is she? Where's Reggie?"

"She's in with the doctor." Sullivan pointed to the hospital room where Reginell was stationed. "Thank you for
coming so quickly."

"Thanks for calling me." Mark took a second to catch
his breath. "What's going on? What happened?"

"We don't know yet," replied Angel. "We just know that
she was in a lot of pain."

"She's been complaining about that lately," said Mark.
"I knew I should've gotten her to a doctor."

"Don't blame yourself. My sister is stubborn. She
wasn't going to a doctor until she was good and ready,"
said Lawson.

They all turned in the direction of Reginell's room
when they heard the door creak open and saw the physi-
cian emerge, having completed his examination of Reginell.

"Hello. I'm Dr. McNamara. Which one of you is responsible for Reginell Kerry?"

"I am," replied Lawson. "I'm her sister and next of kin."

Mark moved ahead of her. "No, *I* am. I'm her husband."

Kina and Angel gawked at Mark with opened mouths.

"You mean fiancé," Lawson said, correcting him.

"No, I mean her husband. We haven't told anybody yet, but we made it official about two weeks ago," explained Mark.

Lawson stumbled back a bit. "So . . . you're married?"

"Yes, Lawson, we're married." Mark edged closer to the doctor. "How is she? What's wrong with my wife? Is she okay?"

The doctor raised his hand a little to calm Mark down. "She's going to be fine. We administered an ultrasound—"

Lawson interrupted him. "Ultrasound? Is she pregnant?"

"No. We found some scar tissue outside of her uterus, which is usually consistent with endometriosis."

"I've heard of it, but I'm not sure I know exactly what endometriosis is," admitted Mark.

"Basically, women have tissue that line the uterus, or womb. Endometriosis occurs when tissue grows outside of the uterus, on other organs or structures in the body, like the fallopian tubes, the ovaries, or the rectum. It can spread to other parts as well," Dr. McNamara explained.

"Is that dangerous?" asked Kina.

"Endometriosis may spread like cancer, but it's benign," explained Angel.

Mark was still worried. "If it's harmless, why has she been in so much pain?"

"The tissue and blood that's shed into the body can cause inflammation, scar tissue, and adhesions. This scar tissue may cause pelvic pain," said Dr. McNamara. "And trapped blood in the ovaries can form cysts."

"Poor Reggie," moaned Kina.

"Okay, so if pain is the worst thing that can happen, she should be fine, right?" asked Mark. "You can fix that with medicine, can't you?"

Dr. McNamara nodded. "We'll try."

Lawson released a deep breath. "Doctor, how did this happen?"

"There's really no way to know that definitely. Endometriosis is actually quite common, especially among women Reginell's age. Risk factors can range from genetics to not having children to damaged pelvic cells resulting from infection."

"So what happens now?" asked Mark.

"Well, we'll need to schedule your wife for a minor surgery called a laparoscopy."

Inexplicably, it stung Lawson slightly to hear Reginell referred to as Mark's wife.

Kina gasped. "Surgery?"

"It's a very simple procedure, but it's the only way to definitively determine if she has endometriosis," Dr. McNamara told them.

Mark was still anxious. "Can I see my wife now?"

The doctor nodded. "Yes, she's resting comfortably, but she's awake."

"I'm coming too," insisted Lawson.

Mark stopped her. "Give me a minute with her first."

"That's my baby sister in there!" cried Lawson.

"But she's his wife." Angel pulled Lawson off to the side. "Let them have a moment."

Lawson reluctantly yielded to Mark's request and watched in the background as he entered Reginell's room without her.

"Wow, Reggie's *married!* Can you believe it?" asked Kina, still in awe.

"Mark is looking like a real husband in there with her too," observed Angel, peeking into the room.

Lawson frowned. "I think we should be focusing on Reggie's health, not her nuptials."

"She'll be fine," Angel assured her. "Depending on the severity of it, Reggie could be treated with something as simple as pain meds or hormone therapy. They may even be able to treat during the laparoscopic procedure."

Kina placed her hand over her chest. "That's a relief."

"The main thing with endometriosis is getting the pain under control and making sure it doesn't spread to other parts of the body. The worst thing about having this condition is the chance that it will make it harder for Reggie to get pregnant," Angel warned them.

"Uh-huh," grunted Lawson. "I wonder why they felt the need to keep the wedding a secret."

"I thought we weren't going to focus on Reggie's nuptials," Angel reminded her.

"We're not. I'm just saying . . . I'm Reggie's sister and I share a child with Mark. I would think they owed me a heads-up."

"Obviously, they thought otherwise," remarked Angel, detecting an attitude from Lawson, as well as noting the distressed look on her face. "You're not upset about them getting married, are you?"

Lawson huffed. "Angel, they were engaged for over a year, so it's not like it's a total shock. I just thought they'd run it by me first."

"Run it by you for what?" asked Kina, probing. "They're grown!"

"You're missing the point!" Lawson shook her head. "Anyway, I think the newlyweds have had sufficient time together. I want to go in and check on my sister."

Angel grabbed Lawson's arm. "Wait a minute. You're okay with this, right? I mean, you're not jealous or anything, are you?"

"Angel, my teenage son has knocked up his teenage girlfriend, my best friend has spent the past few days fighting for her life, and we still don't know if her son is going to make it. I had to watch my baby sister collapse in pain, and now I find out she's married to my son's father. There's really not a lot of space on my plate to add *jealousy* at this moment. All I want to do is make sure that my sister is okay."

Angel let her go. "I'm sorry. You've been through a lot lately. I was being insensitive."

"It's fine. For the record, I'm not jealous of Reggie and Mark. If this is what they want, I'm happy for them. I just wish they had told me. It feels like too many changes coming at me too fast. You know I have to have structure and order. My life has been anything but that lately."

"Sullivan is finally awake, and Reggie is getting the help she needs. I know she and Mark sneaked off and got married without telling you, but look at it this way—you didn't lose a baby's daddy. You gained a brother-in-law!" enthused Kina. "It's a happy day!"

Lawson smiled, when all she really wanted to do was haul off and slap that insipid grin right off Kina's face.

"The important thing is that Reggie now has a husband who loves her and wants to take care of her, and who doesn't want that?" Angel fished her ringing phone out of her purse. "Hello?"

Lawson and Kina watched as a stunned look washed over Angel's face. After a few minutes, she hung up the phone, seemingly in shock.

Lawson moved closer to her. "Angel, is everything okay?"

Angel swallowed hard. "Um . . . no."

Kina placed her hand over her heart. "Oh, my God, what's wrong?"

"That was Duke. He . . . he was arrested."

# Chapter 11

"We may look like we have it all together on the outside, but looks can be deceiving."

*–Kina Battle*

"You have some really great friends, Kina," stated Desdemona when they returned to Kina's house after the visit to the hospital. "You're very lucky."

Kina hung up her jacket. "I don't know about all that," she muttered.

"You don't think so?"

"I know I'm blessed. I have this beautiful home, an awesome son, and winning *Lose Big* has opened all kinds of doors for me and given me opportunities that I never even dreamed of, but life hasn't always been this gravy."

Desdemona followed Kina into the kitchen and took a seat at Kina's maple-top breakfast bar. "Yeah, I heard that you had sort of a strained marriage."

Kina opened the refrigerator and pulled out the left-over chicken from dinner. "More like a *pained* marriage! It was doomed pretty much from the onset."

"Why do you say that?"

"First off, E'Bell and I got married really young. We were only eighteen. We didn't have any money and barely had an education, but I was pregnant. E'Bell's parents were traditional. They put a lot of pressure on him to do the right thing."

"So it was a shotgun wedding?"

Kina thought back. "Not really. I mean, in those days, E'Bell and I were in love. We were the quintessential high school sweethearts. I was the cheerleading captain, and he was the football team's quarterback. We were the perfect couple, until it all fell apart."

Desdemona pulled a small pad from her purse and began taking notes. "What happened?"

"E'Bell, or rather 'Give 'Em Hell' E'Bell, which we all called him, was this hotshot athlete. He was born to play football. Nobody could touch him on the football field. He had colleges all over the country throwing scholarship money at him," Kina said, recalling the past fondly. "Then we found out I was pregnant. Instead of going to college to play ball, he chose to stay home and marry me and raise our son. He ended up a janitor at the same school he used to play for. That did something to him. He had always dreamed of playing for the NFL. Once that dream was shattered, he ended up taking it out on me and Kenny."

"Is that when the abuse started?"

Kina nodded. "He never forgave me for taking his dream from him. He resented us and said we were the reason he was a failure. I believed him and blamed myself too. That's why I stayed with him as long as I did, enduring that abuse year after year. Then I discovered that the reason he didn't go to college wasn't me. It was because he had never actually graduated high school. Unbeknownst to us, E'Bell couldn't read. When I confronted him about it and tried to leave, he beat me within an inch of my life. That's when Kenny shot him. My son was trying to save me and killed his father in the process. To this day, E'Bell's parents haven't forgiven me. They don't believe that he was illiterate or that he tried to kill me. In fact, they think I put my son up to killing him. How ridiculous is that?"

"Wow!" Desdemona released a breath. "You have such an incredible story! This book can pretty much write itself."

"Girl, we all have stories! Sullivan got caught in a big cheating scandal a few years ago. It was only last year that they found out that Charity is the pastor's biological child."

Desdemona was taken aback. "Oh?"

Kina pinched off a piece of chicken and ate it. "Yeah. Sullivan's husband is a pastor and is always busy with the church. Unfortunately, Sully is the kind of woman who requires lots of attention. When she doesn't get it, look out! Don't get me wrong, though. Sullivan has a big heart, and she is a wonderful mother. She loves her babies. That's why we've been so worried about Christian. There's no telling what she might do if he doesn't make it."

"I'll be praying for him. What about Angel? She seems pretty levelheaded."

"Angel's current boyfriend, Duke, is her ex-husband, who cheated on her and left her for his pregnant mistress, whom he later married. She died a few years ago, and now Angel is raising that woman's kids. Angel also took care of Duke's new wife when she was dying, which we all thought was a little odd. But, hey, who are we to judge?"

"It takes a strong woman to be able to do that."

"Or a stupid one! But for whatever reason, she keeps going back to him, no matter how many times he screws up. In spite of all that, I think the biggest drama in our group is between Mark, Lawson, Reggie, and Garrett."

"Why?"

"You see, Mark and Lawson had a one-night stand when we were in high school. Lawson got pregnant, but she never got to tell him, because he moved to Virginia to go to college," related Kina. "Anyway, Lawson and Garrett got together, and he agreed to raise Namon like his own. Fast-forward to five years ago. Lawson and Mark ended up teaching at the same school. She hadn't seen him since the night they conceived Namon, and was afraid to tell him that they had a child together. They had this weird sort of attraction going on, until Mark found out he had a thirteen-year-old son whom he knew nothing about. Boy, was he pissed!"

"I bet!"

"He threatened to take Lawson to court and sue for custody unless she married him."

Desdemona was rapt by the story. "What about Garrett?"

"She and Garrett were engaged but not married yet. I think Lawson was strongly considering marrying Mark. In the end, though, she married Garrett, and Reggie hooked up with Mark. The rest is history."

"Goodness gracious! Has Lawson ever thought about writing a book?"

"It would be more like a continuing drama. Mark loves Reggie, and Lawson is gaga over Garrett, but she and Mark still have this undeniable chemistry."

Desdemona bristled at the thought. "And their significant others don't mind?"

"I don't think they're aware of how deep it is, but there's definitely something there. In fact, they kissed not too long ago. Lawson said it was on impulse and didn't mean anything, but I guess that's easier than admitting the truth."

"Dang, you all have lived nine lives. I'm still trying to get through one!"

"Yeah, we may look like we have it all together on the outside, but looks can be deceiving. We all have had our crosses to bear. Most of us are still carrying them."

Desdemona nodded, steadily taking notes.

# Chapter 12

"The Lord will see to it that you're vindicated."

*—Angel King*

Duke paid the babysitter and thanked her for watching his daughters after he and Angel returned to his home from the police station.

"Well, that's one call I never want to get again!" said Angel once they were alone.

"That's one call I never thought I'd have to make!" replied Duke. "Thanks for coming to bail me out. I'm sorry I put you through that."

Angel set her car keys down on the coffee table, and Duke helped her out of her coat. "I think my heart stopped when I heard you say that you were in jail. Thank God I was able to get you out. I wouldn't be able to stomach the thought of you having to spend the night in that place."

"You and me both!" Duke exhaled and flopped onto the sofa. "Sitting in that holding cell, I couldn't get my mind off what you said before I left."

"What was that?"

"You told me not to trust Mya. I should have listened."

"Don't beat yourself up about it. Not even I could've predicted that she would take it this far!" Angel softly broached the inevitable question that had to be addressed. "Duke, I know your mind is probably racing a thousand different ways right now, so I didn't want to press you at the station or in the car. And I don't want you to think I'm accusing you of anything, but I've got to ask. Exactly what went down between you and Mya in LA?"

Duke ran his hand over his face. "Nothing, as far as I know! I mean, we flew out to LA, and everything seemed cool. We met with our clients and accomplished everything we went out there to do. We came back, and the next thing I know, I'm shackled in handcuffs and being charged with sexual assault!"

"But there had to be something. What could she have against you to substantiate these claims? They can't just take her word for it without any proof, can they?"

"Obviously, they can." Duke rubbed his wrists, still sore from the handcuffs.

"I can't understand why she'd bring up these fake charges against you." Angel sat down next to him. "So did you all argue? Was there some kind of misunderstanding?"

"Your guess is as good as mine. The most she can say is that we had a glass of wine with dinner, and that wasn't a crime the last time I checked."

Angel was a bit unnerved by this new development. "It is if she's underage. I thought you said she's twenty."

"She's twenty-one. She was carded, so no crime there."

"Did you do or say anything that could be misconstrued as sexual harassment? Did you touch her in any way?"

Duke seemed reluctant to answer the question. "We talked. Admittedly, the conversation may have gotten a little flirtatious at times, but it definitely wasn't anything to warrant sexual assault charges."

Angel became quiet and solemn. "So you flirted with her."

"If you can even call it that," argued Duke. "Just a couple of jokes and innuendos here and there. It was all very PG." Duke saw the doubt in her eyes. "You believe me, don't you, Angel? I swear, I didn't touch that girl! Not to brag, but I've never had to force a woman to do anything. And why would I go after that little girl when I have a woman like you waiting for me at home?"

Angel caressed the side of his face. "Don't worry. I believe you."

"Thank you." Duke was comforted. "Even though these charges are completely bogus, I'm hiring a lawyer first thing in the morning."

"I think that's a good idea. I know you didn't do what she's accusing you of, but you still need good representation."

Duke nodded. "Can you believe she had the police come up to my job to arrest me? I was fingerprinted and booked like a common criminal, and I've never even so much as gotten a speeding ticket!"

Angel's heart went out to him. "As terrible as that must've been for you, I'd rather it happened there than here. Can you imagine how frightened the girls would've been to see you taken away in handcuffs?"

"Yeah, I know. I guess I should be thankful that it's my colleagues, not my daughters, who think I'm a rapist."

"Honey, no one thinks that," Angel assured him. "Mya is not going to get away with this. The Bible speaks against bearing false witness, and the Lord will see to it that you're vindicated."

"I'm not worried about being convicted by the Lord. I'm worried about being convicted by the *law!*"

"He's a lawyer in a courtroom. By the time this is over, everyone will know that Mya is lying. We will clear your name in no time, I promise."

"I wish it was that simple, Angel, but the fact is that this nightmare is just getting started."

"It doesn't matter. We're not going to be negative or assume the worst outcome. We serve Jehovah Nissi. The Lord is our banner of love and protection."

"That's exactly what I need Him to be right now!"

"And He will be! I'm sure you're emotionally exhausted." Angel rubbed his shoulders. "Do you want something to eat or drink?"

Duke shook his head. "The only thing I want to do right now is kiss my girls good night, hop in the shower, and pretend this whole scene never even happened."

"Okay, try not to let them see how upset you are. Kids are very perceptive, and you don't want to scare them."

"I won't." He stood up, then leaned down to kiss Angel. "I'll be back in a sec."

"I'll be waiting."

Before going upstairs, he turned around. "You have no idea how much it means to me to have you on my side," said Duke. "What means the most to me is that you never doubted my innocence for a second. I love you for that."

She smiled. "I love you too, baby."

Angel was relieved that Duke had faith in her and her belief in his innocence. Now she just needed to convince herself.

# Chapter 13

"If your intentions aren't honorable, I suggest you leave now, before anyone gets hurt."

*—Kina Battle*

Kina gasped. It took her a moment to recognize the gray-bearded figure at her door the following afternoon. He looked so much like her dead husband that she feared she was looking at a ghost. Her fear morphed into anger when she realized who the unannounced and unwelcomed visitor was.

"What are you doing here?" asked Kina, confused.

"Don't I get a hug?" He enveloped a stunned Kina.

"No, not after not coming around for five years!" She quickly broke away from him. "What do you want, Elvin?"

Elvin Battle, E'Bell's father, had never been an easy man to read, except when it came to his disapproval of Kina's handling of E'Bell's death. He and his wife, Brenda, made no secret of the fact that they held Kina responsible for his son's demise and wanted nothing to do with her once E'Bell was buried.

"You look good! You lost weight. Back to looking like you did the first time my son brought you home." He smiled as if he was as happy to see her as she was infuriated to see him. "How are you, daughter-in-law? How's my grandson?" asked Elvin, evading Kina's question. "I bet he's as big as me now. Is he home?"

Kina crossed her arms in front of her. "Kenny is fine. He's at school. Why all the sudden interest in my son?"

"He's not just your son, Kina. He's my oldest grandson and the only piece I have left of my son E'Bell."

"Kenny is nothing like his father, so don't insult him by drawing those comparisons. Why are you here? In fact, how do you even know where I live?"

"I called around. I hope that's okay." He grinned. "You're a big star now, I see."

"Is that why you're here? You looking for handouts?" quizzed Kina, now furious. "I hate to break this to you, but the money is almost gone, and whatever's left is put up for Kenny's future. So if that's all you came for, you can go." Kina began to close the door.

Elvin prevented her from shutting him out. "I didn't come here for money, Kina."

"Oh, really? You don't show your face for five years and then magically appear after I win a quarter of a million dollars on TV? I wasn't born yesterday, Elvin!"

"I admit I heard about you being on some kind of reality show, but that's not the reason I'm here. Kina, we're family. Don't you think it's time we started back acting like it?"

"No, I don't. Your family disowned my son and me after E'Bell's death. You blamed me for Kenny shooting him."

"We were upset, Kina, and rightfully so. My son was shot and killed, and nobody could give us a straight answer as to why it happened."

"It happened because your son was abusing me. I probably would've died that night if Kenny hadn't been there."

Elvin was skeptical. "I know you *say* E'Bell was abusing you, but—"

"There is no *but,* Elvin."

"I'm just saying that's not a side to him we ever saw, and you never mentioned it in all the years the two of you were together."

"Did you think that he was going to come out and tell you that he was going upside my head every time he got mad or that he'd be crazy enough to beat me in front of you?"

"I know my son, Kina. E'Bell was far from perfect. Like everybody, he had his demons, but I have a hard time believing that it was as bad as you say it was."

"You hardly knew E'Bell at all!" alleged Kina. "You didn't even know he couldn't read, when he was living right there under your roof. How do you expect to know what he was doing once he got out of your house?"

"Look, I don't want to argue with you and upset you. I just wanted to see you and see my grandson. Now that my Brenda's gone, y'all are the only family I got left."

Kina softened toward him. "I, um, heard that your wife died last year. I'm sorry."

"Thank you. I know she would've wanted to see Kenny one last time, but she never got around to it. The last thing I'd want to do is leave this world without at least even trying to get to know my grandson again."

Kina raised an eyebrow. "So that's the real reason you're here? To see Kenny?"

"Yes."

"Why now? Are you dying or something?"

"Not that I know of. I just want to talk to him. It's important that he knows this side of his family." He paused. "I also think it's important for him to get to know another side of his father. He needs to know that his daddy wasn't all bad."

"I haven't been filling his head with horror stories about E'Bell, if that's what you're implying."

"I never said that, but there's a lot about E'Bell that only his mother and I know. I think Kenny needs to know these things. He ought to know that his father wasn't a bad person."

Kina put her hand on her hip. "Things like what?"

"Things like his dad being a Boy Scout when he was younger or leading his football team to the city play-offs when he was thirteen. He should know that E'Bell and his mother used to cook together every Sunday and that the two of us would go fishing during the summer and that E'Bell could build things, that he was good with his hands. He even saved his grandmother's life when he was fifteen. Her house caught on fire. He rushed in and brought her out. He received second-degree burns, but he saved her life."

"I didn't know," revealed Kina, a bit uncomfortable. "E'Bell never said anything about that."

"Maybe you didn't know my son as well as you think, either. Kina, Kenny needs to know the whole story about his father, not just the ending. I'm one of the few people who can tell him the truth about him."

Kina looked down at her watch. "He'll be home in a few minutes. I guess it'll be all right if you wait for him here." She let him in.

"Thank you." Elvin looked around the town house. "Nice place you've got here."

"Thanks."

Elvin sat down. "I'm glad you've been able to make a good life for yourself and my grandson."

"God has been good to us, no doubt about that." Kina stood in front of him, arms folded. "So you still didn't say how you found me. My address isn't listed, and I know none of my friends or family would tell you where I live."

Elvin looked up at her. "Tell me, Kina, do you believe in fate?"

"Not where you're concerned, no," snapped Kina.

He laughed. "You're kind of feisty, ain't you? You've changed from that quiet, timid young girl you used to be."

"I have, so there's no point in you trying to run game on me or my son. If your intentions aren't honorable, I suggest you leave now, before anyone gets hurt."

"I'm here for one reason only, Kina, and that's to get to know my grandson again."

"The jury is still out on that."

Elvin laughed again. "Still don't trust me, huh?"

Kina frowned. "No. Why would I?"

"I told you I'm on the up and up."

"So you say. . . ."

"I guess there's only one way to find if I'm telling the truth." He grinned. "You've got to try me out and see!"

# Chapter 14

"A girl can't even slip into a coma these days without the whole world going crazy in her absence!"

*–Sullivan Webb*

"Reggie's married, and Namon is about to be a daddy?" repeated Sullivan in disbelief after Lawson and Angel filled her in on all she'd missed during the past week. "Good grief! How long was I out?"

Lawson fluffed Sullivan's pillow and stuffed it back behind her. "A few days, but it felt like a lifetime."

"Dang, a girl can't even slip into a coma these days without the whole world going crazy in her absence!" Sullivan took a sip of juice. "How is Reggie, by the way?"

"She's a little nervous about the surgery. She's in pre-op now, and the laparoscopy is scheduled for tomorrow. It sounds like a fairly simple procedure. Hopefully, they can find out what's going on with her, treat it, and everything goes back to normal."

Sullivan nodded. "In the meantime, how are you handling the new normal? Reggie being Mrs. JaMarcus Vinson."

Lawson brushed it off. "I'm fine. Why wouldn't I be?"

Angel gave Lawson the side eye. "Lawson, be honest. I know you felt some type of way when Mark announced that he and Reggie had eloped."

"Yeah, I was surprised, but that's about it. I don't know why you all keep trying to make something out of Mark and me that isn't there."

"Lawson, all three of the blind mice can see there's something there!" quipped Sullivan. "But the state of denial seems to be where you feel most comfortable, so stay there."

Angel laughed. "So when are they springing you out of here?"

"The doctor said I should be ready for release within the next few days. I'm walking now, the concussion is being treated, and my broken rib is healing, but I'm not leaving here without my son."

"Sully, Christian may have to be hospitalized for several more weeks," Angel reminded her. "Is the hospital going to let you stay that long?"

"I'd like to see them try to kick me out!" avowed Sullivan. "I'll go home when Christian does."

"How's his breathing?" asked Angel. "He should be getting stronger every day."

Sullivan smiled. "He is, Angel. I can tell. Of course, I haven't been able to hold him yet, but I go to the neonatal unit as much as I can and sing to him and talk to him. I pray over him nonstop. I want him to know that I'll be here however long it takes for him to get better."

Lawson smiled. "You've turned out to be quite the awesome mom, Sully."

"Thank you. I know you all had your doubts."

"And you should also know that we kept child protective services on speed dial for the first year of Charity's life!" revealed Angel.

"Being a parent changes you. I'm living proof of that." Sullivan glanced over at Lawson. "It'll change Namon and Shari for the better too."

There was a knock on the door. Reginell and Kina poked their heads in.

"Can we come in?" asked Kina.

Sullivan invited them in. "I think I'm the only one at this hospital who gets this much company. If I didn't know better, I'd think y'all loved me."

"Of course we do," Angel confirmed. "And we will make this hospital room as much fun as a middle school sleepover, except instead of talking about boys and braiding each other's hair, we'll talk about men and work each other's nerves!"

"Indeed!" Lawson turned to her sister. "How did the pre-op go, Reggie?"

Reginell settled down at the foot of Sullivan's bed. "It was cool, mostly blood work and paperwork."

Angel checked the door. "Where's your shadow, Kina?"

"If you mean Des, she does have a life outside of tracking my every move. She doesn't follow me twenty-four-seven. Matter of fact, she should start following you all around soon to gather info for the book," replied Kina.

"So what did we walk in on?" inquired Reginell. "It seemed pretty intense."

"I was just telling Lawson that Shari and Namon may turn out to be better parents than she gives them credit for," said Sullivan, recapping their conversation.

"I told her that, but she won't listen. You can't tell her nothing," replied Reginell. "She's still trippin' because her innocent little boy isn't as innocent as she thought."

"Is it so wrong that I was hoping his first time would be on his wedding night, the way God intended?" lamented Lawson.

Sullivan raised an eyebrow. "You mean like yours was?"

Lawson twisted her mouth into a frown. "Very funny. I wish I had waited, though."

"Then you wouldn't have Namon. He was a direct result of you losing your virginity," Kina pointed out.

"Obviously, I don't regret having my son. I was destined to be his mother. However, I do wish I hadn't lost my virginity to a guy I met at a party three hours earlier!"

"Lawson, you are not the first person to have a one-nighter," said Reginell. "I can't speak for you, but I could tell when Namon started having sex. You can always tell with boys. They start acting different. Plus, that facial hair began creeping in, and you know what they say about that!"

Lawson crossed her arms in front of her. "No. What do they say, Reggie?"

Reginell laughed out loud. "It means he must be eating something new!"

Angel tried to comfort her flustered friend. "Don't worry, Lawson. Medical science has yet to confirm that. It's just an ole wives' tale."

"Whatever," said Reginell. "I know for a fact that that's when my first real boyfriend started getting facial hair."

"You still remember your first?" asked Sullivan. "I'm shocked that you can still think back that many men."

"I do believe that this is one of those 'pot calling the kettle black' moments," snarled Reginell. "Besides, I remember very well who I lost my virginity to. It was Montee Jackson, my first love."

Lawson sucked her teeth. "I believe what you meant to say is your first *thug!* That dude was nothing but trouble. He had the rap sheet to prove it."

Reginell sulked. "You all just didn't understand him."

"Neither did the elderly couple he robbed at gunpoint! Nor did the judge and jury who convicted him."

Reginell disregarded Lawson's comment. "I never saw that side of him. He was always kind and gentle with me, especially that first time. We were in the back of that old Caprice."

"The back of an old hooptie?" squawked Sullivan. "How romantic! What did he do for your first date? Take you to the 7-Eleven to pick up snacks?"

"Shut up, Sullivan. I wouldn't expect you to know what it's like to be with a man without getting paid for it. Montee and I were just kids, but we were definitely in love." Reginell shrugged. "At least as much in love as you can be at fifteen. It all seems so insignificant now compared to what I have with Mark."

"I don't think we have to ask if you and Mark waited until you got married," stated Lawson.

"Um . . . we waited as long as we could!" replied Reginell, snickering.

"Which probably means halfway through their first date," commented Sullivan.

"No. We waited until we were sure that this was the real deal. Mark made sure everything was perfect. It was a night I'll never forget."

"I guess we all know Miss Goody Two-shoes over here waited for her wedding night, like a good Christian girl is supposed to," jeered Sullivan, gesturing to Angel.

Angel nodded. "I did but . . ."

Reginell was intrigued. "But what?"

"We . . ." Angel bit her lip and shook her head. "It's too embarrassing!"

"What?" said Sullivan, pressing. "You didn't pray first? Duke was in and out in under two minutes? Did you give him a little sloppy toppy?"

Angel came clean. "No, it's nothing like that. It's just that Duke and I . . . we didn't do things the *traditional* way for the first time."

"Huh?" Lawson was dumbfounded. "How was it non-traditional? Shoot, you waited until your wedding night. It doesn't get more traditional than that!"

"What are we talking about here, Angel? Positions? Toys? A third party?" interrogated Reginell.

Angel exhaled. "He didn't *enter* the traditional way, if you know what I mean."

Kina wrinkled her brow. "Didn't enter the traditional way? There's only one way in and one way out unless . . ."

"Unless someone sneaked in through the back door!" Sullivan howled with laughter. "Dang, chick, I didn't think you had it in you—literally, it seems!"

Lawson's eyes bulged. "Seriously, Angel? That's how you lost your virginity?"

Angel pouted. "Now, y'all are making me feel like a dirty little whore."

Sullivan recanted. "Hey, Duke was your husband. It was your wedding night. Who are we to judge?"

"Besides, with the right guy and a good lubricant . . ." added Reginell, ribbing her.

Lawson covered her ears. "Reggie, please spare us the how-to tutorial. I think we can all figure that much out."

"I'm just saying . . . don't knock it till you try it!" advised Reginell.

Angel turned to Kina. "What about you, Kina? Was E'Bell your first?"

Kina nodded. "Yes, it was after the prom. We were in a hotel, but we had to share the room with his cousin and his prom date."

Sullivan wrinkled her nose. "So it was an orgy?"

"Not exactly, but it wasn't an ideal situation, either. To be honest with you, I wanted to wait until I got married, but I was afraid of losing him if I didn't do it."

"It wouldn't have been much of a loss," muttered Sullivan.

"Sully, even you have to admit that E'Bell was *the man* in high school," said Kina.

Sullivan took another sip from her juice. "Obviously, our standards were much lower then."

"Sullivan, I've got to ask." Angel blushed. "Was Charles a virgin when the two of you got married?"

Sullivan snickered. "Hardly. My husband wasn't always a preacher, you know. That didn't come about until he was well into his twenties. I don't think he was ever a man whore, and, of course, I had to teach him a few things, but he's seen his share of lady parts—trust me!"

"You've got so much to say about everybody else, but what about your first time, Sully?" asked Reginell, probing. "Whose husband deflowered you for a small fee?"

"Yeah, Sully, you've never told me about that," added Angel.

Lawson thought back. "Wasn't it with that guy who lived around the corner from us? I think his name was Steve or Sean—something like that."

"It was Sean." Sullivan seemed reluctant to talk about it.

"How old were you?" asked Angel.

Sullivan lowered her head. "I was young—too young, really."

"We've all gotta start somewhere," said Reginell. "Some of us start in high school, and some of us in preschool, like Sully."

Sullivan swatted at Reginell. "Not that young! To be truthful, I would've preferred to wait, but it wasn't in the cards. I guess I must've started developing early, because Vera's boyfriends started taking an interest in me. I couldn't have been any more than thirteen or fourteen when her new man, Skeet, started coming around. He was a total perv, always looking at me and finding reasons to touch me . . . hugs that lingered too long and kisses that were a little too close to my lips or neck. I don't know how Vera didn't see it. Maybe she didn't want to."

Lawson shook her head. "As a mother, I'll never understand why Vera didn't do everything humanly possible to protect you from those sick bastards!"

"Neither will I," Sullivan concurred. "I mean, I know she was messed up after losing my baby sister and my dad, but still. Anyway, she started leaving me at home alone with him. In my gut, I knew it was only a matter of time before he tried to force himself on me." Sullivan took a deep breath. "I didn't want my first time to be like that, so I told myself that if this has to happen, it'll be on my own terms. I knew that Sean was crazy about me. I just wanted my first time to be with someone who genuinely cared about me, not a random pedophile. I at least wanted to be able to have some control over that much."

Angel hugged her. "No one should have to go through what you've gone through, Sully. I'm so sorry you had to endure that."

"I'm fine. I have a wonderful husband and two beautiful children." Sullivan smiled. "Those sad days are behind me."

As if on cue, Charles came in with Sullivan's wheelchair. "Evening, ladies." He tilted his head toward them.

"How goes it, Pastor?" asked Lawson.

"Beyond blessed, sister. Beyond blessed." Charles shifted his attention to Sullivan. "Are you ready to go see that brave boy of ours?"

"Always," answered Sullivan, beaming.

Charles and an orderly helped Sullivan into the wheelchair. As they headed to the door, one of Christian's pediatricians halted them.

"I'm sorry. I'm going to have to ask that you stay here," he told them.

Sullivan was taken aback. "Why? We were about to go to the NICU to visit our son."

"I know, but we're monitoring a situation in the neonatal unit," he replied. "No visitors are allowed at this time."

"What kind of situation?" Sullivan was apprehensive. "Is something wrong with my baby?"

The pediatrician danced around the question, not giving her a definitive yes or no answer. "His lungs are inflamed due to an infection. Rest assured that we're doing all we can to save your son."

"*To save him?*" repeated Charles. He swallowed hard. "Is his situation grave?"

Sullivan didn't wait for a response before attempting to get up. "Get out of my way! I'm seeing my child."

Charles held her down in the wheelchair. "Sullivan, let the doctors do their job in there. We'll do our job in here. God has our son in the palm of His hand."

Sullivan tried to wriggle out of his grip. "Charles, you're the preacher. You pray, but my son needs me right now! Let me go!"

Angel tried to assuage her. "Sully, there's nothing you can do for him. Don't get in the way. Let the doctors do their jobs."

"We're giving him oxygen therapy and doing all we can," said the pediatrician on his way out. "I'll update you as often as possible."

"I need to go!" insisted Sullivan, tearing up. "He needs me. He needs his mother in there. He needs to feel my presence and my love almost as much as he needs those doctors. I may be the only one who can save him!"

"Sweetheart, God is the only one who can save him," Charles reminded her. "This isn't the time to panic. We need to activate our faith and speak life over our son."

"Come on, Sully. Let's pray," urged Angel. "You see what our prayers did for you. They can do the same for Christian."

They all joined hands in a circle, and Charles led them in a fervent prayer on Christian's behalf. He ended the prayer by asking that the Lord's will be done. Sullivan silently prayed, asking that her son be saved, whether it was the Lord's will or not.

# Chapter 15

"It's not okay. . . . *I'm* not okay!"

*–Sullivan Webb*

"It was bronchopulmonary dysplasia," Angel explained to Sullivan's mother, Vera, an hour later. Both Sullivan and Charles were too grief-stricken to be pelted by Vera's inquisition following the pronouncement of Christian's passing. "It's really not uncommon, especially with preemies who have RDS, or respiratory distress syndrome."

Vera hiked Charity up on her hip. "Angel, I don't know what that means. I need to know in plain English why my grandson died!"

Angel spelled it out as best she could. "He had a very serious lung condition. Since he was born so early, his lungs didn't develop enough surfactant, which is a liquid that coats the inside of the lungs and helps them stay open so the baby can breathe. Without it, the lungs become infected or inflamed and can collapse."

Vera was visibly irritated. "Then what was the breathing machine for? Why was he hooked up to all those tubes if they couldn't help him breathe?"

"Vera, a machine can't do everything," reasoned Angel.

Vera couldn't accept that explanation. "So who fell down on the job, then? Who do we need to cuss out, then sue?"

"Nobody, Vera. This isn't anyone's fault," said Kina.

"Somebody fell down on the job! A baby is dead, and somebody's gotta take responsibility! Where's this God y'all are always talking about?" Vera scanned the room. "Why didn't He come down and do *His* job? See? That's why I don't believe in nobody, nothing, and no God! What kind of God will just sit on His throne and watch a little baby die?"

"God was with Christian then, and He's with him now," replied Lawson. "He's with Sully and Charles too, and He will get them through this."

"Oh, yeah?" Sullivan lifted her head from Charles's bosom. "You know, it's not often that I agree with my mother, but she has a valid point this time. Where was God when my baby was dying, huh? Where was He when I had the accident? Can anybody tell me that? Where was He then?"

Charles tried to console his wife. "Baby, don't talk like that."

Sullivan pulled away from him. "Don't do what, Charles? Tell the truth?"

Charles tried to put it in perspective for Sullivan and Vera and for himself as well. "The truth is that God didn't take our son away. His condition did. Even in the midst of grieving, though, we can still praise Him. We can be grateful that we have Charity and each other and all the people who care about us. We can thank God that Christian is safe in His arms, not hooked up to a bunch of machines and suffering anymore. We still have a lot to be thankful for. It's hard right now, but everything will be okay."

Sullivan was emotionally charged and directed her frustration at her husband. "Charles, can you just be human for one minute *please!* Our son is dead! *He's dead!* I don't want to hear about the so-called goodness of God or listen to another scripture or none of that. Our baby is gone, and I'm not going to stand here and act like it didn't happen or that it doesn't hurt like hell. I'm angry. I feel cheated, and I shouldn't have to pretend like everything is okay. It's not okay." Sullivan pointed at herself. "*I'm* not okay!" She broke down, crying again. "It's not okay, Charles! It's not okay. . . ." Charles folded Sullivan in his arms. Sullivan cried, clinging to her husband and trembling. "Christian is gone. Our baby is gone," she wailed.

Tears slid from Charles's reddened eyes, and he allowed himself to have an honest moment of grief. "I'm not okay, either. You're right. This hurts."

"He was my baby, and I never even got to hold him," whimpered Sullivan.

Vera stood by idly as long as she could. Though she had the maternal instincts of a pet rock, seeing Charles and her daughter in pain moved something in her. She was not one to show emotion. Without warning, she stepped out into the hallway and flagged down a medical assistant she spotted walking toward them. "Hey! You—yeah, you! Hey, we need some help in here!"

Angel was mortified. "Vera, what are you doing? A little tact please!"

The young blond assistant came to her aid. "Can I help you?"

Lawson offered a friendly smile, hoping to diffuse the situation before Vera created an even bigger spectacle. "We're fine."

Vera pointed to Sullivan. "My daughter didn't get to hold her baby. Somebody needs to get him. She needs to hold her baby."

The medical assistant was puzzled. "What do you mean?"

"He died. Y'all had him hooked up to a bunch of machines that clearly don't work, and he died. She never got to hold him. I want y'all to let her hold him before you do whatever y'all gon' do with his body."

The medical assistant was as confused by the request as she was by the person making it. "Umm . . . let me see if I can get a doctor over here."

"Look, what's your name?" asked Vera testily.

"Christy."

"*Christy,* please believe me when I tell you that I will turn this hospital upside down and back round again if you don't find me somebody who will bring my grandson to his mama! I really don't want to have to ask twice. You understand me?"

Sensing that Vera was very capable of keeping her word, Christy uttered, "Yes, ma'am. I'll see what I can do," and made a hasty exit.

"You're gonna get yourself thrown out of here, Vera," warned Angel.

"That's all right. They can do what they want to me, but Sullivan is gonna hold that baby!"

A few minutes later, Christy beckoned Charles and Sullivan and led them into a private nursery. She sat Sullivan down in a rocking chair, and a nurse came in with Christian swaddled in a blanket no larger than a cloth diaper.

She placed the child in Sullivan's arms and smiled. "We wanted you to be able to hold your child."

Sullivan's heart melted the second she received his tiny body. He was so small that he could practically fit in the palm of her hand. Unable to express her gratitude and every other emotion overwhelming her, she simply said, "Thank you."

"How long can we be in here with him?" asked Charles.

Christy smiled. "Take as long as you need." She and the other nurse slipped out quietly.

Sullivan drank him in, studying every fold and layer of his body. "Look at him, Charles," whispered Sullivan, marveling at seeing Christian for the first time without any wires and tubes attached to him. "He's so beautiful, like a little baby doll."

Charles stroked Christian's face with the tip of his finger. "He looks like he's sleeping. He looks peaceful."

Sullivan rocked her lifeless son in her arms, singing to him the songs she would sing to him while he was in the womb. She spoke quietly to him, telling him all the dreams she'd had for him and apologized that he'd never get to celebrate a birthday or ride a bike or fight with his sister or know how much his mother loved him.

After thirty minutes, Christy reappeared at the door. The eye exchange between her and Charles signaled that she'd come to take their son.

Charles kneeled down next to his wife. "Sullivan, honey, I think they're ready for him. It's time to say goodbye."

Sullivan continued rocking and humming to Christian, as if she hadn't heard him.

Charles spoke a little louder. "Sweetie, they've come to take the baby. It's time to let him go."

"I need a few more minutes," pleaded Sullivan. "Please, Charles."

Christy didn't say anything as she took slow strides toward them.

Charles leaned into Sullivan's ear. "Sullivan, I don't want anybody to come take this baby out your arms, but they will if you don't voluntarily let him go. Please, sweetheart, give him to this nice lady. Have faith that we'll see him again."

"When, Charles? At his funeral?" cried Sullivan.

"We'll see him when we get to heaven. He shall wipe away every tear from their eyes; and there shall no longer be any death; there shall no longer be any mourning, or crying, or pain; the first things have passed away," said Charles.

Sullivan refused to release him.

Charles spoke to her in a caring but firm voice to snap her out of her desolate state of mind. "Sullivan, we have another child waiting on us. She's probably scared and confused. She needs her parents to tell her that she's safe and that they love her. We can't stay here. Charity still needs you, baby. We've got to go."

"I'll take good care of him," Christy assured them.

Sullivan looked up at her through watery eyes. "I know he's just another carcass to you. You see death every day, but this is my baby. Don't just toss him aside like a piece of garbage!"

"I won't," vowed Christy.

Sullivan took a deep breath. "Good night, Christian. Sleep well." She kissed him one last time, soaking his blanket with her tears. "Mommy loves you. Mommy will always love you."

She gave the baby to Charles, who kissed him and said he loved him before turning him over to Christy.

Sullivan followed the retreating figures with her eyes, knowing Christy wouldn't turn back, but hoping against hope that she would.

"Come on. We should go. I'm sure somebody else needs this room." Charles tried to help Sullivan out of the rocking chair.

She sat firmly in place. "No, I want to stay."

"You can't do anything for him here. He's gone."

"Charles, just leave me here. I need a minute to myself. Can I have that much?"

Charles yielded. "I'll be right outside the door."

Sullivan waited until Charles was on the other side of the door to look at her now empty hands. There was nothing there except the memory of what it felt like to hold her child. She passed her hands over her vacant belly. To look at her, no one would even know she had been pregnant and carrying a precious life a few weeks prior. It was as if Christian had never existed, and she knew intuitively that a part of her had stopped existing the same time he had.

# Chapter 16

"It should take longer than an hour for your whole world to come crashing down."

–*Angel King*

"It all feels so surreal," said Angel, standing in the hallway outside of Sullivan's hospital room with Lawson, Kina, and Reginell as they waited for Sullivan and Charles to return. "It wasn't even an hour ago that we were laughing and everything was fine and now . . . It should take longer than an hour for your whole world to come crashing down."

Lawson agreed. "I've known Sully a long time, and I don't think I've ever seen her this broken. I pray that she can move past this and accept that God's will takes precedence over ours."

Kina shook her head. "Sullivan can't hear that right now. All she knows is that she prayed and that her precious baby died, anyway."

"We all knew he was a preemie and there was a chance that he wouldn't make it, but he seemed like such a little fighter. I wanted to believe that he'd be a miracle child," admitted Angel.

Reginell sighed. "How am I supposed to go into surgery tomorrow with this on my mind?"

Lawson hugged her. "You'll be fine, baby sister. This was just one of those things, you know?"

Desdemona approached them, carrying a bouquet of flowers. "Hey, I know you all don't know me that well, but when Kina texted me and said Sullivan's son died, I had to come."

"That was very thoughtful of you," replied Angel. "I'm sure Sullivan will appreciate the flowers."

"How is she?"

"She's devastated," answered Lawson.

They looked up and saw Charles wheeling Sullivan back to the room. Sullivan seemed to look right through them through vacant eyes. Her face was ruddy from crying. Neither she nor Charles said anything before disappearing into the room.

"Whoa!" uttered Desdemona. "You can look at her and tell she's really going through it."

"They both are. They were so excited about this new baby, and Sullivan had been praying for a little boy," relayed Angel. "It's heartbreaking."

"I think we should get out of here and give them some space and time to grieve," suggested Lawson. "It's clear they aren't up for visitors right now."

The ladies agreed and began to disperse.

Kina noticed that Desdemona was lagging behind them. "Aren't you coming?"

"I really want to stay and talk to Sullivan," she confessed.

"Why? You don't even know her."

"But I know what she's going through. I've been there. I think it'll help to know she's not alone."

"That's very kind of you." Kina slung her purse strap over her shoulder. "I'm going to head out. Call and let me know how it goes with Sullivan."

"I will."

Kina left. Desdemona waited outside of Sullivan's room until she saw Charles leave, presumably to take Charity to get something to eat.

She knocked softly on the door. "Hello, Sullivan." Desdemona crept into the darkened room. "I'm so sorry to hear about the baby. How are you?"

Sullivan sat up, startled. "Who are you?"

"My name is Desdemona Price. We met briefly a few days ago. I'm helping Kina write her book."

"Oh . . . I remember now. If you're looking for Kina, she's not here."

"I was looking for you." Desdemona set the flowers down on a table near Sullivan's bed. "Listen, if there's anything I can do, please let me know. If you ever want to talk—"

"Why would I want to talk to you?" interrupted Sullivan. "I hardly even know you."

"Sometimes it's better and easier to talk to a stranger. I have no history or preconceived notions about you. I'm not here to judge."

"So, what? Are you a therapist too?" asked Sullivan, cagey regarding any unsolicited advice.

"No." She moved in closer to Sullivan. "I'm just a mother who knows the pain of losing a child." This made Sullivan tune in. Desdemona went on. "I lost my daughter five years ago. She was fourteen."

"I'm sorry . . . really, I am. What happened?"

"She was at a party with some friends. A fight broke out, and a couple of guys started shooting." Desdemona struggled to recount the painful ordeal. "A bullet tore off half her chest. The guy who shot her was only sixteen years old. They even took a class together at school. He said he had never intended for her to be struck by the bullet, but what does that matter? He took her life, whether he intended to or not."

"That's awful. My heart goes out to you and your family."

"Thank you." She squeezed Sullivan's hand. "I know right now it seems like you're going to feel sad and empty forever, but I can tell you from firsthand experience that it does get easier. Now I cry only on her birthday and sometimes during the holidays. Mostly, I think about the joy Madison brought into my life, not the fact that it was cut short."

"At least you have memories of your daughter to comfort you. I don't even have that. All I have is this." She opened her hand to reveal the pair of tiny socks Christian was wearing when he died.

"You still have that beautiful little girl of yours. Besides, you're young. You can try again."

Sullivan shook her head. "No, this was it for me."

Desdemona offered up a smile. "Give it some time. You may see things differently six months or a year from now." Desdemona reached into her purse. "I want to give you my card. You can call me if you feel the need to talk to someone who's been through what you're going through."

"Thank you."

"I know you have a strong support system and a great group of girlfriends. They mean well, but they can't always relate to your pain. I can. Now, you get some rest."

Sullivan curled up into a fetal position and wrapped the blanket tightly around her body. She sank down into the bed and shut out the rest of the world.

# Chapter 17

"I won't set myself up for that kind of heartbreak."

*−Reginell Vinson*

Between tending to Reginell and Sullivan, Lawson was starting to feel like she was the resident nurse instead of Angel. She'd come to Mark's house, which he now shared with his wife, Reginell, following her outpatient laparoscopic surgery.

"Endometriosis," repeated Lawson after hearing Reginell's official diagnosis. "I know that the doctor suspected that's what it was, but I was still hoping . . ."

Reginell slouched down in her bed. "Yeah, me too. Unfortunately, they weren't able to treat it during surgery, so I'm really no better off than I was before."

Mark kissed Reginell on the forehead. "Reggie's doctor is concerned about it spreading to her bladder. We're praying that it won't, though."

Lawson handed Reginell her pain medication. "I still don't understand how this happened."

"I didn't get it from stripping or sleeping around, if that's what you're implying," barked Reginell.

Mark came to Lawson's defense. "Baby, I'm sure she didn't mean it that way. None of us really knows much about this condition, how serious it is, or what the best way to treat it is."

"It's serious, Mark," attested Reginell. "You heard the doctor. I'm not going to die or anything, but there could be long-term consequences."

"Like what?" asked Lawson.

"Like needing a hysterectomy," replied Reginell.

"Only if it spreads or if the pain can't be treated with the medication he has her on, but that's a worst-case scenario," reported Mark.

Lawson knew what Mark and Reginell were both worried about. "If it came to that, I guess that would mean . . ."

Reginell finished her sentence. "It would mean never having children of our own. Even if I didn't have a hysterectomy, endometriosis can still affect my fertility."

Mark could tell that the prognosis was crushing to her. "Hey, I can live with that. I have Namon and Mariah. Heck, I'm about to have a grandchild. I can handle not being able to have any more children. It's not having you that would be devastating."

"Yeah, that's fine for you, Mark, because you have two children," interjected Lawson. "She doesn't."

"We don't subscribe to all that stepkid stuff," Mark informed her. "My kids are *our* kids."

"You know how much I love my nephew, and I adore Mariah, but they're not my children, not biologically. We've been planning to have kids all along. I don't want to give that up," said Reginell.

"Then we've got to explore other treatment alternatives," responded Lawson. "A hysterectomy can't be the only solution."

"No, but it's the only guaranteed solution," acknowledged Reginell.

Lawson wasn't all too keen on the thought of Reginell and Mark having children, but she loved her sister dearly and wanted to see her happy, even if that meant having children with Mark. It was then that the ideal solution sparked in Lawson's head.

"I think I have the perfect solution. In fact, I think it's genius!" Lawson started laughing hysterically. "Isn't it awesome how the Lord works?"

Mark was leery. "I guess that would depend on what the solution is."

"Simple! Reggie may have to have a hysterectomy, which would eliminate the chance of her of ever being able to conceive. However, she still wants a child who's biologically linked to both of you," pointed out Lawson. "On the other hand, we have Namon, who is in no shape, form, or fashion anywhere near ready to have a child. Neither is Shari."

Mark was taken aback. "Lawson, are you seriously suggesting . . ."

Lawson's face lit up. "I think it's the perfect solution, don't you, Reggie?"

"You want us to adopt Namon's child?" Reginell asked, seeking clarification.

"Even if you didn't want to commit to a full adoption, you could just raise the baby until Namon and Shari finish school," proposed Lawson.

Reginell and Mark exchanged puzzled glances.

Reginell shook her head. "Nah, I don't think so."

Lawson gave her sister a stern look. "Why not, Reggie? This could be the solution to everyone's problem."

"Yeah, temporarily, but what happens in four years, after I've grown attached to that baby and love him or her like my own, only to have Namon and Shari come snatch him or her out of my arms?" Reginell shook her head. "I won't set myself up for that kind of heartbreak."

"Well, then adopt the baby outright." Lawson looked to Mark for encouragement.

Mark sided with his wife. "Lawson, Reggie's right. Why would you even assume they want to give their child up? Has Namon said anything to you to make you think that?"

"Do you really think our teenage son wants to be saddled with a child? He may not admit it, but you know he doesn't."

"That may be true, but I still think trying to adopt my grandchild is a bad idea," admitted Mark.

"You haven't even thought about it. Better yet, you haven't even prayed on it. How do you know this wasn't God's will all along?" said Lawson.

"I think it's more Lawson's will than God's!" concluded Mark. "You keep trying to find ways to keep this from happening, but Shari's pregnant, and they are having this child. You've got to find a way to deal with it, like you found a way to deal with Garrett's son."

"I have accepted it. I honestly don't know why you can't at least consider raising this baby as your own."

"Why can't you?" Mark fired back.

Reginell intervened. "Lawson, your best friend just lost her baby. It doesn't seem right that we should be talking about snatching another baby from his or her mother's arms."

"How is Sullivan, by the way?" asked Mark. "I was sad to hear about Christian. Sullivan is crazy, but I know she's also crazy about her kids."

"She's still in the hospital. She's supposed to be going home the day after tomorrow. Physically, she's in a much better place. Emotionally, she's falling apart," Lawson divulged.

Reginell sympathized with Sullivan. "I can't imagine how awful it must be to bury your kid. Are they doing any kind of funeral for the baby?"

"It'll be a quiet, small graveside memorial. But you just had surgery, Reggie. I'm sure she'll understand if you don't come."

"No, I'll be there. Sully and I have our differences, but at the end of the day, she's fam. Plus, my doctor cleared me to resume normal activities as long as I don't overdo it."

"I'll make sure she takes it easy," Mark assured Lawson.

Reginell pointed at Mark. "You see why I love this guy so much? He's always taking good care of his wife."

"While we're on the subject of you being his wife, why all the secrecy with the wedding?" blurted out Lawson. "I mean, we haven't really talked about it. I kind of felt like I had a right to know up front."

Reginell and Mark were both caught off guard by the question, but Reginell was more irked than thrown by it. "Why would we need to tell you anything up front?"

Lawson was exasperated. "Mark and I share a child, Reggie."

"No, you and Mark share a young adult who's in college. At this point, what Mark does in his personal life doesn't really affect Namon, which, in turn, means it doesn't really affect you."

"Okay, I'm going to let the two of you hash this out while I go check on Reggie's dinner," said Mark, all too happy to escape the sparring sisters.

Lawson advanced her tirade. "Don't you think you should've told me about the wedding as a courtesy? I'm the mother of Mark's son, but I'm also your sister."

Reginell tilted her head a little. "Why do you keep trying to insinuate that we *owe* you some kind of explanation or justification for our actions? What Mark and I do is our business, just like what you and Garrett do is yours."

"All I'm saying is that I'd like to be kept in the loop."

"And all I'm saying is that Mark has a wife now, and you need to respect that."

"We are all a part of each other's lives, and *you* need to respect that, Reggie."

"I do, but you've got to learn some boundaries. All this being possessive over Mark and wanting people to keep you looped in and laughing it up with my husband—that's got to stop."

Lawson copped an attitude. "Oh, so Mark and I can't be friends now?"

"I don't tell my husband who he can and can't be friends with. More to the point, we're family, and you and Mark work together. What do I look like saying he can't talk to you and you're his baby mama? But don't overstep, Lawson. Stay in your lane and respect the boundaries. You're my sister and I love you, but don't push me."

"Or what?" challenged Lawson.

"Or I can be real quick to forget I love you and forget we're sisters, and can treat you like I would any other chick in the streets."

"Seriously, Reggie? You're stooping to gutter tactics now?"

"Like I said"—Reginell gave Lawson the once-over—"don't push me!"

# Chapter 18

"I knew I couldn't have stayed with him, but that didn't
make it any easier to let him go."

*–Kina Battle*

Kina watched stealthily from the breakfast nook as
Elvin and her fifteen-year-old son, Kenny, bonded over
a football game on television. It was the third time Elvin
had come over since his initial visit a little more than a
week ago. To her astonishment, he seemed to be genuinely interested in getting to know his grandson.

Kina checked the time. "All right, Kenny. It's after nine
o'clock, and I still haven't seen you crack open that math
book since your granddad got here."

Kenny kept his eyes glued to the television as he spoke.
"Granddad has only a short time to be with us. Math will
be here forever."

Elvin's arms shot up in the air. "Touchdown!" He and
Kenny slapped hands.

Kina moved in front of the television, blocking their
view of the game. "Elvin, did Kenny tell you he's barely
hanging on in math? He has a low C. He needs to study."

"Aw, Ma, I can do that later," claimed Kenny. "We're
looking at the game."

Elvin grabbed the remote control and turned off the
television. "Your mama is right. Them boys that we're
looking at on the TV have their millions, and you don't

even have your thousands! And you won't get your thousands or millions if you don't graduate and get into a good college, and you can't graduate or go to college if you don't pass math."

Kenny sulked. "So are you going to take her side on everything?"

Elvin released a hearty laugh. "No, only when she's right."

"And that's nine times outta ten!" Kina shooed Kenny away. "Now, go get on in your room and study. I'll be back there to check on you in a minute."

Kenny addressed his grandfather before peeling himself off the couch. "Are you still gon' be here when I finish studying?"

Elvin nodded. "If your mama don't kick me out first!"

Kenny left, and Kina took his spot on the couch next to Elvin. "You seem to have made quite an impression on my son!"

"Well, he's made quite an impression on me. He's a good kid."

"Yeah, he goofs off sometimes, but he's sharp and skilled with his hands, just like E'Bell." She paused. "Hopefully, his hands won't be used to abuse people, like E'Bell's were."

Elvin groaned.

"I know you don't like to talk about that, but it's the truth. E'Bell was abusive."

"I believe you," conceded Elvin. "Kenny told me how my son would get drunk and terrorize everybody in the house. He also told me what really happened the night E'Bell was killed. I think in my heart, I always knew it was true, even though I'd hoped I had raised him better than that."

"E'Bell was a grown man who was responsible for his own actions. It had nothing to do with you. I actually think you're a pretty good influence—at least so far. I like seeing you with Kenny," confessed Kina, smiling. "It's good for him to have a man around."

"Maybe it's good not just for Kenny."

"What do you mean?"

There was a twinkle in Elvin's eye. "Maybe having a man around is good for you too."

Kina shifted in her seat. "I don't need a man around. I have plenty to keep me busy right here. Men are an unneeded distraction."

"So you don't miss having a husband?"

"Jesus is my husband."

Elvin laughed. "You single women kill me with that. Jesus is not your husband."

"Well, he's the most important man in my life!" attested Kina.

"I guess that's fair enough. I reckon he should be, but don't say he's your husband. God created man for that."

Kina nodded. "For some, yes."

"But not you?"

"I haven't had much luck in the relationship department. I'm starting to think marriage and a man may not be in the cards for me, but I'm okay with that. I have Kenny and my friends. I've got my church and my career. It's a pretty full life. Honestly, I don't have time for a man."

"Do you mean that for real?"

She tensed up. "I want to."

"Kina, there's nothing wrong with wanting someone special in your life. It doesn't make you less of a Christian. Shoot, I'll tell anybody I'm looking for a wife."

"But Brenda died just a year ago."

"Brenda didn't die just a *year* ago. She's been dead for a year. There's a difference."

"Don't you miss her?"

"Yes . . . every day. But she's gone, and I'm still here. Life goes on. My wife would want me to go on."

"What about the grieving process? Are you going to merely skip over that?"

"Kina, her death wasn't sudden and unexpected like E'Bell's. Brenda was sick for three years. I took care of her and grieved that whole time. I was by her side when she took her final breath. I had time to make my peace with her dying, and so did she. There was nothing left unsaid, nothing more either of us needed to do. When she closed her eyes for the last time, we both had closure."

"You're lucky. It wasn't like that with E'Bell and me," said Kina, recalling the past. "I was so angry with him—angry and sad and in love and hurt and scared all at the same time. I knew I couldn't have stayed with him, but that didn't make it any easier to let him go. E'Bell's death was very hard on me. It was hard on Kenny too. He was in therapy for a couple of years after it happened."

Elvin appeared to be genuinely remorseful. "I'm sorry we weren't there for the two of you, like we should've been, but with Brenda getting sick and all the confusion over how our son died, it was easier to stay away. I see now that it was wrong to do that."

"Thank you. I admit I could've done a better job keeping you in contact with Kenny."

"When you know better, you do better," recited Elvin. "I hope you let me stay a part of his life . . . and yours."

Kina felt flushed and smiled. "I guess we're kind of like a packaged deal. You get one, you automatically get the other one."

"You got a pretty smile, you know that?" observed Elvin. "You ought to smile more."

"I need more to smile about first!"

"I can help you with that!" proclaimed Elvin. "Friday night. The fair is in town this week. I say we go and have ourselves a good time. I guarantee I'll have you smiling all night long."

Kina clasped her hands together. "That sounds wonderful! Kenny loves the fair."

Elvin paused before continuing. "Kenny ain't the one who has trouble smiling. Now, I'll take him to the fair, but that'll be a different night."

Kina blinked back, now realizing that he was asking her out on a date. "So it . . . it would be just me and you?" she stammered.

"Yeah. Why not? You don't mind being seen with a man old enough to be your daddy, do you?"

She reddened. "No."

"Then it's a date. I'll pick you up around seven and have you smiling till midnight. How does that sound?"

It sounded heavenly, but Kina couldn't conceive spending the night on the town with her estranged father-in-law. His spending time with Kenny was one thing. Planning dates with her was a different matter.

Then again, life was short and unpredictable. Kina thought of Christian and Sullivan and how tomorrow was promised to no one.

Kina smiled and uttered three words she hadn't said in a while. "It's a date!"

# Chapter 19

"I don't need you to be my pastor right now! I want you to be my husband."

*–Sullivan Webb*

Lawson, Reginell, Angel, and Kina watched with concern as Sullivan moped around her formal dining room in her nightgown, her hair disheveled, clutching a glass of wine, the day following Christian's graveside memorial and her release from the hospital.

"Sullivan, you have to eat something," insisted Angel. "This isn't healthy."

Sullivan didn't heed the warning. She opened the wine cabinet and snatched down a bottle of Riesling. "How many times do I have to tell you people that I'm not hungry?"

"I see you've been quite thirsty," Lawson noted. "That bottle is almost empty."

Sullivan fumed. "What do you want me to say, Lawson, huh? I just buried my child. It should be understandable that I'd be a little sad and want to numb the pain."

Angel draped her arm around Sullivan. "We know you're having a rough time, but you don't want to go down this road again, Sully. Your drinking didn't solve anything before. It just made everything worse. Look at what abusing painkillers cost me. It's not worth it."

Sullivan clenched her teeth and released a deep sigh. "I'm not you, and this isn't like before. I'm in control now."

Lawson looked down into the empty glass. "Are you really?"

Sullivan cut her eyes toward Lawson and refilled her glass.

"Sullivan, maybe this was for the best, you know?" suggested Angel. "Chances are that Christian would've had a lot of lifelong complications and developmental delays."

Sullivan slammed the glass down on the dining room table. "Do you think I would've hesitated to spend every day of my life taking care of him? It would've been my honor to do that. He's my child, my miracle baby."

Angel attempted to calm her. "I know you wouldn't have, but perhaps God didn't—"

Sullivan cut her off. "Angel, don't tell me about God right now. I swear, I don't want to hear one more thing about God and how this is His will or how we shouldn't question Him. I can't hear that right now."

Lawson interceded. "The Bible says, 'Come to Me, all who are weary and heavy-laden, and I will give you rest.' God is here to comfort you, Sully, if you let Him."

"Yeah?" Sullivan lifted up her wine bottle. "Well, so is this!"

"Sullivan, I know it's difficult, but drinking isn't the solution. Your son is gone, but you still have a daughter and a husband who need you," Kina said, lecturing her.

"How is Charles holding up?" asked Reginell.

Sullivan shrugged. "Okay, I guess."

Lawson was dismayed. "You guess? What do you mean? Haven't you asked him how he's coping with losing his son?"

"You know Charles, Lawson." Sullivan rolled her eyes. "He lets the Lord handle everything."

"Yeah, but I'm sure he needs his wife too. Sullivan, you're not the only one who lost a child here. Your husband needs the same love and support that you do," cautioned Lawson.

Sullivan disagreed. "Charles doesn't need me."

"How can you say that? He adores you!" insisted Reginell.

"Really? So it was *adoration* that told him to ignore my wishes and kill my baby?"

"Sully, you know that's not fair! You can't blame Charles for what happened," said Angel.

"Why not?" Sullivan fired back. "Charles was the one who insisted I drive across town to meet him, despite the fact that I told him I wasn't feeling up to it."

"He was trying to surprise you!" exclaimed Kina.

"Charles also knows I hate surprises. He made the decision to have the doctors take the baby, even though he knew keeping him in the womb even a few days longer could mean the difference between life and death."

"Yes, it could, for Christian and for *you!* You can't seriously fault the man for loving you so much that he refused to risk your life, even to the point of risking his own son's life to save yours. You should be thanking him for loving you that much," maintained Lawson.

"I don't need you telling me how to treat my husband, and I don't need any of you to tell me how I should grieve the loss of my child. I lost that baby, not you! I carried that child. I painted his nursery. I picked out baby names. I felt him kick. I sang to him. I had dreams for him and for our family, and I was the one who lost him. All those dreams and that nursery and that life I was planning were shot to hell in an instant by my own husband making a split-second decision, so don't you dare stand there and tell me how I should feel, how I should grieve, or what I should do!" Sullivan emptied the bottle of wine into her glass and tossed it back.

Angel shook her head. "It breaks my heart to see you in so much pain."

Sullivan released a deep sigh. "Angel, you can't begin to imagine what kind of pain I'm in and what this feels like." She looked up, fighting back tears. "You'd think I'd be used to losing people by now. My father walked out on me, not once, but twice. Seven months after I found my grandmother, I lost her to a heart attack. For all practical purposes, I lost my mother when my baby sister died. My God, when is enough *enough?*"

Angel, Lawson, and Kina rallied around Sullivan in a group hug.

"Sully, you're going to get through this," Angel promised her. "And you don't have to do it alone."

Lawson began praying. "Lord, we come standing in intercession for our sister Sullivan. Lord, only you know the depths of her pain and how heavily it weighs on her heart, but we know that you strengthen us and uphold us with your righteous hand, because your Word says so. We know that we can cast our cares unto you, because you care so deeply for us.

"Lord, be a comforter to Sullivan, Charles, and Charity right now, during their hour of need. Let them be revived by your Word. Help them to remember that Christian's body is gone, but his spirit will live forever and they will see him again. Remind them that the sufferings of this present time are not worthy to be compared with the glory that is to be revealed to us when we get to heaven.

"We thank you for being our refuge in a time of sorrow. We thank you for Christian and for the joy he brought to the people who loved him. We thank you for your wisdom in all things, including the things that we don't understand. We honor and praise you forever. Amen."

The circle broke up. Angel hovered over Sullivan. "Do you feel better now?"

"I appreciate everything you all are trying to do for me, really." Sullivan paused. "But nothing is going to fill this void in my heart, nothing except having my son back, and that's never going to happen."

"No, but you will be happy again," reasserted Angel. "Who's to say God won't bless you and Charles with another baby?"

Sullivan shook her head. "I don't think that's in the cards for us. Christian was more of a miracle baby than Charity was. At least she was conceived naturally. We had to resort to in vitro for Christian. I don't think either one of us wants to go through that again."

Reginell scooped up her purse. "Maybe we should get out of here and leave Sullivan to deal with this in her own way. Besides, I'm not feeling so good."

"Are you in pain again?" asked Kina. "The medication still isn't helping?"

Reginell shook her head. "Not really."

"Reggie, you really need to go get that checked out," Angel advised her.

"I have a doctor's appointment tomorrow. Mark insisted on it."

"Good!" replied Lawson. "I'm glad somebody has been able to get through that thick skull of yours."

"Are you going to be okay here by yourself?" Kina asked Sullivan.

"I told you I'm fine. Time alone to think and to process everything is exactly what I need right now."

Lawson slid into her jacket. "I think being alone is the *last* thing you need, but I know when I'm not wanted, so . . ."

Angel hugged and kissed Sullivan on the cheek. "You call me if you need anything, all right? I don't care what time. If you need to talk or cry or you want someone to come sit with you, you call me, you hear?"

Sullivan smiled weakly and nodded.

Kina squeezed Sullivan's hand. "The same goes for me, Sully. Let me know if I can do anything."

"Actually, you can, Kina. Do you have Desdemona's number? She gave it to me at the hospital, and I must've put it down somewhere. I'd like to give her a call."

"Sure." Kina reached into her purse for a pen and paper and scribbled Desdemona's contact information for Sullivan.

"Thanks." Sullivan tucked the number down into her pocket. "Now, if you ladies will excuse me, I think I'm going to lie down for a few minutes and try to get some rest."

"You take care of yourself, Sullivan," said Lawson. "Take care of Charles and Charity too."

"Did I hear my name?" asked Charles, entering the room with Charity in his arms.

Angel hugged him. "How are you holding up?"

"Blessed be the God and Father of our Lord Jesus Christ, the Father of mercies and God of all comfort, who comforts us in all our affliction, so that we may be able to comfort those who are in any affliction, with the comfort with which we ourselves are comforted by God," said Charles, reciting scripture.

"Amen to that," said Kina.

Sullivan rolled her eyes and lifted Charity out of her father's arms. "I'll take her. I want to spend a little time with my favorite girl before she goes down for her nap."

"And that's our cue," noted Lawson. "We're going to get out of here. Please know that we're praying for all of you, and you can call day or night if you need anything."

The ladies filed out, leaving Sullivan alone with Charles.

"That was nice of them to stop by," said Charles. "I'm sure having them here put a smile back on that beautiful face."

"Why would it?" Sullivan snapped. "Do you think having a few girlfriends over would erase the fact that I just buried my child?"

"No. I was hoping that it would take your mind off of it for a little while."

"Well, it didn't, okay? Nothing will."

Charles spied Sullivan's empty wine bottle. "Except that, maybe?"

Sullivan held her daughter close to her chest. "It's how I cope with things, all right? You deal with things your way, and I'll deal with them my way."

"*Our* way should be the Lord's way, Sulllivan. No good can come of you drinking again."

"Can some good come of me losing my son?"

"Yes, if you let it, if you open your heart to see what the Lord wants us to learn from this or how our loss could help somebody else going through this same struggle."

"Can you stop for five minutes?" shrieked Sullivan.

Charles was confused. "Stop what?"

"Being on the pulpit and talking to me like you're Pastor Webb! Charles, I don't need you to be my pastor right now! I want you to be my husband. I want you to understand what I, your wife, am going through."

"That's what I'm trying to do, sweetheart."

"No, Charles, you want me to pretend for you! You want me to act like all I have to do is throw up a few prayers, shed a few tears at a graveside funeral, have a few laughs with the girls, and everything will be all right. Well, Pastor, everything is not all right!" Sullivan thought before going on. "And I can't tell you when it will be or if it ever will."

# Chapter 20

"Take it from me—what a man says he's going
to do and what a man actually does can be two
vastly different things."

*—Lawson Kerry Banks*

Lawson impatiently stared out her kitchen window the week after Christian's memorial. She'd summoned Namon's pregnant girlfriend to her house following Shari's first prenatal doctor's appointment. Lawson's heart palpitated when she saw Shari's rickety Corolla sputter onto the driveway. Lawson had determined that this would be the day she'd put an end to the madness surrounding Shari's pregnancy. Since Namon was still on campus, taking midterms, she knew that this might be her only opportunity to isolate Shari long enough to drive the plan into action.

Lawson swung open her front door when Shari emerged from the Corolla. "Shari, thank you so much for coming." She invited Shari inside. "Did you tell Namon you were coming by?"

"No, you told me not to."

"I appreciate you honoring that. I just thought we needed some time to talk and get to know each other better without the men around."

Shari appeared apprehensive. "I guess so."

"Please sit down." Lawson offered her a seat next to her on the sofa in the living room. "How did the doctor's visit go?"

"It was all right."

"Did your mom go with you?"

Shari nodded.

"What did the doctor say?"

"She told me I was almost three months along. I'm due in June. Everything seemed okay with the baby. I had to get a lot of blood tests, though, which kinda sucked, because I hate needles."

"Honey, that's nothing! You're gonna be poked and prodded so much between now and June that you're gonna think you've turned into a pincushion! But even that's a cakewalk compared to labor. I was in labor with Namon for eighteen long, excruciating hours."

Shari was a little shaken. "It wasn't that bad, was it?"

"It was bad enough for me to stop at one child!" Lawson poured Shari a cup of tea. "I made us some chamomile tea. It's supposed to be soothing and help relieve the nausea from morning sickness."

"Sounds like exactly what I need!"

"Have you been battling morning sickness?"

"I've been throwing up a lot, but Dr. Brennen said that's normal."

Lawson nodded. "The first trimester can be rough. Actually, all three can be rough, between the backaches and fatigue and false labor pains. Morning sickness is the absolute worst! I don't even know why people call it morning sickness, because it can occur all day long."

Shari's countenance changed. "For real?"

"Yes, my pregnancy was almost as hard as the labor! Don't believe that crap about not remembering the pain after the baby gets here. I remember every twinge and contraction. Even at sixteen, I never wanted to go through that again!" Lawson saw fear register in Shari's eyes. "I'm not trying to scare you. Every pregnancy and labor is different."

"I'm worried if I keep getting sick, I'm not gonna gain enough weight for a healthy baby."

"I wouldn't worry too much about that. If you keep eating and taking your vitamins, I'm sure you'll fatten up in no time." Lawson paused, looking Shari over. "Then again, you're such a petite thing. Carrying all that extra weight might be rough on your little body. Getting off that weight after the baby is born might be a challenge too. But you're a pretty girl, so people probably won't even notice if you're a little overweight for a while after the baby is born."

Shari gulped and blinked. "You mean the weight doesn't come off as soon as you have the baby?"

"Honey, please! I'm still trying to lose my baby weight from having Namon! But enough about that. How are *you* doing, Shari? I imagine it's hard to focus on school with everything you have going on."

"Sometimes," admitted Shari. "I try not to let it get to me, though."

"I'm sure you do, but it can't be easy seeing everyone around you living carefree lives and having fun being regular college students. It's only going to get more complicated once the baby gets here. It's hard to study or hang out or find any free time when there's a newborn in the house."

"I know, but Namon has promised that he'll be here to help."

"Men promise lots of things, sweetie. I love my son, and I think the world of him, but Namon is eighteen years old. His mind is going in a million directions right now. I know he says he'll be there for you and the baby, but I can't promise you that he's going to live up to his end one hundred percent."

"Namon said that he loves me and our baby and that he'll always have our backs, no matter what."

Lawson nodded. "I'm sure he meant every word of it . . . while he was saying it. Take it from me—what a man says he's going to do and what a man actually does can be two vastly different things."

"Namon has never lied to me—"

"That you know of," Lawson interjected before taking a sip of tea.

"If he says he's going to be there for me and our baby, I believe that he'll keep his word."

"And if he doesn't, then what? Are you prepared to be in this alone? What if the two of you break up and he starts dating someone else? Are you ready to deal with his new girlfriend? As someone who has to deal with that very issue with my stepson, Simon, I can tell you from experience that it's not easy."

"Mrs. Banks, Namon and I love each other. We want to be together for the rest of our lives. We're not thinking about dating other people."

"Of course you aren't right now, but what about a year or five years or ten years from now? I know at your age, being a couple for six or seven months seems like a long time, but it's really not. It's also hard to know what real love is at eighteen."

"It's real," asserted Shari. "I know it. I can feel it."

"I understand. I've been there. I thought it was love at first sight when I met Mark, but I was wrong. The man for me was Garrett, not Mark." Lawson reached for Shari's hand. "The fact of the matter is that you and Namon both will meet other people. One day, one of those people will turn out to be the mate whom God has created for you."

"How do you know Namon isn't my soul mate?"

"How do you know that he is?"

The question silenced Shari for a moment. "If I had to raise this baby by myself, I think I could do it. My mom raised us."

"Think about it, Shari. Was your mother really the kind of mother you needed, one you could model yourself after?" Shari shook her head. "I've been a single parent. It's no picnic. It's long nights and not having any money, never having enough rest or time to yourself. It's making sacrifices every day and not having your own life. Are you ready for that?"

"People always say what a blessing having a child is."

"It is a blessing when two people love each other and are committed in marriage, the way God intended, but His plan was never for the woman to have to struggle alone to raise a child. Do you really think being an eighteen-year-old single parent in college is really what God wants for your life? Do you honestly think this pregnancy was a part of His plan and purpose for you?"

Shari looked confused.

Lawson pulled back, wondering if she was being too harsh. "Look, I'm not saying that your baby is a mistake. He or she may turn out to be a tremendous blessing. I can't imagine not having Namon in my life, but at the same time, it breaks my heart that he's had to suffer for my bad decisions. I wasn't able to give him the life he deserved because I was broke. We struggled for a very long time. I had to put my dreams of going to college on hold so I could raise him. It was tough for a lot of years."

"But it's okay now, right?"

"It's better, but it's not okay. There's still a lot of tension between Mark and Garrett where Namon is concerned. That'll probably never be fully resolved, and Namon is caught in the middle."

"Yeah, he's told me that he feels torn sometimes. He doesn't want to hurt Garrett or make him feel like he doesn't appreciate him, but he also wants to have a relationship with his biological father because they missed out on so much time together."

"That's true. Namon was a teenager when he met Mark. Mark carries around a lot of guilt because he wasn't there for his son. He probably always will. So you see, there hasn't been an easy way out for any of us. It all could've been avoided if I'd waited to have children."

"But then you wouldn't have Namon."

"I think I would've still had a child when the time was right, and I would've much rather done it when I was emotionally prepared and financially able to give my child everything he needed. I hated watching him suffer and having to go without new shoes and other things that his classmates had. I was also ashamed that I had to rely on public assistance to take care of him. Nobody wants to be on welfare and have that stigma attached to them. That's certainly not what I wanted for my child or myself."

"But it's just a hand up to help you get on your feet, right?"

"Honey, it took me thirteen long years to get on my feet! That's a long time to have to struggle."

Shari exhaled. "I can't even imagine that far out."

"To be honest with you, I had it easier than a lot of other people. At least Namon was healthy. What if he had been a special needs child? That's a lifelong commitment. Have you thought about the possibility of this being a special needs child and what that would mean for your life?"

Shari shook her head.

"You know, a week ago I attended the funeral for my best friend's son. It was sad and tragic, but if there is a blessing to be found in that, it's that he is no longer suffering. He was born premature, and he probably would've had complications for the rest of his life. His parents would've had to spend the remainder of their lives taking care of him. Thankfully, if they had to, they have the resources and support to do that, but do you? Would you even begin to know how to take care of a child who's autistic or blind or has Down syndrome or any number of complications?"

"I hadn't even thought about that," admitted Shari. "I have a cousin with epilepsy. It's tough on her whole family. She can't drive or work a real job. She can't even live by herself because her seizures are so severe."

"It's a lot to consider. You're virtually a kid yourself, Shari. This isn't the kind of thing you should have to be thinking about right now."

Shari exhaled. "It's all so confusing."

"I know it is. I was confused when I was pregnant too. I felt trapped and like I had no options. You have options, though, and you have me here to help you make the best choice for you and your baby."

"I appreciate that. Thank you."

"You know, Shari, I think that you're a fine young lady. You're smart, beautiful, and talented. You have your whole life ahead of you. Don't you want to know what it's like to travel and see the world? Be able to work anywhere or pick up and move whenever you get ready? You and Namon are teenagers. Yes, you care very deeply about one another now, but people change. The kind of guy you like at eighteen isn't the same kind of man you want at twenty-five. You don't want to tie yourself down to a permanent situation at this time in your life."

At this point, Shari's enthusiasm about her baby had deflated, and she was more confused than she had been since failing her pregnancy test. "I don't know what the best thing to do is."

Lawson looked her in the eyes. "Be honest with me, Shari. Do you really want a baby right now? Don't worry about the politically correct answer. Be honest with me and honest with yourself. Do you truly want this baby?"

"If I say no, what kind of person does that make me?"

"It makes you human! Honey, you're eighteen years old, a freshman in college, with no job, no money. Frankly, I'd be more concerned if you were happy about all of this."

"But this is my responsibility. I made the choice to have sex with Namon, and I have to live with that decision."

"So you deserve to be punished for the next twenty years because you had a lapse in judgment? That's not fair to you, it's not fair to Namon, and most of all, it's not fair to this baby, who will have to suffer because his parents took on a responsibility they couldn't handle. This isn't about punishing you for having sex, Shari. That's a done deal, and there's nothing you can do about that now. All you can do is learn something, rectify the situation, and move on."

"How do I do that?"

Lawson placed her hand on top of Shari's. "By listening to your heart and doing what's best for everyone involved."

"You think I should put the baby up for adoption?"

"That's an option, but if you carry this baby to term, do you really think you'd be able to give it up? You'd be so caught up in the emotions and guilt that you probably wouldn't be able to make any rational decisions. Let's suppose you were able to give up the child. Most black children who end up in foster care don't get adopted. They grow up being shuffled from place to place, often ending up in even worse situations. Is that what you want for your baby? Can you live with that?"

"No, but that leaves only abortion as an option."

Lawson nodded slowly. "I'd never tell you to have an abortion, but, yes, that is an option."

"I would be lying if I said I hadn't thought about it. I mean, it would be a solution to all my problems."

"Like I said, it's an option, but so is adoption and so is keeping the baby."

"Just tell me what you think I should do!" implored Shari.

"I can't make that decision for you. It wouldn't be fair, because I don't have to live with the consequences. You're going to be the one taking care of this child and up at two in the morning, feeding it, clothing it, putting your life and your aspirations on hold, not me. No one can make this choice for you, Shari, not even Namon. And you can't be worried about what other people have to say or what they're going to think, because it's your life, your decision, and your body."

"What about Namon? How would he feel if I aborted his baby?"

Lawson thought for a moment, framing her response carefully. "Namon is a kind, honorable young man, and he'd never come out and tell you to have an abortion. He loves you. His conscience wouldn't allow him to ask you to do that, but, sweetie, do you really think my son is ready for a child at this point in his life? Truth be told, I think he'd be relieved, even if he wouldn't admit it."

Shari wrinkled her brow. "Really?"

"Yes. Namon is so scared and confused. He wants to do right by you and the baby, but he's been given this wonderful opportunity to go to college at his dream school. He loves being on campus and learning so much. He knows how proud of him we all are. He was very proud of himself until all this happened. Now he feels like he's let everyone down, including himself."

"So I'd be doing him a favor if I had an abortion?" Shari wondered aloud.

"I don't know that I'd call it a favor, but I think you'd be taking a great deal of stress off of him and you'd be giving both of you a chance at a real future. This way, if things don't work out between the two of you, you can go your separate ways without any regrets. If you two wind up together, you'd know it's because you want to be together, not because you had a child and felt obligated to each other."

"I think I'd be scared to do it."

"It's a relatively quick and safe procedure. It takes about ten minutes, and they'll put you to sleep if you want them to."

"Oh, that's good, I guess."

"Shari, I'm not trying to trivialize it, because this is a huge decision, but it's not some big, scary procedure. However, it is more expensive the longer you wait, so I wouldn't take too long in deciding."

Shari shrugged her shoulders. "It doesn't matter. I don't have the money to pay for something like that."

Lawson placed a hand on Shari's shoulder. "Sweetie, if you don't have enough money to take care of this yourself, how are you going to have enough money to take care of a baby?"

Shari's lip began to quiver, and tears started streaming down her cheeks. "I don't think I can handle all this. I'm not ready to be a mama."

Lawson took Shari in her arms. "Don't cry. It'll be okay."

"No, it won't!" she sobbed. "I don't have any money. How am I going to take care of this child?"

"I can't answer that for you."

Shari pulled away from Lawson and composed herself. "I've seen enough episodes of *Teen Mom* to know how this'll turn out. Namon and me are not ready for this kind of responsibility. I don't know what we were thinking."

"You weren't thinking. That's the problem."

Shari took a deep breath. "I think I should do it . . . you know, have the abortion."

They were the words Lawson had been waiting to hear. "Are you sure?"

Shari nodded.

"If this is something you really want to do, I'll pay for it."

"But I can't pay you back."

"You can pay me back by staying in school and learning from this situation. That's all the payment I need," Lawson assured her.

"I don't know where to go or how I'm going to get there or anything."

"Don't you worry about anything. I'll take care of everything. I'll set your appointment, I'll stay with you during the procedure, and I'll pay for it. All I need for you to do is look me in the eyes and tell me you're one hundred percent positive that this is what you want to do." Lawson held her breath, waiting for Shari to respond.

Shari paused. "I want to do it. I want to have the abortion."

Lawson released a sigh of relief. "I think you made the right decision. I'm going to be there for you every step of the way, I promise."

"What am I going to tell my mom?"

"Sweetie, you're eighteen. Legally, you are an adult and don't have to tell your parents anything. In fact, I wouldn't say anything to anyone if I were you. You've made your decision, and you're comfortable with it. You don't need anyone trying to talk you out of it."

"What about Namon?"

"I don't think you should say anything to him either, not until after it's over."

"Why not? Namon would freak out if he knew I had an abortion and didn't tell him. I can't do that to him."

"I won't lie to you. I think initially Namon may be upset, but he'll get over it in time. Eventually, he'll see that you did this for him as much as you did it for yourself."

Shari's anxiety began to surface again. Her palms grew sweaty. "I don't know. . . ."

Lawson could sense that Shari was faltering, and she wasn't about to let that happen. "Shari, I know my son much better than you do. Once he's had time to think about it and process everything, he'll understand why you handled it this way. If you want, I'll talk to him after the surgery and help explain it in a way that he can clearly perceive. We can tell him together."

Shari relaxed again. "For the first time in weeks, I finally feel like things are going to be okay."

"They are. You should be proud of yourself. You've made a very grown-up choice today. I applaud you for weighing the pros and cons and coming to a decision that is best for everyone involved."

"Thank you for helping me."

"No, you came to this decision all on your own," insisted Lawson. "I let you know what your options were, but you came to this decision by yourself, right? You don't feel like I coerced you, do you?"

"No," Shari answered slowly. "It was my decision, I suppose."

"It was *all* your decision," stressed Lawson. "But that's good! It shows you're moving into adulthood. You're thinking like an adult and making good decisions for yourself. That's what being in college is all about." Lawson noticed the pained look on Shari's face. "I know it's scary, but you'll be fine. You have plenty of time to have babies, but next time it'll be on your own terms and when you're ready for it. There's nothing wrong with acknowledging that you're not ready to be a mother. God will forgive you. He's already forgiven you. Namon will forgive you, and so will your parents. Then we all can put this behind us."

Shari bit her lip. "I'm scared."

"Don't be. You're not the first woman this has happened to, and you won't be the last. You're going to come out of this wiser and stronger, you'll see."

"Thank you for being so kind to me, Mrs. Banks. I love my mom, but with everything going on with her, she can't really help me understand things the way you can. I hope one day I can be a great mother like you are." She reached out for Lawson.

As Lawson hugged Shari, guilt began gnawing at her. There was no denying that she'd completely manipulated Shari, but if Lawson had to end one child's life in order to save the life of her own child, so be it.

# Chapter 21

"We've been together too long to let one low-life hussy
destroy what we have."

*–Angel King*

The ladies all flocked to Lawson's house after being
summoned for a prayer vigil for Reginell, whose doctor
had recommended that she have a hysterectomy because
the endometriosis had spread to other parts of her body.

"I must say, you're handling this remarkably well,
Reggie," Angel praised her following their prayers. "I'm
proud of you."

"What's there to be proud of?" grumbled Reginell.
"The endometriosis has spread, and the pain meds aren't
working. The only option is for me to have a hysterectomy."

"Yeah, but that doesn't make you any less courageous
for going through with it," said Desdemona. "My cousin
had one a few years ago, and it was a very tough decision
for her to make. She thought it made her less of woman
or something."

"Doesn't it?" asked Reginell. "I won't be able to give my
husband any babies."

"The ability to bear children makes you a female, not
a woman," opined Lawson. "You have to look no further
than Shari to see that."

Reginell sulked. "It's not even just that. I've been reading up on it. Hysterectomies can cause depression, emotional distress, and mood swings."

"Reggie, trust me—a woman doesn't have to have her
uterus taken out for that to happen. My mood switches up
real quick if there's no chocolate around or if they run out
of my favorite dipping sauce at Chick-fil-A!" said Kina.

"I can handle that part, but there are a lot of sexual side
effects too. I read that it's not as good after a hysterectomy."

"That's not necessarily true," argued Angel. "Each
woman's body responds to the procedure differently."

Kina was curious. "What are the side effects?"

Reginell made a face. "Vaginal dryness, for one. Who
wants that?"

Desdemona nodded. "I didn't want to bring that part
up, but the hysterectomy totally changed my cousin's
sexual routine. She said it was never the same after that.
Her husband actually said that making love to her was
like walking through a cave! There was no feeling, no
muscle tightening. It was like she was hollowed out. He
said it was awful. Eventually, they both just gave up, and
he married someone else."

Reginell's eyes widened. "A cave? Mark can't deal with
something like that! My man likes it tight and right."

Lawson was indignant. "Why would you say that to her,
Des? She's scared enough as it is!""

"I think she should be prepared," replied Desdemona.
"My cousin wasn't. When dealing with something like
that, experience is *not* the best teacher."

"I agree. Reggie needs to know if her lush nether re-
gion is about to turn into a tumbleweed! A bad sex life
will cause a person to stray," admitted Sullivan. "I know
firsthand."

Lawson stomped her foot. "Will y'all stop trying to
scare her?"

Desdemona apologized. "I'm sorry. I shouldn't have brought it up. I'm sure your husband would never do that, Reggie."

Reginell nodded, still not wholly convinced.

Desdemona continued. "He loves you. Anyway, it's not as if there's anyone around here who could take his attention away from you, is there?"

No one said anything, all trying their best not to look at Lawson.

"No, Desdemona, there isn't!" confirmed Lawson, feeling the heat from Desdemona's question and her past with Mark. "And anyone who dared to mess up my sister's happiness would have to answer to me. Mark and Reggie will be fine, so don't start putting stuff in her head."

Desdemona looked over at Reginell. "As long as you know who you can and can't trust around your husband, there shouldn't be an issue. I'm sure your female intuition will kick in to discern any perceived threats. You'll know in your gut if another woman is after your husband."

"So what's going on with you, Angel?" asked Kina, eager to take the focus off of Reginell and Lawson. "You got kind of emotional while Lawson was praying. Is everything all right?"

Angel shook her head. "Things haven't been all right for a few weeks." Finally admitting it brought her to the brink of tears.

Sullivan rushed to Angel's side. "Girl, what's wrong with you?"

"Is this about Duke?" asked Lawson. "We didn't want to pry, but you never said anything about his arrest. Is that what's bothering you?"

Angel nodded. "I haven't wanted to talk about it. Things are a mess! I can barely hold it together."

"What happened?" asked Kina.

"Duke's assistant accused him of sexually assaulting her."

Reginell gasped. "Rape? Are you for real?"

"Technically, it's sexual assault," Angel informed her. "Attempted rape, to be exact."

Desdemona was still confused. "Is there a difference?"

"Yes, rape is forced intercourse," Angel expounded. "Assault doesn't have to include penetration."

"Oh, so I guess that makes it okay, then," grumbled Sullivan.

"It's definitely not okay for her to trump up false charges!" Angel exclaimed. "Her lies could cost Duke his freedom, his kids, his job—"

"His woman . . ." interjected Sullivan.

"I'm not going anywhere," proclaimed Angel. "Duke is innocent. All he did was maybe flirt with the girl a little bit. He acknowledged that much. However, flirting is not illegal."

"Then that would mean he's not guilty, but he's still far from innocent!" stated Sullivan.

"Humph, humph, humph!" Reginell shook her head. "You think you know a guy. . . ."

"We *do* know him, Reggie, and we all know Duke would never do anything like this." Angel looked to her friends for confirmation. "We all know that, right?"

Lawson reassured her. "Of course we do. Duke may be a lot of things, but he's not a rapist. Everybody knows that."

Sullivan cut her eyes to Lawson. "Do we?"

Kina winced. "Sully, don't. . . ."

"I'm just saying . . . why would the girl lie about something like that?"

"Because she's a vindictive, angry, soulless wench for one!" answered Angel. "Who knows? Maybe she wants money or is mad because Duke rejected her and so she wants payback. There could be any number of reasons."

"Maybe . . . ," said Sullivan. "But it takes a lot of guts to come forward with something like that, especially knowing that you'll be criticized, judged, and scrutinized by lawyers and police officers and that you'll have to face a judge and juror, not to mention your assailant."

"I can't believe you're taking this woman's side, Sullivan," said Lawson. "Duke is our friend, and he's a good Christian man and father."

"I'm not on anybody's side. I just think she deserves the benefit of the doubt."

"And Duke doesn't?" stormed Angel.

"Angel, I've been assaulted before. It's horrific," Sullivan revealed. "I just don't see a woman in her position lying about something so serious."

Angel was vexed. "So you think Duke is lying?"

Sullivan shook her head. "I don't know, but he did admit to flirting with the girl. Maybe things got out of hand."

"It's not improbable," stated Reginell. "Me and just about every chick at the club where I used to dance has had some guy take things too far. I know several dancers who've been raped. At the same time, I know a lot of chicks who've lied about guys too."

"Reggie, strippers can't claim sexual harassment. That's part of the job description!" said Lawson.

Sullivan frowned. "No woman signs on to be sexually assaulted. I don't care what the job is."

"Sully, Duke may be a flirt, but he'd never betray me," Angel declared.

"Are you serious? He left you for another woman, then cheated on her with you while she was dying, I might add!"

"He and I were never intimate while he was still married to Theresa!" insisted Angel.

"I just don't want you to have blinders on where Duke is concerned. You know I've liked Duke ever since we were in college, and I don't want to believe he'd hurt anyone like that, but you've got to be realistic. What if he did it, Angel? What will you do?" quizzed Sullivan.

"I can't. . . ." Angel shook her head. "I can't even consider that possibility."

"How can you not?" asked Desdemona.

"I can't believe that I've been planning a future with the kind of man who is capable of doing something like that. He has daughters, for God's sake! I know Duke. If anyone ever raped or assaulted them, he'd kill him, so I can't imagine that he'd do that to someone else's daughter. He couldn't have assaulted that woman. I know he couldn't!"

Sullivan hugged her. "I know you love him, and you want to believe in this man you've spent almost half your life being in love with. Unfortunately, sometimes people do things that we'd never expect them to do, things we had no inkling that they were even capable of. I've seen it in my own marriage. You can't put nothing past anybody."

"I feel a headache coming on. I think I need some fresh air. Excuse me." Angel slipped out the back door and took solace alone on Lawson's deck.

"Don't you think you were a little hard on Duke?" Lawson asked Sullivan.

"Absolutely not! I pray that Duke didn't hurt that girl, but if he did, I hope they throw the book at him. No woman deserves to have her innocence or dignity stripped away because some horndog can't accept that no means no!"

Desdemona went out on the deck unnoticed a few minutes after Angel took refuge there. She sighed, making her presence known. "It's sad."

"What is?"

"How sometimes the people closest to you don't want to see you happier than they are."

"Don't be confused. These are not happy tears," said Angel, wiping her eyes with the back of her hand.

Desdemona dotted Angel's eyes with a napkin. "I know. I'm sure it hurts to hear your friends say things like that about the man you love. I'm sure they aren't trying to be hurtful, but you and Duke probably have the kind of relationship they all wish they had. Even if they don't realize it, there may be some jealousy there, and subconsciously, they say cruel things about him because they don't want to see the two of you happy together."

"I don't think they're jealous, Des."

"I'd certainly hate to think so. I just find it strange that they aren't more supportive. Personally, I think it's commendable that you're standing by your man. That's what a woman is supposed to do," asserted Desdemona.

"Thank you."

"You're so lucky to have someone in your life whom you can trust. I haven't had the best luck with men, so I'm a little gun-shy. It would probably be a lot harder for me to have that kind of faith in my husband or boyfriend."

"Duke and I have been through a lot together. I know him better than anyone else does. I know he wouldn't do anything like that."

Desdemona nodded slowly. "I wonder why your friends aren't more understanding. They should have your back."

"They do. It's just . . . it's complicated. They've been here for the good and the bad. They know what kind of merry-go-round our relationship has been."

"I guess they're concerned because they know he's been unfaithful to you before. If he cheated when you were married to him, maybe they feel there's no telling what he'd do now that you're not. In my opinion, it takes a strong woman to be able to ignore the fact that he's stepped out on you and deserted you in the past. Not many women could get over that, but you have. You've accepted his children like your own, including the one who was conceived during your marriage. I admire that kind of strength."

"Believe me, I'm not strong at all. It's God's strength that keeps me sustained. You can do anything with God's help, even forgive."

"Indeed. I guess your friends don't see it that way. They look at Duke, and all they see is the lying and sneaking around, the selfishness, and all the hurt you endured because of him."

"Even though we're not married yet, we're very much one in our hearts. Duke, me, and the girls are a family. I know he's not perfect, and he's made his share of mistakes. We both have, but we have learned from our mistakes and have grown from them."

"That's awesome, Angel, really. I think it's sad that your closest friends have such a low opinion of the man you've chosen to spend your life with. I think it's admirable that you can look past all his mistakes and betrayals and see a man worth fighting for."

"I'm not perfect, either. He's overlooked my screw ups too."

"I'm sure he has. Listen, don't let this situation get you down. This is just a small roadblock on your way to happiness."

Angel smiled a little. "You're right. We've been together too long to let one low-life hussy destroy what we have."

Desdemona agreed. "You've talked to this other woman, right? You know she's a liar."

"Well, no. Obviously, I think she's a liar, but I haven't talked to her."

"So you're just blindly taking your boyfriend's word for what happened? I'm not saying there's anything wrong with that. I mean, sure he's lied about other things, but he wouldn't lie about something this important, would he? He certainly wouldn't be unfaithful to you, knowing how much you trust him."

"Of course not." As Angel responded, she couldn't help but think of all the times Duke had cheated and betrayed her trust.

"Then you have nothing to worry about. To tell you the truth, I wish I was more like you. I'm kind of like Sullivan in that regard. I don't put anything past anyone. I probably would've been on that woman's doorstep, trying to find out what happened, the minute I heard about the charges. Then again, I've been burned, so I'm a little more suspicious than you. As long as you believe him, that's all that really matters. And you do believe him, don't you?"

Desdemona's words started to take hold and plant seeds of doubt. Angel shivered and hugged her body. "It's getting kind of cold out here. I'm going back in," she said, unable to definitively answer Desdemona's question one way or the other.

# Chapter 22

"You're a pastor, but that doesn't give you the right to play God!"

*–Sullivan Webb*

"Thank you for coming over," said Sullivan, offering Desdemona a seat beneath the sun on the terrace outside her bedroom. "And you came bearing gifts!"

"Wine is always the perfect gift." Desdemona poured Sullivan a glass of wine and extended it to her. "When all else fails, it rarely disappoints. I'm glad I was able to come."

"You're the only one I felt like I could talk to." Sullivan took a sip from the glass. "They just don't understand me."

"Who? Your friends?"

She sighed. "My friends . . . my husband."

Desdemona poured a glass for herself. "Unfortunately, we're a part of a sorority no one ever hopes to be initiated into. Your friends don't know what it's like to lose a child, Sullivan. We do. We know the pain and the emptiness that come along with it. We know what it's like to rack your brain for hours, trying to figure out what went wrong or what could've been done differently. We've been to hell and back. They haven't."

Sullivan nodded in agreement and swallowed another mouthful. "They think I should just get over it and move on. They want me 'back to normal,' whatever that means. What they don't get is that *this* is it. *This* is my new normal. Nothing will ever go back to being the way it was before I lost Christian."

Desdemona refilled Sullivan's glass. "It's pretty quiet around here. Where's your husband and your little girl?"

"Charity is on a playdate with Lawson's stepson. She and Garrett took them to Gingerbread Village. Charles is over at the church, of course."

"And he left you here alone to grieve?" Desdemona shook her head. "Men can be so selfish sometimes, even the good ones."

"Charles isn't like that. In fact, he's probably the most selfless person I know."

"I'm sure he doesn't mean to be selfish, Sullivan, but you're his wife. You're falling apart, and you need him. He's the one who should be here comforting you, not me."

"No, you've got Charles all wrong. He's a wonderful husband to me and a doting father to Charity. Right now, he's just—"

"Busy?" queried Desdemona. "Preoccupied? Got a lot on his plate? Sasha's father and I have our differences, but he was there for me when our daughter died. I don't think I could've made it without him. He was my rock. If a no-account bastard like Ricky Harris knows how to be there for me, there's no justification for a man of God like Charles not to be there for you."

"It's not that simple, Desdemona."

"It *is* that simple, Sullivan. Don't make excuses for him just because you're married to the guy."

"You make him sound like a deadbeat, but nothing could be further from the truth. Charles is the best man I know. He's kind, considerate, loving. At this very moment, he's at the church, supporting the seniors at their annual holiday brunch."

"So the seniors at church take precedence over his family?" Desdemona asked in disbelief. "I'm sorry, Sullivan, but I can't pretend this is okay. Your husband's top priority should be you and your daughter."

"We are!" argued Sullivan.

"Just not today, right?" Before Sullivan could respond, Desdemona stopped herself. "You know what? I shouldn't have said anything. I was way out of line. I apologize."

Sullivan was quiet a moment. Her mood became pensive. "No, it's okay. You . . . you brought up a valid point."

"Look, Sullivan, I'm not trying to stir up trouble between you and your husband."

"You're not. In fact, I think you're right. Charles *should* be here. I guess I'm so used to him putting the church before me and our family that I've just accepted it."

"You shouldn't have to do that. He vowed to forsake all others for you, including the church."

Sullivan nodded. "You know, I've always felt like I was in competition with Mount Zion Ministries for Charles's time and attention. It's been an issue since the beginning of our relationship."

"If it means anything, I think you're handling it remarkably well."

"Actually, I've handled it quite terribly. A few years ago, I had an affair, and it nearly ruined our marriage. I fully accept my responsibility in all that, but I don't think it would've happened if I felt wanted and appreciated at home."

"That's how it usually is. Men cheat just because it's there and because they can. Women, however, stray because they're missing something at home."

"I was definitely missing something. In a lot of ways, I still am, I guess."

"Yeah, you're missing your husband, on top of having to face every parent's nightmare. You lost your son. I'm sure it doesn't help that your husband had a hand in that."

"No, it doesn't."

"Has he even acknowledged what he did? I mean, Christian might still be alive if he had chosen differently."

"He keeps rationalizing, saying that he did what he thought was best and that he wanted to save me, but how can he not know that I would've wanted to save my son instead?"

"It really makes you question how well your husband knows you. And for him to do that—to be the kind of person who'd endanger the life of his child—it's got to make you question how well you know him too."

Later that afternoon Charles found Sullivan in Christian's half-decorated Noah's Ark themed nursery, staring out the window.

"Some more flowers were just delivered," he told her. "They're from some of my family members up north."

"That's nice," she responded drily.

"Charity still with Lawson and Simon?"

Sullivan nodded. "They should be back around eight, but Lawson asked if Charity could sleep over. Apparently, the kids are having a blast."

"That's good. I'm glad she's having a good time. How about you and me doing the same? You know, it's been a while since I've taken my lovely wife out. How about we take one of those dinner cruises you like?"

Sullivan turned her nose up at the idea. "A dinner cruise in November?"

"Yes, if that dinner cruise is in Aruba!" He strode up behind his wife and wrapped his arms around her. "Why don't we get Charity first thing in the morning and take off for a few days to get away from this sadness for a while? I think a change of scenery would do us a world of good."

"Do you really think a day at the beach is gonna make me forget that my son died three weeks ago?"

"No, but it's important for us to remember that there's still plenty to be thankful for. Christian will always be in our hearts, but it's time to start the healing process."

"What you really mean is that it's time to move on, don't you?"

"I think it's time to honor our son's memory by embracing life, not focusing on death. We still have each other, and we still have Charity. We've got a good life, Sullivan. We can't lose sight of that. I think staying here, especially in this room, will only keep reminding you of what we lost."

"This room is all I have left of my child. Being in here makes me feel closer to him."

"But I don't think that's healthy. That's why . . ." Charles took a deep breath. "That's why I'm calling some people out to come and redo this whole room."

Sullivan whipped her head around to face him. "What?"

"Sweetheart, we can't leave this room set up for a baby who's never coming home. I was thinking of fixing it up as a studio for you so you can start back doing your artwork. I think it'll be good for you to start painting again."

"How many coats of paint do you think it'll take to cover up losing our child? Why are you so bound and determined to pretend like Christian never happened?" Sullivan shook her head. "This room is staying just like it is, Charles. Stop trying to erase our son."

"That's not what I'm doing. I don't want to erase him. I want to save *you*."

"You mean like you did after the accident? You're a pastor, but that doesn't give you the right to play God! You didn't have to let them take my baby. You could've saved him!"

"Then I would've lost you."

"*And?* I would've laid down my life for the life of my son. You know that!" Sullivan dropped her head. "Charles, there are only two things in my life that I'm good at—screwing up and being a mother. Giving life to those children gave me purpose. You didn't take just Christian. You took the only part of me that's worth something."

"Sullivan, God created you for a higher purpose than just popping out babies. There's a special call for your life. That's the gift that God gives to all of us. If you needed Christian in order to fulfill God's purpose for your life, God never would've allowed him to die."

"I guess we'll never know which one of us is right, will we? You made sure of that when you put your wishes ahead of Christian's needs."

"You keep blaming me for our son dying. Do you know how that makes me feel? I loved him too!"

"You didn't love him enough, Charles." Sullivan wiped her eyes. "Every time I look at you, I'm reminded of that. You didn't put him first. You never put your family first."

"I put God first, Sullivan, but you're a close second. Charity is right behind you. How can you question that?"

"How can you stand there and say you put us first when I have to compete with the church for the least bit of attention from you? Yeah, you may want to believe that you prioritize us, but that church is your wife, Charles, not me. Frankly, I don't know how much longer I can stay in this kind of marriage."

"Everything I've ever done has been for you! All I've asked for in return is your love and respect. I don't always get it, but that's all I've ever asked for you."

Charles fell silent. No words passed between them for several minutes. At long last, Charles said, "I can't make you stay, Sullivan."

"What?"

"Maybe you're right. Sweetheart . . . I'm tired. I love you. Sometimes, I believe I love you more than I love myself, but there's only so much I can do to make you love me enough to stay in this with me and fight for our marriage and our family. I haven't thrown your mistakes in your face, and I never will. We've all fallen short. However, your actions speak volumes, Sullivan, and they don't always communicate that you're as vested in this relationship as I am. And, quite honestly, I need a wife who's going to fight as hard for me as I'm going to fight for her. I can't be in this by myself. I don't want you to leave. God knows I don't! But this time, I won't stop you."

Defeated and exhausted by Sullivan, Charles made his way to the door.

Sullivan stopped him. "Charles . . ." She reached out for Charles's hand but let it fall by his side. She had no idea what she was going to say. His words were jarring. Never had Charles been willing to walk away from their marriage without a fight, not even after her affair with Vaughn went viral or when Charity's paternity was in question. This time, with Christian's death and Sullivan's verbal attacks, perhaps he'd had enough. She wondered if they both had.

Charles said one last thing to her before leaving. "I'm having the room done over next week, Sullivan. If you don't like it, you don't have to stay."

# Chapter 23

"I think we have two very different definitions of what
constitutes fun."

–*Kina Battle*

"There it is! Isn't she a beauty?" asked Elvin in awe.

Kina's frightened eyes zoomed upward to the top of the
Spin Cycle, a ninety-foot roller coaster that zipped into
the air, spinning the riders through multiple loops before
descending back to earth. "And you want me to get on
that thing?" she asked incredulously.

"Heck, yeah! I've been waiting to hop on that train
since we got here!"

Kina backed away from him. "How about I just stand
here and watch? I'll keep my feet on the ground and of-
fer moral support. I sort of have this thing about staying
alive."

Elvin chuckled. "Kina Anne, you ain't even lived till
you've ridden on one of these babies! Come on!"

Kina protested nonstop as Elvin dragged her to the
front of the line. Elvin had stayed true to his promise to
take her to the fair and had kept a smile on Kina's face
while they trekked through the fairgrounds, tossing rings
on bottles and shooting at balloons, trying to win one of
the pelicans that Kina had coveted since she was a child.
Kina had even allowed herself to be subjected to the hu-
miliation of the "Guess My Weight" game for the chance

to win one, but there wasn't a stuffed pelican in the world big enough to make her happy about going through the Spin Cycle.

"Don't worry. It'll be fun," promised Elvin as Kina was strapped in.

"I think we have two very different definitions of what constitutes fun," said Kina, her heart pounding as the engine on the ride revved up. The roller coaster then zipped through the air, tossing them across the seat.

"Help me, Jesus!" cried Kina, digging her nails into Elvin's arm.

Elvin released a hearty laugh. "Open your eyes, Kina! I got you."

Kina shook her head, keeping her lids tightly shut. "I don't want you! I want Jesus!" After another minute of stomach flipping and heart dropping, the ordeal finally came to a halt.

Elvin peeled Kina's fingers off of him. "All right, it's over. You can breathe now."

"Oh, God! Oh, God!" panted Kina, clutching her pounding heart as Elvin helped her off the ride.

"Here. Grab my hand." He lifted her out of the seat. "You know I wasn't going to let anything happen to you, right?"

Kina exhaled, thrilled to be back on solid ground. "I did feel rather safe . . ." She stopped herself from adding, "In your arms."

"Taking care of you and Kenny is my pleasure. You're my family."

"Thank you."

"You want something to eat?" asked Elvin as they passed a food stand.

"I'd love a candy apple, but I'm afraid it'll turn into tossed cookies if I eat it right now."

Elvin laughed. "One day you're going to look back on this day and thank me."

"That day will be a day a long time from now!"

"Sometimes, you've got to step out of that comfort zone and try something new. You might be surprised by what you find." He elbowed her. "Admit it. You know you liked riding on that thing."

"Okay, it wasn't *terrible*," conceded Kina, sitting down on a nearby bench. "The important thing is that I survived."

He sat down too. "I think you've proven to everybody what a survivor you really are. I admire you, Kina. You won that weight-loss competition and weren't afraid to compete in front of the whole world. You've been doing an outstanding job taking care of your son, and you survived E'Bell. I want to say again how sorry I am that we didn't believe you about being abused like that."

"It's okay. I should've spoken up sooner. If I had, maybe E'Bell could've gotten some help and would still be alive today. I'd give anything for my son not to have to carry the guilt of killing his father."

"He shouldn't feel bad about that. He was protecting his mother. Many people would consider him a hero."

"I'm one of them."

Elvin took Kina by the hand. "I want you to know that we didn't raise him to be that way. I never raised a hand to his mother, and I never would to any woman. Don't think he got that from me."

"I know he didn't. You're a kind, gentle man. I know you wouldn't hurt me. I mean, I—I know you wouldn't hurt any woman in a violent way," she stammered.

He caressed her hand. "I would never hurt you, either."

Kina cleared her throat and eased her hand away from him. "You know what? I think I'm ready for that candy apple."

Elvin sensed she was uncomfortable and patted her on the hand. "Coming right up."

Kina was relieved when he left. Her heart and mind were racing. She felt something she had no business feeling for her late husband's father.

"Snap out of it, Kina," she scolded herself out loud. "He's literally old enough to be your father! Heck, he's a grandfather and E'Bell's dad, and he's . . ." She sighed. "So sweet and sexy!"

Elvin came back with her candy apple. "I got the biggest one they had."

She happily received it and ripped the plastic covering off of it. "Thank you. Candy apples are the sole reason I even bother coming to the fair." She bit into it.

"Yeah, I'm a huge fan of them myself."

Kina extended it to him. "Have some."

"You're making it look so good over there, I think I will." Their fingers touched as Elvin leaned in to bite the apple. He stared at her intently. "It's better than I thought it would be."

They both bit into the apple at the same time, their lips almost brushing against each other.

"Sorry about that," Kina apologized quickly.

Elvin shook his head. "I'm not."

Then he pulled Kina in for a kiss. Instead of pushing him away, she found herself kissing him back.

It was better than any pelican and candy apple put together.

# Chapter 24

*"I'm asking you to tell me what happened . . .
woman to woman."*

*—Angel King*

"Are you sure you can't be persuaded to join us for dinner?" Duke asked Angel before heading out.

"Please come!" pleaded Duke's eight-year-old daughter, Miley. "We're getting La' Berry after dinner. It's your favorite!"

Angel pretended to ponder the request. "Hmm . . . as much as I love frozen yogurt, I have to pass, but I'll make a deal with you. If you let me off the hook today, we're go to La' Berry after school one day next week—all you can eat!"

Miley seemed satisfied. "Deal!"

"And what do I get?" asked Duke's preteen daughter, Morgan. "I'm not eating dairy this week."

Angel kissed her on the cheek. "You get to raid my make-up drawer!"

"Awesome!"

"All right, now that that's settled, we better go before you end up promising these ladies your kidneys," Duke joked and then gave Angel a quick peck on the lips. "Are you going to hang around here until we get back?"

"I don't know. I have a few errands to run, but I'll call you," replied Angel.

That wasn't entirely true. Angel had only one errand to run, and that was going to see Mya.

Against her better judgment, she'd broken into Duke's cell phone and confiscated Mya's phone number. She'd called, requesting to speak to her face-to-face. To Angel's surprise, Mya had agreed to meet with her at a local coffeehouse.

Angel's nerves were already on eggshells when she arrived at the coffeehouse. Seeing the biracial beauty approaching the table did little to calm them.

"Thank you for meeting me. I wasn't sure if you were going to show up," Angel said.

"I started not to." Mya sat down across from Angel. "I know why you asked me here, and you can save your breath. I'm not dropping the charges."

"I didn't come to ask you to do that, although you should know the kind of havoc your accusations have heaped on our lives. Duke can't eat. He can't sleep. The girls are worried sick about their father—"

"Oh, cry me a river!" snapped Mya, giving no credence to Angel's claims. "Do you think I've been sleeping soundly? I have nightmares, Angel, about what your boyfriend did to me! I was afraid for my life. He took more from me that night than you'll ever understand."

"That's why I'm here. I need you to help me understand. I need to know what happened."

"I'm not talking to you about that. You can hear all about it in court."

"I don't want to hear it with lawyers and the officers of the court involved. I'm asking you to tell me what happened . . . woman to woman. Mya, you can talk to me. Whatever you say will stay in this room. I promise you that."

Mya released a coarse laugh. "So you expect me to fall for this BFF bull? I may just be an administrative assistant, but give me some credit, all right? I'm not stupid enough to think that you're my friend or that I can trust you any further than I can throw you."

"I'm not here to dig up information for Duke's case. I'm here because I love him, but before I commit my life to this man again, I need to know what happened."

Mya smirked. "What's the matter? Don't you trust him? If he says I'm lying and I made the whole thing up, why don't you believe him?"

"I do believe him!" proclaimed Angel. "I trust Duke. You know what? Never mind . . . this was a mistake." She stood up. "I shouldn't have wasted your time or mine."

Mya exhaled. "Wait. . . . Sit down. I'll tell you what you want to know."

Angel slowly returned to her seat. "Are you going to tell me everything that happened that night?"

"I'm going to tell you what you need to know." She thought for a moment. "I will say this. Duke has been nothing but the consummate professional whenever we've been at the office. He's always treated me with the utmost respect, but the minute we got on the plane, he made it very clear that we were no longer on the clock."

"What do you mean?"

She tilted her head down. "What do you think I mean?"

Angel gulped. "Are you saying that Duke made a play for you?"

"He did more than that! Once we landed, he took me out for dinner and drinks. He told me that whatever happened in LA stayed in LA. He confessed that he'd wanted me since the day I walked into his office."

"And what was your response?"

Mya tossed back her hair. "I told him the feeling was mutual."

Angel felt sick.

"You still want to hear it?"

Angel shook off the nausea. "Go on."

"We went up to his room. We started kissing, touching, and one thing led to another." She paused. "I'm sure you don't want me to give you all the details," she added quickly. "Once we were practically naked in bed, I changed my mind. I didn't want to go through with it, and I told him that we were making a huge mistake. I guess he felt like we'd gone too far to stop. When he saw that I wasn't trying to give it to him, he decided to take it."

Angel shook her head. "I don't believe you."

Mya shrugged. "I'm sure a judge will see it differently."

"Duke is a family man. He's a father and a Christian. Why would you want to destroy his life this way? What is it that you're after? Money? Revenge?"

"Justice."

"This whole case comes down to your word against his. There's no proof that he tried to attack you. I don't know about you, but Duke has a gang of people who can vouch for his character and good standing in the community."

"Hmm . . . maybe, but that's not what's bothering you," replied Mya, guessing what was gnawing at Angel. "You don't care whether it was consensual or not. You want to know if Duke came after me, if he was willing to cheat on you."

"No. What I want to know is why you're insisting on slandering a good man's name with this garbage! We both know he didn't try to rape you. In fact, I doubt that he was even in the room with you at all. When the truth comes out and you're revealed to be the liar that you are, I pray that God has mercy on you, because we sure won't!"

Mya nodded slowly, sucking her teeth. "What about the bull?"

"Huh?"

"He's a Taurus, right? I'm assuming that's why he has a bull tatted on his chest. It's right here, isn't it?" She pointed to a place above her breast. "How could I possibly know that?" She waited for Angel to reply and rose when it became clear that Angel had no response. "I think I've answered all your questions now. I'll see you and Mr. King in court."

# Chapter 25

"In all fairness . . . you married her baby's daddy. . . . I say this makes you even."

*—Sullivan Webb*

Lawson closed and locked the door after the last of her ministry members filed out of her house. Sullivan, Angel, Reginell, Kina, and Desdemona stayed behind.

"That was nice of the women's ministry to have a special luncheon for Sullivan today, wasn't it?" commented Desdemona, referring to the thoughtful gesture on the part of Mount Zion's Women of Virtue.

"Yeah, the whole church has been concerned about her and Charles. They wanted to do something to try to cheer her up." Lawson stowed the last covered dish in her refrigerator. "Look at all this food they brought over. Sully probably won't have to cook again till Christmas!"

"I'm just thankful I was invited to come," said Desdemona. "I've really been enjoying getting to know all of you and attending church with Kina. Savannah is becoming more like home every day."

"No thanks necessary. We've enjoyed having you," Kina told her. "And it was very nice of you to volunteer your home to host it in, Lawson," added Kina.

"They did all the work. All I had to do was open the door . . . and, of course, make sure the honored guest showed up." Lawson nodded her head toward Sullivan, who sat many feet away, watching Charity and Simon play.

Desdemona lowered her voice. "Did anyone else notice that Sullivan was kind of quiet through the whole lunch? She mostly kept to herself or interacted with the kids."

"She's still struggling a little bit," remarked Angel. "Between the accident and all the hormonal changes from her pregnancy and losing Christian, that's to be expected."

"It's been over a month, though. How long is she supposed to be like this?" wondered Lawson.

"Well, at least she isn't drinking today," observed Desdemona. Then she whispered, "She was hitting the bottle pretty hard the last time we spoke."

"Really?" Lawson was concerned. "We really need to keep a closer eye on her. We can't let her sink into a full-blown depression."

"We can start by lightening the mood around here." Angel called over to Sullivan. "Don't you want to come join us at the grown folks' table?"

"I'm fine," she replied.

"Sully, come on," invited Reginell. "You know how much you love to gossip. Kina was just about to spill some hot tea, weren't you, Kina?"

Kina was confused. "Was I?"

"Yeah. Earlier today Des said that you've had a 'gentleman caller' hanging around, and I want to know who it is!"

Desdemona sat down next to Kina. "I wasn't putting your business out there, Kina. Reginell asked me why you've been so chipper lately, and I told her it may have something to do with your new friend."

"Well, he's definitely not new, and I don't know if I'd call him a friend."

Angel leaned in. "What's going on?"

Kina nodded. "It's true. I've kind of been seeing somebody. Well, not really *seeing* him as in dating, but . . . I don't know."

Lawson held up her hand. "Wait a minute. Backtrack. Who are you sort of seeing?"

"Elvin Battle."

"Elvin?" Lawson thought for a moment. "Hold up. Are you talking about Daddy E'Bell?"

Kina huffed. "Do we have to call him that?"

"Would you prefer Big Daddy or perhaps Dirty Daddy?" joked Angel. "It sure seems like you're headed that way!"

Sullivan's ears perked up. "Huh? What did she just say?"

"Kina has been picking fruit off the family tree, it seems," Lawson quipped.

Kina elbowed her. "I have not!"

"Kina, are you gettin' it on with E'Bell's daddy?" Sullivan joined them at the table. "What's up with all this inbreeding? First Reggie, Lawson, and Mark. Then Angel and Duke's cousin, and now Kina and her father-in-law! Is 'Help! I'm in love with a family member!' your new pitch to get a reality show?"

"I'm not in love with him, and technically, he's not any kin to me," argued Kina.

"But he's very much kin to your child and dead husband," Lawson pointed out.

"Elvin is nothing like E'Bell, though. I mean, he is, but only his good parts."

Sullivan wrinkled her nose. "E'Bell had good parts?"

"Yes, Sullivan, like being hardworking and funny and protective."

"*Protective?*" squawked Angel. "Do I have to remind you that this is the same man who regularly used your face as a punching bag?"

"He wasn't all bad, y'all. There were some happy times between Kenny, E'Bell, and me. When he wasn't drinking or smoking weed, E'Bell was a pretty good husband."

Lawson shook her head. "But how often was that, Kina? Every thirty-first of February? I know we don't like to speak ill of the dead, but that doesn't mean you should start sugarcoating your marriage. E'Bell was a terror to you and Kenny, and I doubt that the apple falls too far from the tree."

Angel frowned. "Plus, weren't you the one who said you find the whole notion of sleeping with relatives . . . What was the technical term you used . . . ? *Icky*, I believe it was. What's he doing here, anyway? I thought E'Bell's side of the family excommunicated you and Kenny after the funeral?"

"They did, but E'Bell's mom passed away a year ago. I think that prompted Elvin to want to reach out to the rest of his family. He's been great with Kenny."

Angel smirked. "And how's he been with you?"

Kina blushed. "He's great there too, but it's nothing serious. I'm not expecting him to be anything more than Kenny's granddad and a friend. We're just hanging out. It's all very platonic."

"But do you want it to stay that way?" inquired Desdemona.

"Yeah. I mean, wouldn't his mom dating his grandfather be confusing to Kenny?"

Lawson laughed. "No more confusing than Namon's dad being married to his mother's sister!"

Reginell rolled her eyes.

"He did kiss me, though," confessed Kina in a low voice.

"What?" Lawson blurted with a mixture of shock and amusement.

"It was one kiss. It just kind of happened, but I don't anticipate it happening again."

Lawson was skeptical. "So you say . . ."

"Girl, don't listen to Lawson! If he makes you happy, I say, Go for it. Besides, we've all made rather questionable dating choices," admitted Angel. "Sully, you remember that guy you dated junior year?"

"I dated several guys junior year."

"I'm talking about the weird one. What was his name?" Angel thought back. "Julian something . . ."

"Oh, yeah, Julian Floyd. He was weird. He had a thing for sniffing women's underwear."

Lawson frowned. "And you let him smell yours?"

Sullivan shrugged. "To each his own. The craziest thing about it was that he liked to smell them after they'd been in the hamper a couple of days. He said time gave them a nice heady aroma."

"Eww! I work with teenagers. I hear things that make me gag all day long, but I do believe that's the grossest thing I heard all week!" Lawson exclaimed.

"You've had your share of weirdos too, Lawson," Sullivan reminded her. "What about Sage?"

"Sage?" repeated Reginell. "You mean like the plant? Who names their kid that?"

"No one," said Lawson. "He said Sage is the name Mother Earth gave him. However, his real mother, Joycine, named him Orlando Parker. We dated before I started going out with Garrett. And he wasn't *weird*. He was introspective."

"And cheap!" added Sullivan. "Who gives someone a water jug and a leaf as a birthday gift?"

"It was not just any leaf. It was the first leaf that grew in spring on the tree outside my house. The water jug was actually fresh rain sealed in a jar that had been recycled for twenty years, and it happened to be my twentieth birthday at the time."

"Like I said," continued Sullivan, "a water jug and a leaf!"

Angel beamed. "This feels like old times! It's good to see you like this, Sully."

Sullivan nodded. "It feels good to laugh again."

Lawson wrapped her arm around Sullivan. "It'll get easier day by day. You'll see. Keep leaning on God, and when you need some laughs, lean on us."

"So, Lawson, how's your son?" asked Desdemona, changing the subject.

"He's good. Um, school is going well. I'm still not thrilled about this baby of his, but I'm coming around. Mark has been a great help with me coming to terms with it."

Reginell narrowed her eyes at Lawson. "Oh, has he?"

Lawson sighed. "Yes, Reggie, we talk. Mark knows how I feel about the situation. He's just been trying to help."

"Shouldn't your husband be the one helping you?" snarled Reginell.

"He is, but I see Mark every day at work. Of course, we're going to talk about whatever is happening with our son."

"Just be careful," cautioned Desdemona. "You know what happened the last time you and Mark were alone together."

The tension in the room thickened.

"You mean when she got pregnant with Namon?" asked Reginell. "That was almost twenty years ago." Reginell could sense something was amiss. "That is what you're talking about, right? The one night they shared when Lawson was sixteen and they conceived Namon?"

"Don't listen to me," said Desdemona, brushing it off. "I was just talking."

"Talking about what, though?" Reginell's curiosity was piqued. "What part am I missing?"

Desdemona apologized. "Lawson, I-I'm sorry. I thought Reggie knew about the kiss."

Angel and Kina winced.

Reginell was taken aback. "What kiss?"

Lawson exhaled. "It was nothing, Reggie."

"You let me be the judge of that," Reginell snapped. "Now, what's this about a kiss? Did you kiss Mark?"

"It happened months ago," blurted out Desdemona. "I'm sure it didn't mean anything to Lawson or your husband."

"Des, I really think this is something that should be discussed between my sister and me," said Lawson.

Desdemona bit her lip. "Of course. We should leave."

"No, wait," insisted Reginell. "I want to hear this. What happened between you and Mark, Lawson?"

"We kissed, all right?" Lawson revealed. "It was nothing major, just a stupid kiss."

Reginell turned to Desdemona. "You said this happened months ago, right?"

Desdemona nodded.

Reginell faced her sister. "So this kiss happened while Mark and I were together?"

"You weren't married yet," added Kina.

"So you knew too, Kina?" Reginell was stunned. "Dang, did everybody know except me? I guess the wife really is the last to know!"

"Reggie, that kiss happened a long time ago," explained Lawson. "It was right after Kina busted you at the strip club. You and Mark weren't even speaking then."

"So!" spat Reginell, disinclined to accept that as an excuse.

"Plus, Garrett and I were going through such a rough time dealing with Simon and Simone. Mark and I leaned on each other for support."

"It sounds like y'all did a lot more than just lean!"

"Look, we were both heartbroken and upset, and it just happened. We both knew it was a mistake and stopped before it went any further."

"Is that supposed to make me feel better, Lawson? My husband cheated on me with my sister!"

"In all fairness, Reggie, you married her baby's daddy," pointed out Sullivan. "I say this makes you even."

"It's not about getting even or going behind your back," asserted Lawson.

"Then why did you do it? And if it wasn't a big deal, why did you keep it from me?"

"Because I know you have a tendency to make mountains out of molehills. The kiss was nothing."

"I'm sure Mark reached out to Lawson only because he was hurt," offered Desdemona.

"So that's it?" asked Reginell. "When my husband is hurt, he reaches out for you instead of me?"

"Reggie, don't do this. You know Mark and I have been close for years. We share a child together. I don't think it's that big of a stretch that he'd reach out to me from time to time, but he's never crossed the line with me."

"Except for when he kissed you," retorted Reginell.

Lawson groaned.

"You know, for some people, kissing is more intimate than sex. In fact, the only other thing that's more intimate is sharing a child together. It looks like you and my husband have all of your intimacy bases covered!"

Desdemona interceded. "I know that Lawson and Mark share a powerful connection through their son and that it can be tough for you because that's a part of himself that he doesn't share with you, Reggie, and never will, because of your hysterectomy."

"I don't think pointing that out is helping," noted Kina with a raised brow.

"My point is that Mark loves you," continued Desdemona. "You're the one he chose to spend his life with. Your sister loves you too. I don't think she'd ever do anything to hurt you or disrespect your relationship again.

Let's just pray that it was a one-time mistake and lapse in judgment."

"If the kiss was so insignificant, why didn't either of them bother to tell me? Why the secrecy?" Reginell wondered aloud.

"Reggie, come on now. Is there really an easy way to tell anyone, especially your sister, that you shared a passionate kiss with her husband and not expect an all-out war?"

"Des, I can answer the question myself, thank you," grumbled Lawson.

Desdemona shrank back. "Sorry . . . I was just trying to help."

"The reason I didn't say anything is that we knew it was a mistake and regretted the kiss as soon as it happened."

"That's understandable," said Kina. "Sometimes people just get caught up in the moment. I know that's how it was for me and Elvin."

Desdemona dove back into the conversation. "Right. Just because you kiss someone doesn't mean it has to lead to sex or even has to mean anything."

"Oh, it means something, all right!" hissed Reginell.

"What? More threats, Reggie?" muttered Lawson.

Reginell leapt up and got in Lawson's face. "I don't make threats! Don't come for me, Lawson. You ain't about this life!"

"I think you need a time-out." Desdemona dragged Reginell outside before the argument escalated any more.

Reginell began pacing, trying to calm herself down.

"You all right?" asked Desdemona.

"Yeah, I'm good." Reginell stopped and took a deep breath. "I bet you must think I'm real ghetto for carrying on like that."

"No. I didn't want to say this in front of everybody, but I understand why you got upset. A person can only take so much disrespect."

"Yeah, but when all is said and done, Lawson is my sister, though. I should go back and apologize."

Desdemona stopped her. "I don't think so. Your relationship with your husband supersedes yours with Lawson. Doesn't the Bible say you should leave and cleave? You have every right to fight for your marriage, even if it means fighting your sister. Right now Lawson is acting like the other woman. You can't stand on the sidelines, waiting for her to seduce your husband. If you don't put a stop to it, that's exactly what's going to happen."

"Honestly, Des, I don't think either one of them would take it that far."

"You didn't think they'd take it as far as the kiss, either, did you?"

Reginell admitted that she didn't.

"Reggie, you just had that hysterectomy. Your sex life isn't what it was while you're in recovery. Your husband is vulnerable right now, and she could easily take advantage. It wouldn't take much—a slight touch here and a flirtatious smile—for Lawson and your husband to give in to their flesh. They've been physically intimate, and they've been intimate emotionally. You can't turn a blind eye to it."

Reginell nodded slowly. "You're right."

"I hate that I am, but I don't want to see another happy family destroyed. Keep her away from you, and definitely keep her away from your husband!"

Reginell and Desdemona rejoined the other ladies. The moment Reginell set eyes on her sister, the rage she'd felt when she left the house came flooding back. She envisioned Lawson and Mark kissing, then pictured the two of them rolling around in the bed she shared with Mark, laughing about how they'd been able to deceive her.

Without warning, Reginell lunged forward and socked her sister in the face.

"Reggie!" shrilled Desdemona.

"Oh, my God!" shrieked Kina. "What did you do that for?"

They all huddled around Lawson.

"It's gonna be hard tryin'a kiss my husband with your lip swelling up like that!" taunted Reginell, standing over her sister.

Angel was horrified. "Reggie, what the devil is wrong with you? That's your sister!"

"I don't care what she is! I told her to back up off my man. She can learn the easy way, or she can learn the hard way."

"Reggie . . ." began Lawson, but she stopped when her mouth started filling with blood.

"You don't have to say anything." Reginell rubbed her knuckles. "*Now* we're even."

# Chapter 26

"You don't so much as take a leak without thinking about it first. Nothing 'just happens' with you. There's always a plan, always an agenda."

—*Reginell Vinson*

"You should've called first," warned Mark when Lawson turned up at his front door two days after the blowout with Reginell. "Wow. She really did a number on your lip, didn't she?"

Lawson touched her distended bottom lip. "It'll heal, but I'm not as worried about my lip healing as much as I am the rift between my sister and me."

"For the record, I don't think what she did to you is cool. I told Reggie I don't want to be the source of any friction between the two of you. I've done everything I know to do to assure her that nothing is going on between us, nor will there ever be again."

"Is she home? Can I speak to her?"

Mark let Lawson into the house. "She's in the back. I was just about to head out to pick her up something to eat, unless I need to stay here and referee."

Lawson raised her right hand. "We'll be fine, I promise."

"All right. I'll be back in ten minutes."

Lawson made her way to Reginell and Mark's bedroom, where she found Reginell cleaning.

"Hi, Reggie."

Reginell threw up a hand to say hello.

"So are we going to talk about this?" asked Lawson.

"Talk about what?" Reginell continued busying herself with mundane tasks to avoid giving Lawson her full attention.

"Just tell me what I can do to make this right. I hate fighting with you."

Reginell slammed a drawer shut. "Who's fighting?"

"You were when you gave me this busted lip! Reggie, you won't even look at me. We need to talk about it."

"Talk about *what*?" Reginell asked again. "You want me to apologize? Fine. I'm sorry your lip got in the way of my fist. I was really aiming for the nose."

"We need to talk about the kiss . . . I know it bothers you."

Reginell shrugged. "I'm over it." She paused and looked up at her sister. "Unless it bothers you that you kissed my husband and neglected to tell me about it."

"You're making it sound like we had some sordid affair, but it was nothing like that. It was just one stupid kiss! It just happened. We weren't thinking—"

"Wrong!" blurted out Reginell. "You were thinking. You're *always* thinking. You're my sister. I know you better than anyone, and if there's anything I know about you, it's that you don't so much as take a leak without thinking about it first. Nothing 'just happens' with you. There's always a plan, always an agenda."

"Not that time, Reggie."

"Just admit it. . . . You kissed him because you wanted to. You didn't care that we were together or that you had a husband. You wanted what you wanted, which happened to be my husband."

"He wasn't your husband then."

"What about Garrett? Wasn't he your husband at the time?"

Lawson was reluctant to answer. "Barely."

"But he was still your husband, though, right?"

"I'm sorry that it happened. It was wrong, but I wasn't out there kissing myself that day. Mark is just as much to blame. More really, because he initiated it."

"I've dealt with him, but that part of it isn't any of your business." Reginell shook her head. "I shouldn't even be surprised, really. You've never wanted Mark with me. You've never thought I was good enough for him."

"That's not true, and you know it."

"What I know is that you've tried to undermine my relationship from day one. That's why we didn't tell you about the wedding. You're too stouthearted to be supportive."

"Don't get it twisted, Reggie. If I didn't support this relationship, there wouldn't be a relationship!"

Reginell frowned. "What's that supposed to mean?"

"You know exactly what it means. Who did Mark propose to first? If I wanted him—better yet, if I didn't want him with you— you wouldn't have him!"

Reginell laughed. "Are you still trying to play that tired 'he wanted me first' card? He may have *asked* you to marry him, but he married me," Reginell sneered and held up her left hand. "I'm the one with his ring. He never wanted you, Lawson, just Namon."

"Then why are you so worked up about the kiss?"

"Don't flatter yourself into thinking it's because you're some kind of threat to my marriage. You're not. Everything Mark wants is right here, and he can't get enough of it! The problem is that you kissed him. What kind of person does that to her sister?"

"Are you kidding? Reggie, you married my child's father, and you have the nerve to stand there and ask me about a freakin' kiss?"

"There it is. Just admit you're still jealous because Mark chose me over you."

"Reggie, this isn't about being jealous! This is about you, my sister, who could've had any man she wanted—and let's be real . . . you've *had* just about every man you wanted—but chose to pursue the one man on this entire planet who has a lifelong connection to me. He's the one person anybody with any sense of loyalty would've avoided."

"Mark approached me, not the other way around."

"You could've turned him down. You could've said no. I know that's not a word you were used to saying in your past line of work, but you could've at least tried for me and for your nephew!"

"Why? You had a man. Who or what Mark does ain't none of your business."

"You're right, but I'm not talking about Mark. I'm talking about you."

"What I do ain't your business, either!"

"You owed me more, Reggie."

"I don't owe you *jack!*"

"Reggie, I've been the closest thing you've had to a mother since Mama died when you were fifteen. I took care of you. I made sure you were fed and had a roof. I was there for you when no one was there for you. I defended you and bailed you out of trouble more times than I can count. I've earned your respect and your consideration. You do owe me that."

Reginell calmed down. "Lawson, I love you, and I am thankful for everything you've done for me, but this isn't gonna work."

"What isn't?"

"You, me, Mark . . . all trying to coexist peacefully. It's just not possible."

Lawson was rattled. "What are you saying?"

"I'm saying that I don't want you coming around any-more."

"What?" Lawson was dumbfounded. "Reggie, I'm your sister!"

"You are, and nothing will change that, but Mark is my husband. We're newlyweds, and we're still trying to figure this marriage thing out. I think we have a better chance with that if you stay away."

"You're just upset about the kiss—"

"I am upset about the kiss, but I'm also upset about you not respecting my boundaries with Mark, you finding reasons to call and talk to him, and you trying to use Na-mon to get to him. I'm sick of all of it."

Lawson tried to reason with her. "I really believe this is just the hormones talking. You're still recovering from the surgery, and your body is still adjusting. You said yourself that mood swings are one of the side effects."

"If that's what you need to tell yourself, fine. But I'm telling you to back off. Stay away from me. Stay away from my husband."

"For how long?"

"I don't know." Reginell shrugged her shoulders. "I'll let you know."

"What does Mark have to say about this?"

"That's not your concern, Lawson. Mark is going to go along with whatever I want. He doesn't care about what you think or what you want. You worrying about what my husband has to say or what he's feeling is why it's come down to this."

"It's not like that, Reggie. I love Garrett. I don't want your husband."

"If you don't want him, staying away from him shouldn't be a problem. You can see yourself out. You know the way."

"Reggie—"

"We've said all we need to say, Lawson. Now, get out."

# Chapter 27

"Our marriage has been held together with prayer,
Band-Aids, and borrowed time for a while now."

*–Sullivan Webb*

Sullivan made the drive to her mother's house against
her better judgment. Vera could rarely be counted on for
sound advice even if Sullivan managed to catch her while
sober. Nevertheless, desperate times called for desperate
measures. If Sullivan showed up on Vera's doorstep, it
had to mean she was desperate.

"How many times do I have to ask you not to smoke
around my child?" asked Sullivan when Vera answered
the door with a lit cigarette in her hand.

"You can ask as many times as you want, but that
doesn't mean I have to listen. Your rules apply to your
house, not mine." She let Sullivan and Charity inside.

"I know that you love your granddaughter. Can you not
smoke for her sake please?"

Vera grunted and crushed the cigarette in an ashtray.

Sullivan joined her on the sofa. "I take it Cliff's not
home."

"You just missed him."

"When? Three years ago? The only proof that I have
that he even still lives here with you is that I can still smell
the stench of his cigars."

"How about the stench of the new car he just bought me, the one sitting out on the driveway? Is that proof enough for you?"

Sullivan shook her head in pity. "Anyway, Cliff and his mysterious whereabouts are the least of my concerns right now."

"Oh, my grandbaby is getting so big!" Vera gathered Charity up into her arms. "How's that husband of yours?"

"It's funny you brought him up. Charles is exactly who I wanted to talk to you about." Sullivan paused, giving another moment of thought to her question. "Do you think I could make it on my own? You know, be a single mother and raise Charity myself?"

"Why? Is Charles sick or something?"

"Sick of me, maybe."

"Girl, what are you talking about?" She momentarily stopped smothering Charity with kisses. "You messin' around on him again?"

"Vera, give me some credit."

"I don't believe in credit. I believe in showing me who you are and taking you at your word! You've already shown me who you are. Heck, with that Internet video, you showed the whole world."

"Well, I'm not having an affair, if that's what you're worried about. This is far worse."

"How so?"

"I think Charles has given up on me," Sullivan confessed aloud for the first time. "I think we've both given up. Losing Christian did something—*broke* something—in our relationship. Our marriage has been held together with prayer, Band-Aids, and borrowed time for a while now. It may be time to face the truth about our situation."

Vera shook her head. "You thinkin' about leaving Charles? You're a bigger fool than I thought you were!"

"I know you're saying that because he's rich, but contrary to your warped beliefs, money ain't everything."

"If that was the case, I'd tell you to divorce him, take half, and rack up more in child support and alimony." Vera put Charity down. "Sullivan, it ain't too many men I have more than an ounce of faith in, especially not so-called preachers. Just look at your triflin' daddy. But Charles is different. Charles is the real thing. He's a good man."

"Charles *is* a good man, but no man's irreplaceable. You taught me well, remember? I could have a new and improved Charles in no time."

"Humph! That's what you think!" Vera laughed a little. "You're always asking me why I keep Cliff around. Yes, he's a lyin', good-for-nothing piece of . . . I won't say it, because the baby's right here. But out of all the no-good pieces, he's about the best one I could find, so I'm holding on to him."

"You could do so much better than Cliff! Anybody is better than Cliff. In fact, having *nobody* would be better than living with Cliff!"

"It ain't that simple. I'm old now. I can't pull 'em like I used to. Times are hard for an old ho like myself! And you gettin' old too! You're going on thirty-five, and thirty-five is a world away from twenty-five. If you know like I know, you better keep your behind at home!"

"But I'm not happy. Neither is Charles."

"*Happy?* You act like being happy is like being black! You can't choose the color of your skin, but you can choose whether or not to be happy. Shoot, if I was waiting on Cliff to make me happy, I'd be waiting forever! Girl, you better make yourself happy! Give me that big ole house you're living in and that BMW you're driving and a man like Charles, and I bet you I can be happy!"

"See? There you go, making it about materialistic things again. What good is the house and the car if the man I'm married to doesn't understand me?"

"You worry about the wrong things, Sullivan. You always have. One thing I know about Charles is that he could've slammed the door on me a long time ago, and I wouldn't have blamed him if he had. I'm sure you done bad-mouthed me so bad that he's looking to see if I leave hoof prints behind when I walk by. But he's never shown me anything except kindness, even after I showed out at your Christmas party and announced to the world that good ol' Pastor Sammy Sullivan was your daddy. You don't find that kind of man every day, and that ain't got nothing to do with money. It's just the goodness in him."

"I'm not denying that he's a good man. I just don't know if he's the right man for me. What if being married to me is keeping him from the woman God really wants him to be with? What if he's keeping me from the man I'm destined to be with?"

"If you have a man who knows everything you've done—all your crimes, all your shortcomings, all your whorish ways—and he still wants to be with you, then that's the right man for you. It's hard to find somebody who accepts you the way you are." Vera thought for a moment. "I'd like to think that's how this Jesus is y'all keep yappin' about, and Charles is the closest thing you're going to find to Him on this side of heaven. You best hold on to him. Believe me—there are plenty of women who are a whole lot less trouble than you are who'll have no problem sweeping up your leftovers."

Sullivan yanked her hair in frustration. "I just don't think I can get over what he did to our son. I wanted that baby more than anything, and Charles took him from me, literally had him ripped from my body. When he did that, a part of me died too. There's an empty space inside of me that will never be filled again. How do I get over something like that?"

"Sullivan, let me tell you something. Christian is dead! He ain't thinking about you, and he ain't coming back. That's all there is to it. Now, you can sit over here and be mad with Charles, lose your husband, have some other woman walking around in that big old house of yours. And you know what? That baby will still be dead! You've got to suck it up and move on."

"Do you have to be so cruel, Vera?"

"Silly rabbit, I'm doing you a favor. I know what you're going through. I lost a baby too, same way you did, in a car accident. And I blamed her daddy the same way you're doing with Charles. The difference is Samuel Sullivan was trying to kill my baby. It nearly killed Charles to risk your child's life. The only reason he did it—*the only reason he did it*—was to save your pathetic, selfish, ungrateful self. Now you have the nerve to sit up here and crucify this man for loving you more than he loved his own flesh and blood. You ought to thank God Charles hasn't left *you!*"

# Chapter 28

"One day, when he has children of his own that he's actually ready for, he will understand what I did and why and will thank me for it."

*−Lawson Kerry Banks*

"Take a deep breath," Lawson told Shari, coaching her, in the car outside the abortion clinic. "You can do this."

Shari nodded and did as she was told.

"We're going to go in here. When you come out, all your problems will be behind you and you can go back to your regularly scheduled life, complete with your education, your freedom, parties, and just being a normal college student. You ready?"

"Yeah." Shari opened the passenger door and stepped out.

Before they could reach the clinic's entrance, they were met by Namon, who was livid.

"I don't believe this!" he bellowed. "Seriously, Ma? You were going to have her go through with this without even telling me?"

Lawson's heart sank. "Namon, what are you doing here?"

"Shutting down whatever you had planned." He grabbed Shari by the hand. "Come on, Shari. Let's get out of here!"

Shari clasped her arms around Namon's neck. "I was so scared. I didn't think you were gonna come."

Lawson narrowed her eyes and pitched her stony gaze at Shari. "You called him?"

"She texted me and told me what was going on," replied Namon. "She was terrified."

"Namon, don't be mad at me," cried Shari. "I was just trying to make things easier on you."

"Regardless of what you may think, Shari made this decision on her own. She's doing what she thinks is best for everyone involved," insisted Lawson.

Namon pulled away from Shari and confronted his mother head-on. "And just who convinced her that this was best? I've seen you do some questionable things, but this . . . baby killing? Not just any baby, your own grandchild! Who does that?"

"Namon, this baby is a mistake, and everybody knows it," said Lawson. "We're just trying to make the best of an already difficult situation."

"*We?*" Namon shot back. "There is no *we!* There's just you and you being lowdown enough to try to trick Shari. How could you do that?"

"Babe, can we just get out of here?" pleaded Shari. "I hate this place."

"Yeah." He turned to leave, with Shari in tow.

"Namon, wait!" commanded Lawson. "We've got to talk about this."

Namon faced his mother. "I ain't got nothing to say to you." Then he turned on his heels, and he and Shari headed to his car, climbed in, and drove away.

Lawson walked briskly back to her car, got behind the wheel, and hurried home. When she pulled into the driveway, Namon and Shari were getting out of Namon's car. Lawson followed Namon into their house, trying to plead her case. Namon ignored her, stormed into his room, and began packing his belongings.

"How long do you think you can go without talking to me?" said Lawson as she entered Namon's bedroom.

Namon didn't say anything.

"Namon, I'm your mother. You can't keep giving me the silent treatment. You're acting like a child."

"Might as well. You treat me like one. You obviously don't think I'm capable of making my own decisions."

"Honey, it wasn't like that at all. I was just trying to protect you."

"I don't need your protection, not like that."

"You're angry now, but when you have a child of your own, you'll understand that."

"And you did your best to make sure that wouldn't happen, didn't you?"

Having heard the commotion, Garrett barged into the room. "Hey, what's going on in here?"

Namon looked up at his stepfather, incensed. "Were you in on this too?" he demanded to know.

"In on what? Lawson, what is he talking about?"

Lawson exhaled. "Shari asked me to take her to get an abortion. Then, at the last minute, she got cold feet and told Namon all about it. Now he's taking it out on me."

Garrett sighed heavily. "Please tell me you didn't coerce that poor girl into that," he implored.

"Of course she did," answered Namon.

"Regardless of what you think, I didn't bully Shari into having an abortion. It was her decision."

"No, you just coaxed her into doing it," retorted Namon. "She told me what happened."

"It didn't take much convincing. Unlike you, Shari knows that the two of you aren't ready for a baby."

"Thankfully, we have several more months to get ready."

"You're gonna need a lot longer that, my son!" exclaimed Lawson.

Garrett stepped in. "Nay, I know that you're heated right now. What your mother did was deplorable at best, but she's still your mother. As much as I don't agree with what she did, I know in her heart, she did it to protect you."

Namon stopped packing for a moment. "Ma, can I ask you something?"

"You can ask me anything. You know that."

"Wasn't there a time when you didn't want me?"

"Absolutely not!" asserted Lawson. "Namon, I loved you before I even knew you."

"Come on, Ma. You were sixteen. What sixteen-year-old is thrilled about being pregnant? You told me yourself that Grandma wanted you to put me up for adoption."

"Yes, but the moment I felt you kicking inside of me, I knew that there was no way I could give you up. I already loved you."

"Then why would you try to destroy my baby and your grandchild? Don't you think I love my baby too?"

"Namon, you're not old enough to know what you're getting yourself into. And is Shari really the kind of girl you want to be tied down to for the rest of your life?"

"You were younger than me, and you barely knew my father!"

"That's beside the point. Look at Shari's background, baby. Her dad's in and out of jail, and her mother is a drug addict. Her brothers and sisters have been lost to the streets. Is this the kind of family you want to bring a child into? Those people are going to be leaching off of you for the rest of your life!"

"I don't care about that. I love Shari."

"You love her right now. There was also a time when you loved Power Rangers and cartoons, but you grew out of it. The same thing will happen with this relationship, which is supposed to happen. It's a part of the growing process. You don't want to hinder your growth by tying yourself down to this girl for life."

Namon was riled up again. "Stop telling me what I want and quit trying to control my life!"

"Hey, chill out," ordered Garrett. "I know you're upset, but that's still your mama."

"I know you think I'm trying to control you, but that's not what I'm doing. Namon, you're not thinking clearly. As your mother, it's up to me to do it for you when you can't do it for yourself."

"I see we're not going to agree on this." Namon hesitated. "So I've decided to move in with my dad."

Lawson was bowled over. "What? When did you decide that?"

"I talked to my pops on the way over, and he's cool with it."

"Oh, is he now?" She was irked. "Nobody discussed it with me!"

"Nobody had to. I'm eighteen. I'm barely here as it is. This is just making it official."

Lawson vigorously shook her head. "You're not moving out of this house, Namon!"

Namon scooped up his duffel bag. "Ma, it's done. I can't stay here anymore."

"Why? Because I won't cosign on your bad decisions?"

"No . . . because I can't stand to look at the woman who tried to take my child away from me."

Lawson's eyes fell downcast.

Namon gently placed his hand on her shoulder. "I'm not saying this to hurt you. I still love you. I just can't be around you right now."

"Namon, who's the one who's been there for you, huh? Who clothed you? Who fed you?" interrogated Lawson. "Who tucked you in at night and drove back and forth to all your games and practices? Who has been your rock? And you say you can't stand to look at me?"

"Bye, Ma." Namon kissed her on the cheek and left the room.

"Namon, get back here!" she called after him. "We're not done!"

"Let him go, babe," urged Garrett in a low tone.

"He needs me," Lawson protested. "He's acting out, and that ole duplicitous hussy has her hooks in him and is trying to turn him against me."

"I don't think that's it. He's scared, Lawson. He's trying to do the right thing, but he's not altogether sure what that is. Factor in hormones, academic pressure, and an overbearing mother—"

"*Overbearing mother?*"

"Yeah, babe. You're suffocating the boy! He can't breathe or think with you on his neck like this. It's no wonder he's pulling away from you."

"I'm just the only one with the guts to be honest with him. The rest of y'all are worried about trying to be his friend, while I'm focused on being his parent, which is what God called me to be. I'll be Mommy over homie any day."

"You're going to end up pushing him away and losing him forever if you don't fall back a little."

"That's a chance I'm willing to take in order to save him. One day, when he has children of his own that he's actually ready for, he will understand what I did and why and will thank me for it."

"Do you honestly think he's ever going to thank you for trying to kill his unborn child?" Lawson looked away. "I didn't want to say anything in front of Namon, but what you did was cold, Lawson. It was cruel. A man's child is his soul. Even though Simon was conceived under all the wrong circumstances, I wouldn't give him up for the world. That's my child. He's a piece of me. I imagine Namon feels the same way."

"Why can't anyone see that all I did was what any mother in my situation would do? I will do anything to protect my child!"

"And now you see that he will do anything to protect his."

# Chapter 29

"Maybe you'd be less stressed if you didn't have so many lies to keep track of!"

*–Angel King*

"Should I even bother to ask why you've been giving me the cold shoulder lately?" asked Duke when he, Angel, and the girls returned from church that Sunday.

"Who said I was giving you the cold shoulder?" replied Angel.

Duke grabbed his newspaper and sat down. "Whatever."

Angel absently channel surfed.

"Do you mind turning that down please?" requested Duke. "I'm reading."

Angel cut him with her eyes before blurting out, "You lied to me, didn't you?"

Duke muttered something under his breath and continued reading the paper.

"So you're just going to ignore me?"

"At this moment, yes."

"Why?"

"Because whatever it is you're talking about is just going to heap more stress onto an already stressful time in my life."

"Maybe you'd be less stressed if you didn't have so many lies to keep track of!"

Duke lowered his newspaper. "Lies? Angel, what lies are you talking about now?"

"I thought you didn't want to talk about it," she retorted.

"I don't want to talk about it. I want to get it over with—preferably sooner rather than later."

Angel paused. "You said that you never touched her."

"Touched who?"

Angel smacked her lips. "Who do you think, Duke?"

"Man, are we seriously going to rehash this for the thousandth time? We've been over this more than once. I never assaulted her, I never sexually harassed her, and I never did any of the things she's accusing me of! You know that."

"I thought I did. For the record, I truly believe you when you say you didn't assault her, but what I don't believe is that absolutely nothing happened in that room."

"What?"

"Are you telling me that you weren't attracted to her? That you didn't have every intention of sleeping with her that night?"

"No, I wasn't, and no, I didn't."

"But you kissed her, right?"

Duke dropped his head.

"You flirted with her, you bought her drinks, you took her up to your room, you kissed her, and you wanted to take her to bed. You wanted her, didn't you?"

Duke was irritated. "Where are you even getting this crap from?"

"I got it from the horse's mouth."

He looked up. "Are you talking about her deposition? That piece of garbage has more lies and holes in it than Swiss cheese!"

"I'm not talking about that. I went to see her."

He glowered. "Why?"

"I was trying to clear your name, Duke! I wanted the truth."

"So did you want the truth, or did you want to clear my name? Because right now, you seem to think that those are two different things."

"I don't hear you denying it."

"No, what you don't hear is me *dignifying* it! Angel, when have I lied to you? What have I done to make you feel like you can't trust me to be honest with you?"

"Are you kidding me? This wouldn't be the first time you've ever lied and cheated on me, Duke! You left me, remember? You walked out on me and married your mistress, so it wouldn't be a far stretch to think you might be capable of cheating."

"So we're back on that, huh? You're going to use something that happened twelve years ago against me? You don't trust me. After everything we've gone through, Angel, you still don't trust me."

"If I don't trust you, it's *because* of everything we've gone through."

"I've apologized to you, and I vowed that I'd never hurt you like that again. I meant that. And if we're looking at track records, yours isn't squeaky clean, either, baby girl."

She was taken aback. "What's that supposed to mean?"

"Oh, you're going to stand there all wide-eyed and innocent like you didn't go after my cousin a few years ago—carrying on with him right under my own roof? You wanna talk about that? What about all the sex chat rooms you were frequenting, to the point that Miley had to get stitches because you were too busy getting your rocks off on the Internet to watch her."

"I can't believe you brought that up!" snapped Angel.

"And I can't believe you're using something that happened a decade ago as an excuse to side with the woman who's trying to have me locked up! You betrayed me too,

Angel, but once you said that you'd never hurt me that way again, I believed you. I didn't second-guess that for a minute. I wish you could show me the same courtesy."

"I have shown you that courtesy. I'm here, aren't I?"

"Don't say it like you're doing me any favors," muttered Duke.

"Okay, if Mya is lying, how does she know about the tattoo on your chest? Can you answer that?"

"Why bother when you've already decided that I'm guilty?"

"I didn't say that."

"You didn't have to. I see it in your eyes, and I can hear it in your voice."

Angel exhaled. "I just need to know that the man I'm going to marry is being up front with me. I can't get into another union with you having doubts."

"That's a little premature, isn't it, considering I haven't asked you to marry me?"

She was stumped. "Duke, we've been talking about getting remarried for years. We were engaged."

"Yeah, until you started messing around with my cousin and dumped me. Then you went out and slept with ole boy and got pregnant by him. And who was there to pick up the pieces after your abortion? I was—no questions asked. I haven't so much as touched another woman other than you since my wife died. If anybody ought to be questioning somebody's loyalty, it's me!" he declared.

"Yet as hard as it was to tell you the truth, I was honest with you about all of that. All I'm asking is that you do the same."

"I've done that. My story hasn't changed from the first time I told you what happened. All that's changed is that you talked to Mya. Now you can choose to believe the woman who's out to get me instead of the man who loves you."

"The only thing I'm asking is that you tell me how she knows about the tattoo. How could she know about it, unless you were somewhere together, presumably in the hotel room, with your shirt off?"

Duke stood up. "Angel, I've got enough I'm trying to deal with without adding your allegations on top of Mya's. I think you should leave."

"You're kicking me out?"

"I'm giving myself a break! I can't deal with you right now."

Angel stood akimbo. "Is it that you can't deal with me or you can't deal with the truth?"

"I need a woman who is going to stand by my side, not monitor and question my every move. I need a woman who trusts me more than some vindictive trick with a score to settle. If you can't be that person for me, so be it."

"So that's it?" she asked. "We're over?"

When he didn't answer, Angel grabbed her jacket and headed to the door. She looked at him before going out. "Then I guess it's over."

# Chapter 30

"I'm no better than Vera. I didn't protect Christian any
more than she protected me from those pedophiles she
rented my body to for name-brand shoes."

*—Sullivan Webb*

Lawson received a happy surprise on her doorstep that
Saturday afternoon. "So what brings you to these parts?"

"Would you believe me if I said I was just in the neighborhood?" asked Sullivan.

Lawson let her in. "Of course not. It's no secret that you
hate slummin' back into our old neighborhood, unless
expressly forced to, so what's up?"

Sullivan shrugged. "I just needed to get out of the
house. I was starting to feel like the walls were closing in
on me."

"I understand. Where's Princess Charity?" Lawson
picked up a few of Simon's toys off the floor.

"She's with her ever-doting daddy. They have a whole
day of fun planned."

"You didn't want to join them?"

"I got the impression from Charles that my presence
wasn't necessarily welcomed. He didn't come right out
and say it, but I could tell. Christian's death has taken
its toll on my marriage. We're not in a good place at the
moment."

"Aww, I'm sorry, Sully."

"It's okay. I know I haven't exactly been the life of the party lately at home or anywhere else."

"No one faults you for that. You lost your son. People have to grieve in their own way."

Sullivan perked up upon seeing Simon in his playpen. "So you're babysitting today, I see."

"Yep. Garrett had to work, so I'm on diaper duty."

"Aw, Lawson, he's adorable!"

"Humph. Don't let the cute face fool you!" Lawson lifted Simon out and sat him down on the sofa between herself and Lawson. "This little guy is a handful."

"He's getting so big," observed Sullivan. "He's looking more and more like his daddy."

"Yeah . . . that took some getting used to," confessed Lawson.

"Why?"

"The more he grew to look like him, the less I could pretend that there was a chance he wasn't Garrett's baby."

"I know he wasn't conceived under ideal circumstances, but I'm glad you haven't let that stop you from loving him."

Lawson kissed Simon. "It's not his fault his parents were selfish, irresponsible idiots for one night. Oh, wait. Am I talking about Simone and Garrett or Namon and Shari?"

"Well, you could just as easily be talking about yourself and Mark," joked Sullivan. "But you know, Lawson, that grandbaby you have coming can be as much of a blessing to your life as Simon and Namon are. Things any better between you and Reggie?"

"Nope! Still banished from the Vinson compound."

"She'll come around eventually. She's just hormonal right now."

Lawson simpered. "Here's hoping . . ."

"How are things with you and your other son these days?"

Lawson sighed. "He's not even returning my texts, much less taking my calls."

"Most men don't take abortions lightly."

"I was only trying to help him. He's young and naive. He has no idea what he's getting himself into."

"It still wasn't your call to make, my dear."

"So I'm supposed to just stand back and watch while he ruins not only his life but that girl's and their baby's life too?"

"Yes. He's an adult, Lawson. You gave him life, but you can't run it for him after a certain age."

Simon began to get fussy.

Lawson groaned. "I guess it's time for somebody's lunch. He gets very temperamental about his peas and carrots." She picked up Simon.

"Why don't you leave him in here with me? I'll watch him," offered Sullivan.

"Are you sure? He can be kind of cranky."

"Please. I have a two-year-old at home. I know how to handle cranky!"

Lawson laughed and handed him off to Sullivan. "I'll be only ten minutes."

"Take your time," Sullivan called after Lawson as she headed into the kitchen.

Simon started fussing again.

"Oh, don't you start that, mister!" Sullivan lifted Simon into the air. "Aren't you a cutie patootie!" She smiled as she listened to him squeal with laughter. She brought him back down and began stroking his hair. "You're strong and handsome, just like my Christian would've been. He looked like his daddy, just like you look like yours. He had his dad's big ole puppy dog eyes. I bet he would've grown up to be a kind and brilliant pastor like his daddy too."

Sullivan smirked, talking more to herself than to Simon. "Maybe he would've been a troublemaker who could melt your heart with a wink or a smile, like his mama." She went on dreamily. "I can see his big sister, Charity, giving him a hard time for taking her place as the baby in the family, but she would've loved him. She would've protected him from bullies and monsters under the bed."

Sullivan faced Simon, her eyes watering, and spoke to him head-on. "Make sure your parents always protect you, you hear me? That's the most important job parents have. And make sure that they know how blessed they are to have you every day. Make sure they hug and kiss you every day, because some parents never get the chance to hold and love their babies."

Lawson returned with Simon's lunch, startled to see Sullivan experiencing an emotional meltdown. "Sully, are you okay?"

"Not really." She sat Simon down on the sofa and wiped her eyes. "I should go."

"You're not going anywhere in this state. I'm calling Charles."

Sullivan stood up. "No, please don't. I'm fine now."

"Darling, you're many things, but *fine* isn't one of them. Look at you. You're crying!" Lawson handed her a napkin.

"Thank you." Sullivan blotted her eyes. "I'll be okay. Holding the baby and thinking about Christian at that age got me kind of misty-eyed." She tacked on a smile. "I'm fine now, I promise."

Lawson wasn't convinced. "Just stay a little longer and keep me company. Simon's vocabulary is restricted to *ball, food,* and *no.* It makes for very limited conversations."

"Lawson, I can't. . . ." Sullivan broke into tears and sank down on the sofa.

Lawson held her. "My God, you're a wreck! Please let me call your husband."

"He can't help me. He can't make this guilt go away," sobbed Sullivan.

"Guilt over what? What are you talking about?"

Sullivan tried to compose herself. "Nothing . . ."

"Come on, what's this really about, Sully?"

"We didn't protect him." Sully lowered her head. "I didn't protect my baby, and neither did Charles."

"Of course you did! You did everything you could for that boy."

"No, I didn't!" Sullivan took a deep breath. "Lawson, I wasn't wearing a seat belt when I had the accident. The belt made me so uncomfortable, and I wasn't that far from the church. I just figured . . ." She vigorously shook her head. "I should've had on my seat belt. I should've protected him!"

"Honey, I don't think it would've mattered. The other driver ran a red light. Your seat belt wouldn't have stopped that."

"I know, but maybe I wouldn't have gotten thrown from the car and wouldn't have had to deliver him early. But as usual, I was selfish. I didn't think about him when I got in that car. I did what was most convenient for me. I'm no better than Vera. I didn't protect Christian any more than she protected me from those pedophiles she rented my body to for name-brand shoes."

"Sully, don't compare the two. You not wearing a seat belt and your mother allowing you to be molested is not the same thing."

"No, this is worse. I'm still here. I didn't die, but my baby is gone. I failed him in the worst possible way. So did Charles when he made the choice to deliver him."

Lawson seized Sullivan by the arms. "Sullivan, listen to me. You did not kill your son. Neither did Charles. It was a tragic but freak accident. You hear me? *An accident!* You're letting the devil get to you. That's how he operates. He doesn't show up in a blaze of fire with a pitchfork and a red bodysuit. He gets into your head and starts suggesting things that make you have these kinds of crazy thoughts. The whole game plan is to destroy you and your family, because if he can do that, he can fracture our church and its impact on the city. You've got to work against that."

"How do I do that?"

"You fight. You fight for your marriage. You fight against this grief that's trying to take hold of you. You pray and meditate on the Word. You stop drinking, and you stop blaming your husband and yourself for what happened."

"Then that leaves only one person to blame for what I'm going through right now and the pain I suffered through as a child. And that's God. Tell me how am I supposed to trust a God who would do this to me?"

# Chapter 31

"Everybody can relax now. I'm almost myself again."

*—Sullivan Webb*

"This place is amazing!" exclaimed Desdemona as she walked out of a Zumba class with Sullivan. "Thanks for showing me around your gym. I may have to come out here more often."

Sullivan wiped her forehead with a towel as they entered the gym's weight room. "I try to come work out at least three times a week. You're welcomed as my guest anytime."

"Thanks. I may take you up on that since it appears that I'll be in Savannah longer than I anticipated."

"What's going on with Kina's book? How much longer do you think you'll be sticking around?"

"It's tough to say. Kina and I have different ideas about what direction we think the book should go in. I hope to have everything wrapped up in the next month or two, but we'll see. It's moving along slowly but surely."

"Hmm . . . *slowly but surely,*" repeated Sullivan. "Sounds like my marriage."

"Are you and your husband still having problems?"

Sullivan gripped a set of push-up bars and started planking. "It's no worse, and it's no better."

"Well, it's going to take some time to get over your son's death and the role your husband played in it."

"I suppose. My mother thinks that I'm being petty and that I'm crazy to still be upset about that."

"Sullivan, come on. This is the same woman who allowed her boyfriends to sexually abuse her daughter. She's not exactly a pillar of wisdom. You have the right to deal with this in your own way. Besides, your marital problems didn't start with losing Christian. You said yourself that your husband doesn't understand you or prioritize your marriage."

Sullivan lowered her body for push-ups. "I do wonder if I'm expecting too much from Charles sometimes. I don't doubt that he loves me. Shouldn't that be enough?"

"I can't answer that for you, but if you have to ask, that in itself is very telling." Desdemona grabbed an exercise ball and got down next to Sullivan on the floor. "I must say, even if you're aren't feeling great, you haven't let it affect you on the outside. You look fabulous these days."

"I'm feeling pretty good, especially compared to a couple of months ago. I still have my moments when I just want to grab my babies and run off somewhere and never look back."

Desdemona was caught off guard. *"Babies?"*

"Yes. In those fantasies, Christian is still alive, but moments like that are far and few. I'm stronger now. Even though I still miss him every day, I'm able to think about Christian without bursting into tears."

"That's wonderful! Your friends were worried about you for a minute there."

"Yeah, I know, but everybody can relax now. I'm almost myself again."

"So what changed?"

"I don't know. Time, I guess. Staying active, being around Charity. Spending time with Simon has helped too."

"How so?"

Sullivan smiled. "He's such a cute kid. I love watching him and Charity play. They act like brother and sister. Seeing them interact makes me smile. I imagine that's how Charity and Christian would've looked growing up together."

"I bet that's a beautiful sight."

"It is. Take a look." Sullivan whipped out her phone and showed Desdemona pictures of the two children playing together. "That's them at the park. . . . Here's one at Lawson's house. . . . There they are asleep on the floor."

Desdemona scrolled to a picture of Sullivan and Simon making faces at the camera. "That's a nice picture of you and Simon."

"Yeah, I was teaching him the art of taking the perfect selfie. See, here's another one."

Desdemona viewed the shot of Sullivan and Simon striking similar poses. "Aw, that's adorable! Has Lawson seen these?"

"Girl, have you seen that dinosaur Lawson calls a cell phone? I think it's the same one we had in college, and she refuses to upgrade. I doubt she can even receive pictures on that prehistoric thing." Sullivan put the phone away.

Desdemona laughed. "I think it's a positive sign that you're feeling better, but don't rush the grieving process. It's okay to take time to mourn your son. He was a part of you. Don't beat yourself up or feel bad for crying and missing him or for going to his nursery for comfort."

"There is no nursery for comfort," revealed Sullivan. "Charles had Christian's room renovated. The walls have been painted, and all his furniture and toys donated to charity. To see it now, you'd never know that it was once a room for our baby."

"For real? That seems harsh."

"He didn't think it was a good idea to leave it the way it was. He said it was keeping me from healing."

Desdemona scrunched up her face. "And you were okay with that?"

"I didn't have any say in it."

"Sullivan, that room was all you had left of your son. It's like your husband took your child away from you all over again," replied Desdemona. "It's not fair, especially since you haven't tried to dictate how he should and shouldn't grieve."

"It did kinda feel that way," admitted Sullivan. "Seeing strangers come in and box up his things was hard. I was able to take some comfort in knowing that it was all being donated and that somebody's child would benefit from it. I don't know. . . . Maybe Charles is right. I have been able to cope better, not having to be reminded every time I pass by that room."

"That's not the point. It shouldn't have been his decision alone. You live in that house too, and you were the one grief-stricken by losing your child. To do something that drastic without consulting you seems controlling and wrong. He wasn't thinking about your feelings, and once again, he didn't put your needs first. He just did what the heck he wanted to do."

Sullivan sat on the floor, stretching and thinking. "It does kind of seem that way, doesn't it?"

Desdemona nodded. "I don't want you to think I'm trying to cause dissension between you and Charles. I honestly hope that you can work through this, but you have as much right to be respected and heard as he does. That's all I'm saying."

As Desdemona made her way to the elliptical machines, Sullivan sat pondering, asking herself who was right in this situation. Vera had cautioned her not to be quick to give up on her marriage, but anyone with a modicum of sense knew not to trust anything Vera had to say. Desdemona had brought up some good points as well. Charles *had* bulldozed her concerning Christian's room, and how many times had she told him she felt like she was living in the shadows of his ministry? Biblically and spiritually, Charles was the head of the household, but where did that leave her? She wanted to turn to God, but how could she when felt like He'd abandoned her when she needed Him most?

# Chapter 32

"What did you think I was going to do with Simon?
Snatch him up and sell him on the black baby market?"

*–Sullivan Webb*

"Well, this is a surprise!" exclaimed Lawson. "You're
becoming a regular around these parts. Come on in."

Sullivan walked into Lawson's house and handed her
some shopping bags. "Here. You can thank me later."

Lawson began digging through the bags. "What's all
this? Christmas isn't for another week."

"A few super cute outfits for Simon. I was shopping
for Charity and found myself wandering over to the boys'
section. It was all half off, and you know I've never been
one to turn down a good sale!"

"That's true. Where's Charity?"

"Tuckered out and home with Charles. She obviously
didn't inherit my shopping stamina." Sullivan looked up,
surprised to see Desdemona sitting in Lawson's living
room. "Oh, hi, Des. You here to interview Lawson?"

Desdemona held up her notebook. "Yep, gettin' all the
goods on Kina."

Sullivan sucked her teeth. "I can give you a book all by
myself on that subject!"

"I thought you and Kina were in a good place now,"
said Lawson.

"We're in a *better* place. *Good* may be pushing it." Sullivan's mood brightened when she laid eyes on Simon. "Hey, Simon! Come give me a hug!"

"Somebody looks happy to see Mr. Banks," remarked Desdemona as Simon ran to Sullivan's waiting arms.

Sullivan planted a big kiss on Simon's cheek. "Are you kidding? This is one of the highlights of my day!"

"They've become quite close," Lawson informed Desdemona.

Desdemona scribbled something in her notebook. "Interesting . . ."

"I'm sure you two have lots to talk about. Why don't I take Simon outside and let him run around the yard and burn some of this energy off so you two can talk?" suggested Sullivan.

"Sully, you don't have to do that," replied Lawson.

"It's my pleasure. Besides, it's warm outside today, and running behind toddlers is one of the ways I get my cardio in!" Sullivan reached for Simon's tiny palm. "Come on, Si. I've got five pounds to lose, and you and Charity are my versions of SlimQuick."

Lawson smiled as she watched Sullivan lead Simon outside. "She certainly seems like she's in a good mood, doesn't she?"

"Yeah . . . you sure she hasn't been drinking?" asked Desdemona. "That could also account for her jovial mood."

"I didn't smell any liquor on her. I think she's slowly coming back to herself. It's great to see."

"Really? That's not been my assessment at all," remarked Desdemona.

Lawson faced her. "Why not?"

"You know Sullivan and I have been spending a good bit of time together lately. From my observation, she's still very much in a disconsolate state. I think she needs help, Lawson."

"I thought she was getting better." Lawson watched from her living room window as Sullivan played peeka-boo with Simon, and added forlornly, "Maybe I was just seeing what I wanted to see."

"That's often the case when people around us are hurt-ing and have the potential to be destructive. We look for any glimmer of hope and run with it. Hoping the person is getting better is a lot easier than facing the possibility of their getting worse." Desdemona joined Lawson at the window. "*Humph.* Doesn't that concern you?"

"Doesn't what concern me?"

"How attached Sullivan is to Simon."

"No, Simon is my stepson, and Sullivan is my best friend. I don't expect her to treat him like a leper."

"I'm not saying that, but the gifts and the unannounced visits . . ." Desdemona shrugged. "I think it's a bit much."

Lawson turned away from the window. "What are you getting at?"

"Sullivan just lost her child. Now she's fixated on yours. It's not healthy."

"Yeah, I admit that Sullivan has been having a hard time dealing with Christian's death, but I don't think she's fixated on Simon, not the way you mean."

"You're probably right. You know Sullivan way better than I do." Desdemona paused. "But she has said and done some things that I think are cause for concern."

"Like what?"

"She has pictures of the two of them together on her phone, and she talks about him a lot," revealed Desde-mona. "It sort of makes me uncomfortable to tell you the truth."

Lawson was now alarmed. "What is she saying about him?"

"She's talked about how much she misses her baby and how being with Simon makes her feel close to Christian.

She said that when she holds him, she fantasizes about him being her baby. She also talks about wishing she could take off somewhere with her kids and never come back. Her *kids,* plural, so she's not just talking about Charity."

Lawson refused to let her mind go there. "Come on, Des. Kidnapping? That's a pretty far stretch even for a writer like you!"

"Is it? Did you know that she'd been taking pictures of him?"

Lawson disclosed that she didn't.

"Sullivan is obviously going through postpartum depression, in addition to mourning her son," said Desdemona. "The fact that she's self-medicating with alcohol only adds fuel to an already volatile situation. You've all said that she isn't in her right mind these days. It wouldn't take much for her to snap."

"Okay, yes, she has been sad and has been drinking a bit much," conceded Lawson, "but I don't think she's a danger to anyone other than herself."

"Are you willing to risk this child's life to find out? People snatch up babies every day. How could you forgive yourself for putting Simon in harm's way? How would your husband forgive you?"

"I can't ban my best friend from coming over. I know how that feels. I could never hurt Sullivan that way."

"But you can risk her becoming dangerously obsessed with your child?" Desdemona squinted her eyes, trying to make out clearly what she was seeing. "Oh, my God, what is she doing? Is she leaving with Simon?"

Lawson looked out the window, startled at seeing Sullivan taking Simon to her car. "What the . . ."

"Oh, my God!" cried Desdemona. "Lawson, you've got to get out there. You've got to stop her before she does something crazy! Go!"

Frantic, Lawson dashed out of the house. "Sullivan, wait!" she yelled. "Stop! Put him down!"

Sullivan looked up. "Lawson?"

"Give him to me!" Lawson raced to the car and whisked Simon away from her. "Where are you going with him?"

"Nowhere." Sullivan closed her car door.

"Don't you ever take him without asking me again, you hear me? *Ever!*" shrieked Lawson.

"I wasn't taking him anywhere. I was getting Charity's ball out the car for Simon to play with."

"Oh," said Lawson, embarrassed. She set him down.

"What did you think I was going to do with Simon? Snatch him up and sell him on the black baby market?" Sullivan asked half-jokingly.

Lawson exhaled. "I didn't know what was going on. Clearly, I overreacted."

Sullivan put her hand on Lawson's shoulder. "Are you all right?"

"Girl, I just got one of those Amber alerts on my phone. They always make me nervous. I guess I'm a little on edge."

"I'd say more than a little. Did you really think I'd take him without telling you?"

"No," replied Lawson, hoping to convince herself as much as she was hoping to convince Sullivan. "But sometimes people get forgetful or caught up in the moment. . . ."

"Yeah, but I'd never forget to ask his parents before leaving with him."

"I know. I'm sorry."

Sullivan let it go. "It's fine."

Lawson forced a smile. "So are y'all about to play some kickball?" she asked, attempting to lighten the mood.

"We were, but I think I should go on home. It's getting late," said Sullivan, not wanting to show that she was a little hurt.

"Sully, you don't have to leave. I was trippin'. I'm sorry."

"No, you're being a protective mother. As a parent, you can never be too careful."

"Thanks for understanding."

Sullivan gave Lawson a quick hug. "I'll call you later."

Lawson waved as Sullivan pulled out of the driveway and then headed down the street.

Desdemona appeared at her side once Sullivan was out of sight. "Looks like you got out here in time."

"In time for what, Des? To stop an innocent ball game?" Lawson sighed. "Sullivan is no more of a threat to Simon than I am."

Desdemona nodded. "I hope it's true for your sake and this precious boy's."

"You don't know her, that's all."

"I might not know Sullivan that well, but I do know what it's like to lose a child. I wouldn't wish that on anyone."

Lawson agreed. "Yeah, Sullivan's been through a lot the past few weeks."

"Actually, I was talking about you. I'd hate to you see you and your husband go through that because you trusted a loose cannon." Desdemona could see the terror written on Lawson's face. "You better watch your back around her." She looked down at Simon. "His too."

# Chapter 33

"I can't blame you for reaching out to somebody else."

*—Reginell Vinson*

Mark crept up behind his wife, who was studying in their solarium, and stole a kiss from the side of her neck.

Reginell smiled and laid her schoolbooks to the side. "What are you doing home so early?"

"I was missing you, so I sent the basketball team home early and rushed back here to see my gorgeous wife."

"Did you see anyone else today at work?" Reginell hedged.

"No, the rest of the staff is out for Christmas break, but, babe, you know we work together. I can't help but run into Lawson."

"No, I didn't mean it like that," she assured him. "I was wondering how she was doing."

"Why don't you call and ask her?"

Reginell shook her head.

"Reggie, it's obvious you miss her. I know she misses you too. It's the holidays. Why don't y'all squash this already?"

"My sister doesn't know when to back off. It has to be that way for a while."

"I hate feeling like I'm the reason the two of you are not communicating."

"You're not, not really. Lawson has a problem maintaining boundaries. Look what she did to Namon and Shari! She wants to orchestrate our lives the same way. She needs to accept that we're married now. She can't run amuck in your life, like she used to, and she can't keep trying to control mine."

"Couldn't you just tell her that?"

"Lord knows I've tried, but Lawson never owns up to being wrong about anything. I doubt this time will be any different."

Mark sat down next to Reginell. "I think it's time I owned up to being wrong about something."

"What?"

"The kiss."

Reginell groaned.

"Baby, we haven't really talked about it, and it's the catalyst for everything getting so bad between you and your sister."

Reginell picked up one of her books. "I don't want to talk about this right now."

"We have to. You can't keep blaming Lawson for what happened. Some of that anger should be directed at me."

"How can I be mad at you? You'd just discovered in the worst possible way that I'd gone back to the stripper pole after I'd swore to you that I was done with that life. I can't blame you for reaching out to somebody else. I'm thankful that it was only a kiss."

"But it's more than that kiss that's got you upset. It's the way I am with Lawson."

"She initiates all of it, not you."

"But I let her," revealed Mark. "Reggie, I love you, and you're the only woman I've ever truly loved, but I can't deny that I do have this . . . *thing* with Lawson."

"*A thing?*" repeated Reginell, baffled. "Are you saying you have feelings for her?"

Mark went on. "Lawson and I get each other in a lot of ways. I have a ton of respect for her and . . ." His voice trailed off.

"And what?" Reginell could feel her heart pounding as she braced herself for his revelation.

"I guess a part of me has always wondered what would've happened between us if I'd known about Namon from the beginning. I can't lie. We had an instant connection the night we met and conceived him. We had that same connection when we met up again five years ago. It was strong enough for me to ask her to marry me."

"You said you did that for Namon."

"I did, but I wouldn't have even entertained the idea of marrying Lawson if there wasn't something there. It was that same pull that drew me to her the day we kissed."

"You realize this doesn't do much to convince me that you don't have lingering feelings for my sister, don't you?" asked Reginell, already on edge.

"I admit, it sounds bad, but I'm trying to be honest with you and get you to see that it's not all on Lawson. I'm as responsible as she is."

"So, basically, what you're saying is that you still have it bad for my sister," responded Reginell. It was crushing to hear that her husband of a few months was already pining away for another woman. The fact that it was her sister made it that much more excruciating. "Thank you for letting me know it's not all on Lawson. You have feelings for her too. You can't imagine how relieved that makes me feel," she added with sarcasm.

"Reggie, that's not what I'm saying." Mark kneeled down in front of her. "Lawson and I do share a bond. We have a child, we work together, and we're in the same profession. We're friends. While I do have a connection to her, it's nothing you ever have to worry about. I don't want her. I don't want anybody but you. You have to believe that."

Reggie sulked. "Why do you want me?"

"Huh?"

"I'm serious. Why did you choose me over Lawson? You said yourself that you have a connection and you have so much in common. You have a child and a soon-to-be grandchild," said Reginell. "So why me? Lawson is the smart one, the responsible one. She can talk to people, she's confident, and she's pretty. Why settle for the sister when you can have the golden child?"

"Babe, I have something with you I could never have with Lawson." He wrapped his hands around her. "Obviously, I'm attracted to you because you're smart, you're funny, beautiful, unbelievably sexy. . . ." Reginell blushed. "But from the moment we met, my spirit connected with your spirit. Do you remember that day in Lawson's living room?"

Reginell nodded. "I felt it too, but I didn't think I could ever be good enough for you."

"You never have to worry about that. Reggie, I want you because I know that my heart is safe with you. I can bear my soul and be completely open with you. I can sleep at night because I know you've got my back no matter what. You accept me just like I am—kids and baby mamas and all!"

They both laughed.

Mark cupped her face in his hands. "I don't believe there's such thing as a perfect mate, because none of us are perfect. However, I think God places people in our lives who make us better. You're that for me. I'm able to see God through our relationship."

"Really?" uttered Reginell, touched.

"Yeah. Being with you and having Namon and Mariah has helped me to learn how to put someone else first. It's made me more forgiving and gentler. It's made me more like Christ. And the fact that God took His time to create something as magnificent as you for me to love and take care of lets me know how much He loves me. I intend to spend the rest of my life showing you and showing God how thankful I am that He trusted me with your love."

"What about my hysterectomy?" she asked, her voice breaking. "I can't give you any kids. I can't even be intimate with you the same way I was before."

"I have my baby right here." He squeezed her. "And intimacy has nothing to do with sex. Intimacy is how we are together and the way we love each other. As far as sex is concerned, it may take us some time to get back to swinging from the shower rod, but I can wait. I love you, and what we have is so much deeper than sex."

Reginell slung her arms around his neck. "Baby, I love you so much. Hearing you say those things about me . . . No one has ever loved me the way you do."

"Reggie, you never have to even think about me going after your sister. I love you too much."

"I couldn't ask for a better Christmas gift than you." Reginell pulled back from him. "You're the best man I've ever met."

"I wouldn't be half the man I am if it weren't for you." He kissed her. "Baby, now that you've made up with me, make up with your sister. Y'all don't need to be fighting like this and bringing that drama into the New Year."

Reginell shook her head. "I love my sister, but I think we crossed a line of no return. Even if we made up today, nothing would ever be the same between us. Too much has happened."

"Promise me you'll pray about it, okay? Lawson is the only sister you have."

"And you're the only *husband* I have! I get where you're coming from with it, and I know you wouldn't cheat on me, especially with Lawson, but I still think she wants you. That much hasn't changed. Until it does, I've got to treat her like any other enemy."

# Chapter 34

"I haven't had a man warm my bed in a very long time.
Frankly, I'm not sure if I'm ready to go there again."

*—Kina Battle*

It was a Christmas of firsts. It was the first Christmas
Kina had in her new town house, the first Christmas Kina
didn't spend with her cousins Lawson and Reginell, due to
their sibling rivalry, and the first Christmas Kina shared
with Elvin and Kenny.

After the presents had been opened and the football
game had been watched on television, Kina, Elvin, and
Kenny gathered around the table for dinner.

"Kina Anne, you sho' know you can do some cooking!"
extolled Elvin, sucking his fingers. "That was one fine
meal there!"

"If you like my Christmas dinner, you ought to come
back next week for New Year's," boasted Kina. "I make a
mean pot of collards."

"Is that an invitation?" Elvin winked at her.

Kina winked back. "If you want it to be."

"I'd love to come back that night." Elvin swallowed
hard. "Truth be told, I'd love to come back every night."

Kina froze, not sure how to respond to that. "Um, Kenny, why don't you run downstairs and take the clothes out
the dryer for me?"

Kenny chuckled. "Real subtle, Ma. Is that your way of getting rid of me?"

"Boy, I don't need an excuse! If I want you to go . . ." Kina dropped the act. "Yeah, it's my way of getting rid of you, so would you be a good boy and take the hint?"

Kenny slid his chair back. "Let me know when the coast is clear."

Kina waited until Kenny was gone before laying into Elvin. "Now, what's this about coming back every night?"

"I think it's something we should consider."

"Moving in together?"

"Yeah. Why not? I think you could use a man around here, and I want to get to know my grandson and be in his life. I want to be in your life too."

"Elvin . . ." Kina was still blown away by the proposal. "We're not even a couple! All we've done is go out a few times and share a few kisses. Sure, I've known you for fifteen years, but the reality is that we don't know each all that well. Do you really think living together would be a good idea?"

"I recognize that we haven't been around each other that long, but, Kina, I don't think I've been imagining what's happening between us."

"No, you haven't," she admitted.

"Granted, a lot of people like to take their time and muddle through this and that, but I'll be sixty in four years. I ain't got time to waste that way. I follow my gut, and my gut tells me that this is right."

"I follow the Holy Spirit, and He hasn't said anything like that to me. The Bible is very clear about sexual immortality and the marriage bed being undefiled. I couldn't blatantly go against the Lord's Word like that. Elvin, I enjoy having you around, but living together? As a Christian, I can't sanction shacking and fornication."

"I don't mind crashing on the couch for as long as it takes for you to get comfortable having me in your bed."

"Who knows how long that could be? It could take years," mused Kina. "I haven't had a man warm my bed in a very long time. Frankly, I'm not sure if I'm ready to go there again."

"It could be that you're not ready because you haven't opened your heart up to the possibility of finding love again." He clasped Kina's hand. "I know you're scared, and I know you've been hurt. Most of it has been at the hands of my own son, but don't let fear keep you from giving us a chance. This feels right to me. You can't tell me you don't feel it too."

"The main thing I'm feeling presently is mass confusion."

"Kina, we were two lonely people who found each other against all odds. Where's the confusion in that?"

Kina concluded that there was none. "So if we did this, and by no means am I saying we are, would I be your roommate or your landlord or—"

Elvin cut her off. "You'd be my lady."

"As in we'd be a couple?" she asked for clarity.

"Of course. This would be one step toward building our future together."

"How long have you been thinking about this?"

"Not that long. But coming over and spending time with you and Namon has shown me what I've been missing in my life since my wife died. I want that back. I want my life to have purpose again. I miss having somebody to come home to and a woman to take care of."

"What about Brenda? What about E'Bell? You're his father. Being with you romantically wouldn't be right."

"Says who? Kina, your husband is dead. So is my wife. How can our being together hurt either one of them?"

"I'm sure a lot of the members of your family wouldn't approve of us having a relationship."

"What does that matter? They don't have a heaven or hell to put me in or take me out of!"

"How would we even begin to explain this to Kenny?"

"That boy of yours is smarter than you think. He's not blind. He knows what's been going on around here."

"Then he knows more than I do, because I had no clue," voiced Kina. She was still hesitant. "This all feels so rushed. You showed up out of the blue a few weeks ago, we've had a couple of dinners, and now you're talking about moving in. What's the big hurry?"

"There's no hurry, but why wait, baby? Why wait on love and happiness, huh?"

"Love?" repeated Kina.

"Yeah," replied Elvin. "We're both old enough to know what we want." He tilted her chin up and captured her in his gaze. "And I know who I want. That's you, Kina. I don't know if you've noticed or not, but I've been falling for you since the first time I came over."

While her ex-girlfriend Joan had professed her love for Kina, no man had even hinted at being in love with her since she met E'Bell in high school. Kina felt a declaration of that magnitude at least deserved her consideration and attention.

Kina was flattered. "I'm sorry for not being more eloquent and gracious with all this. Truly, I'm at a loss for words."

"You only need one word—yes. Say yes, Kina. We both know that time ain't promised to nobody. Let's make the best of it and go for happiness while we can."

"What if it doesn't work out?"

"What if it does?" asked Elvin. "If we're honest with each other, I can't make you any more guarantees about the future than you can make me, but I'm willing to try. I'm willing to find out what's out there for us. Imagine waking up together, trips, late nights in front of the fireplace, spending holidays with one another. It can be a New Year and a new start for the three of us. All I need is for you to say yes."

"You make it sound so easy . . . and wonderful."

"Because it is. You only have to reach out and grab it." He pulled Kina into a loving embrace. "So what's it gonna be, Kina?"

# Chapter 35

"I know you would never hurt him intentionally, but unintentionally is a different story."

*—Lawson Kerry Banks*

"Sorry I'm late. Traffic was a beast today," explained Lawson as she joined Sullivan at their favorite Spanish restaurant a few days into the New Year. "Did you order?"

"Not yet." Sullivan gave Lawson a hug. "Happy New Year!"

"Same to you. It was kind of weird not seeing any of you over the holidays. What did you and Charles do?"

"We had a quiet Christmas at home. We tried to make things as merry as we could for Charity, but it was hard. We'd planned to be opening gifts with both of our children. Of course, we spent New Year's Eve at Watch Night and kicked back New Year's Day. Were there any Christmas miracles at the Banks household?"

"None worth noting. Reggie and Mark were no-shows at my house on Christmas, and I'm assuming Namon spent the day with them. He didn't call, but he did include me on a mass 'Merry Christmas' text. That's the closest thing I had to an actual miracle."

"What about Simon?" asked Sullivan. "Having him there should've made for a lively Christmas."

"Simone flew back home for the holidays, so Simon was with her most of the time. Garrett and I ended up going to see his family in Alabama."

Sullivan adjusted Charity's bib. "Is Simon still with his mother?"

"No, Garrett has him. Simone dropped him off before she flew back to New York last night."

"You should've brought him with you. I wanted to see him."

Lawson's suspicions were raised. "You sound disappointed."

"I am. I thought he and Charity could have a little play-date. Plus, I had something I wanted to give him." She held up a gift bag.

"That's sweet, but you don't have to keep buying him presents."

"I know, but I love doing it. Besides, you know I'll use any excuse to shop."

Lawson picked up a menu. "Well, I'll be sure to give him a big hug and let him know that it's a gift from his auntie Sullivan when I take it to him. Thank you."

"No. I want to give it to him myself. I'll come by the house tomorrow. I want to see his face light up when he sees it."

"He-he has an, um, doctor's appointment tomorrow," spluttered Lawson.

"Okay. How about this weekend?"

"We'll probably be busy. Garrett was talking about driving up to Atlanta to take him to Legoland." Lawson stared at the menu, unable to look Sullivan in the face while lying.

"Oh, that sounds like fun! Let me know if you decide to go. Charity and I might tag along too. In the meantime, I could just follow you home and bring him the gift today."

Lawson looked down at her feet. "Um . . . this is awkward."

"What?"

"I don't think you should be buying him gifts, Sully."

Sullivan grinned. "If you're worried about me spoiling him, don't be. He's one. He won't even remember it, and he'll probably have more fun playing with the box than the actual gift."

"It's not just that." Lawson exhaled and set the menu down. "I don't want you to see Simon today."

"Why not? Is he sick or something?"

"No, but I think you may be."

Sullivan fluttered her eyelashes. "Excuse me?"

"Sullivan, I don't think it's healthy for you to spend so much time with Simon."

"Why not?"

"I'm scared you may be becoming a little . . ." Lawson held her breath before finishing. *"Obsessed."*

"With what? Simon?"

"Look, I'm not saying that it's inconceivable that you would be somewhat clingy where he's concerned. It wasn't that long ago that you lost your son. Anybody can see why you'd develop a fixation with Simon. I just think it's best that you don't come around right now, for his sake and yours."

"My God, Lawson, I bought the kid a gift. I didn't claim him as a dependent on my income taxes!"

"I'm not just talking about the gifts. What about all the visits and the pictures you've been taking of him without my knowledge or permission?"

Sullivan was dumbfounded. "What pictures?"

"The ones you have on your phone."

"Those were innocent selfies!" argued Sullivan. "You wanna see them?"

Lawson shook her head. "It's not innocent when you factor it in with the gifts and the visits and everything else."

"Lawson, I'm never alone with him for more than five minutes. What could I possibly do to him behind your back in that length of time?"

"Children have been taken from their homes in less time than that," said Lawson.

Sullivan was horrified. "So you think I'm going to kidnap him or something?"

Lawson nervously bobbed her knee up and down. "I don't know."

Sullivan studied Lawson's face. "You're serious, aren't you?" she asked incredulously.

"I know you would never hurt him intentionally, but unintentionally is a different story." Lawson tried to smolder the fire erupting in Sullivan's eyes. "I'm not saying that it'll always be this way. Only for time being. You understand, don't you?"

Sullivan crossed her arms. "Not at all!"

"It's no different than you not wanting Kina around Charity and Charles after Charles's stroke."

"So this is your way of getting me back for that?"

"Of course not."

"Need I remind you that your cousin actually did prove herself to be a threat? She did everything in her power to destroy my family, and she did it on purpose. My situation is nothing like that."

"Yes, it is. Kina had just lost her husband, and you've lost your son. You both responded by acting out in a lot of destructive ways. Sully, these days, I never know which version of you I'll get. You're sad. You're elated. You're angry. You're sweet. You're drunk. You're sober. You're just as unpredictable now as Kina was then."

"I won't deny that I've been all over the place since the accident, but I've been feeling better lately, Lawson. It's mostly because I've been spending time with Simon."

"I've noticed, but that concerns me even more. Getting closer to Simon shouldn't be the reason you feel better." Lawson folded her hands together. "I think you need to use this time to focus on your own baby, not someone else's."

"Lawson, spending time with Simon hasn't made me delusional. It's given me hope. It reminds me that my son is happy and is playing like Simon is, only he's doing it in heaven. Otherwise, I'd be focusing on the fact that his body is decaying in a cold, dark grave six feet underground, where I can never get to him or hold him or see him. I know I've been lost without Christian, but I'd never do anything to Simon or any other child, nor am I sitting around trying to replace Christian with anyone else. That's crazy! And the mere fact that you think I would . . ." Sullivan shook her head. "I have to be honest. It hurts, Lawson."

"Sullivan, you are my oldest and closest friend. You know I wouldn't do this unless I was genuinely concerned."

"Concerned about me or Simon's safety?"

"Both," admitted Lawson.

"I see." Sullivan snatched up her purse. "So my best friend thinks I'm a baby-snatching nut job! It's eye-opening to know what your friends really think of you."

"I *am* your friend, which is why I want you to get help and don't want to see you get attached to a child who doesn't belong to you. Plus, I'm his stepmother. It's my responsibility to look after Simon as much as it is Garrett's and Simone's."

"Look at me, Lawson!" commanded Sullivan, raising her voice and looking her squarely in the eyes. A few nearby patrons took notice. "This is me—*Sullivan!* When have you ever known me to endanger anybody's child? You know me, or at least I thought you did."

Lawson lowered her voice, hoping that Sullivan would do the same. "People change, and I think Christian's death changed you, Sully. I'm sorry, but I can't say definitively that you can be trusted around children right now."

Sullivan rolled her eyes and announced, "This coming from a woman who tried to abort her own grandchild" loud enough to gain the attention of the restaurant's manager. She fumed and began gathering up Charity's belongings. "But I forgot that when it comes to you, it's always *different*."

"I'm not perfect, either, Sully, but I have to do what I think is best for Simon."

Sullivan stood up. "You do that, okay?"

A manager approached their table. "Is everything all right over here?"

"It will be." Sullivan slung her purse over her shoulder. "I'm out of here!"

The manager seemed satisfied and left their table.

Lawson tried to stop Sullivan. "Wait. Don't you think we need to talk about this?"

"So is it you I should be talking to or a shrink? I'm confused, but that's probably because I'm so darn crazy, right?" Sullivan unbuckled the high-chair strap and lifted Charity out of the seat.

"I never said that."

"Right. You don't have to worry about me coming around with all my grief and psychosis ever again. Consider Simon safe. Now, if you'll excuse me, Charity and I are going to the park. It's such a lovely day today. I'm sure I can find at least one child left unattended whom I can take home and pretend is my dead son. Good-bye."

"Please don't leave like this!" pleaded Lawson. "We're best friends. Don't go away angry."

"You don't want me to go away angry, but you do want me to go away, don't you?"

"I never said that," Lawson called after her. "Sullivan . . ."

Sullivan ignored her and marched Charity out of the restaurant without looking back.

Lawson sat down. She grappled with the fact that she had alienated not only her son and sister, but now her best friend too, and was left to wonder if being right was worth being lonely.

# Chapter 36

"When you know better, you do better."

*–Lawson Kerry Banks*

Kina stared out the window from the passenger seat of Lawson's car as they rode to choir rehearsal together later that week. "How did you know you were ready to move in with Garrett?" she asked.

"Ha, that's easy—when I got fired from Macy's and could no longer afford to pay the house note by myself! But that was a long time ago. We hadn't even accepted Christ into our lives back then and knew nothing about fornication and God's plan for marriage." Lawson briefly took her eyes off the road to look over at Kina. "Why do you ask?"

"Elvin wants to move in."

Lawson's mouth gaped open from shock. "Did he propose?"

"Not marriage, only shacking up."

"How do you feel about that?"

"I'm not sure," admitted Kina. "This whole situation is so new and unexpected. I haven't had time to process it, but he thinks we share something special."

"You do—your son and his grandson! Other than Kenny, what do you all have?"

Kina turned to Lawson. "Feelings."

Lawson blinked back. "Kina, are you falling for this man?"

"Maybe . . . I don't know. I like being with him, and he's a good influence on my son."

"But is that enough to build a future on or take such a drastic step? Cohabitation is a very big deal, Kina, and it has both emotional and spiritual consequences."

"That's what's bothering me. I know what the Word says about shacking, and I'm really trying to live my life the right way, especially after living it so wrong over the past few years."

"You can't ever go wrong letting the Bible be the final authority on all decisions. You don't even seem to be at peace with the idea of Elvin coming to live with you. Your peace and God's Word should align. If they don't, you know you're out of His will."

"Yeah, but what if Elvin's the one? What if this is my last chance at happiness?"

"Kina, as long as you're still breathing, there's no such thing as your last chance at happiness. If it's meant to be, it'll be, and you won't have to give up your principles to make it happen," pointed out Lawson.

"That all sounds good, but the truth is I *have* been lonely. And as much as I try to deny it, I want to be in a relationship. I want to be in love again."

"You can have all that without living in sin, Kina."

"Living together before marriage worked out for you and Garrett."

"That's because he moved out once we understood God's take on it. When you know better, you do better."

"I'm weighing it out. Desdemona thinks I should go for it."

"Oh . . . does she?" Lawson's face fell.

"Yeah." Kina noticed the change in Lawson's demeanor. "What was that look about?"

"Nothing, really. I'm just wondering how much we should be listening to her."

"Did she give you some bad advice?"

Lawson spoke with reservation. "Kinda. I had a big fall-out with Sullivan the other day."

"Why? What happened?"

"We all know how hard Sully's taken Christian's death. Des noticed that Sully seemed to be developing a weird attachment to Simon, and suggested that Sully might be too emotionally unstable to be around children, specifically my stepson. Des really had me kind of freaked out and worried that Sully might try to take him, so I panicked. I told Sully I didn't want her around Simon anymore."

Kina raised an eyebrow. "That sounds a little extreme, Lawson."

"It didn't at the time. Needless to say, the conversation did not end well."

"Knowing Sullivan, I'm sure it didn't!"

"Anyway, she stormed out, and I haven't heard from her since. I've called and left messages, but she's obviously not trying to hear anything I have to say."

"I can't say I'm shocked, Lawson. Most people don't take to kindly to being called crazy."

"I didn't say she was crazy."

"Didn't you, though? You barred her from your stepson. Isn't that a clear sign that you think a person is crazy?"

Lawson quietly mulled over Kina's questions.

"Speaking of babies, how's Namon? Is Shari's pregnancy coming along okay?"

Lawson shrugged. "I have no idea. He's not speaking to me, either."

"Wow, you're on a roll, aren't you? Is there anyone else who is estranged that you want to tell me about?"

"Hmm . . . did I mention that Reggie and I are still at odds?"

*"Still?"* Kina shook her head. "This is bad, cuz! When it comes down to it, family is all we've got."

"At least my marriage is intact. Garrett is one person left in Savannah who still loves me."

"Aw, I still love you too." Kina reached over and pinched her cousin's cheek. "That'll never change."

Lawson smiled. "Thanks, sweetie. That's a lovely sentiment. But based on everything that's gone down in the past few months, I've learned to never say, 'Never.'"

# Chapter 37

"Do you have any idea how many times I've been asked, 'Why do you hang out with that whore? Don't you know what kind of person she is?'"

*–Angel King*

Angel shook her head as she watched Sullivan spike her orange juice with champagne after they returned to Sullivan's house following their morning run. Just when she thought Sullivan had been making emotional strides, she seemed to be spiraling out of control again.

"Do you think you should be drinking this early?"

Sullivan rolled her eyes. "I don't know. Do you think having one irksome mother is enough without you throwing your placenta into the mix?"

"Dang, Sully, it was merely an observation! If you want your liver to be looking and functioning like a shriveled-up shrimp in a few years, that's fine with me."

Sullivan took a few sips. "We've all got to die of something, right?"

"We don't have to speed up the process with bad decisions." Angel lifted the glass out of Sullivan's hand. "Anyway, I need to talk to you about something, and I need you to be sober."

Sullivan snatched it back. "Angel, I'm not getting into an argument with you about my drinking. I get enough of that from Charles."

"I'm sure he's concerned, like the rest of us. Are you two any better these days?"

"We've gotten better at avoiding each other, if that's what you mean. Of course, we keep up the facade at church, the way a nice first family should, but once we get home . . ." She swallowed a mouthful. "I have my life, and he has his."

Angel was disappointed. "I wish you could get through this impasse. Christian's death should've brought you closer together, not torn you apart."

"Instead, it only highlighted and magnified problems that were already there. Charity may be the only thing holding us together these days."

"I'm praying for you, Sully, for real. I'd hate to see another Christian family fall apart. We should be able to hold it together if no one else can."

"Church folks are regular people, Angel."

"Church folks are. Christians are covered by the blood of Jesus. Our lives should reflect that."

"I suppose. . . ."

"But your relationship with Charles isn't the only one I'm worried about these days." Angel sat down. "Lawson told me what happened."

"If your objective is to *not* drive me to drink, don't mention that person's name around me."

"Sully, she means well. . . ."

"She all but called me a psychotic, baby-thievin' lunatic and banned me from seeing her stepson."

"She's trying to do the right thing and protect him."

"But from me, Angel? I've been her best friend for over twenty years, and I've never done anything to hurt her. Why would I start now? The mere fact that she even thinks that I'm so far off in Toontown that I can't distinguish between my son and hers says a lot about this friendship, if you can even call it that. I'm done with her."

"I think this is the mimosa talking."

"To tell you the truth, I wouldn't even be drinking right now if it hadn't been for that fight with Lawson," Sullivan confessed. "I'd stopped drinking. I was starting to pull my life back together. I was feeling like the old me again. I guess there's something about your best friend, who also happens to be the person who knows you better than anyone else, saying that you're a head case that can shoot all those warm, fuzzy feelings straight to hell."

"I know that what she said hurt you, but this"—Angel pointed at Sullivan's glass—"is not the solution."

"Then what is?"

"Leaning on your family. Most importantly, leaning on God. I don't see you doing much of that these days."

"Well, I guess there's nothing like losing your child to send those warm, fuzzy faith feelings straight to hell too."

"Is your faith that weak that one tragedy can make you turn your back on everything you know to be true about God? Or your friendship with Lawson, for that matter?"

Sullivan shook her head. "There are simply some things that can't be undone, regardless of how much faith or history you have."

"If that were true, we'd all be in trouble! Faith in Duke and our love and believing that God brought us together are what has sustained us through the tough times."

"I thought y'all broke up."

"We're on a break," explained Angel. "That's not the same as a breakup."

"If your man being a rapist isn't grounds for a breakup, I don't know what is!"

Angel turned sullen. "Duke is not a rapist, Sullivan. I wish you'd stop saying that even as a joke."

Sullivan finished off her mimosa. "Who said I was joking?"

"If it wasn't a joke, it would make you one cruel, heartless witch for saying that to me."

"For speaking the truth?"

"What truth? He was charged, not convicted. " Angel flung her hand. "I'm not going to get into this with you today, Sully."

"Why not?"

"Because you're two sips away from inebriation and you're talking crazy."

"Oh, so now you've jumped on the 'Sullivan is crazy' train too?"

"I didn't say you were crazy. I said you were drunk."

"Angel, you know it takes more than one watered-down mimosa to get me drunk. Plus, I haven't said anything about Duke that I haven't told you already."

"Sully, how would you feel if I called the man you love a rapist? That's not a word you play around with."

"Duke may not be a rapist, but he is a liar and a cheater, right? You do own up to that much, don't you?"

Angel raised an eyebrow. "Are we talking about Duke, or are we talking about you?"

"Whatever," muttered Sullivan.

"Regardless, cheating on me with one person doesn't make Duke a rapist."

"One person that you know of," retorted Sullivan. "Even in college, we all knew that Duke wasn't exactly stingy with the peen. He's dipped it in practically every available hot pocket from D.C. to Georgia!"

Angel took offense. "That's completely unfounded and unnecessary, Sullivan. You don't know Duke the way I do."

"Maybe not, but I *do* know that you drove all night from D.C. to my apartment in Savannah because you didn't have anywhere else to go after Duke left you for Theresa. I *also* know that we found you in the bathroom, passed out and overdosing on pills after you tried to kill yourself, and I also remember having to help you pick up the pieces when you lost your baby after finding out your husband had fathered someone else's child."

"Sullivan, you're talking about things that happened over a decade ago. You've changed since the whole Vaughn affair fiasco. Don't you think it's possible that Duke's changed too?"

"*You* don't even think he's changed, Angel," argued Sullivan. "Otherwise, you wouldn't have gone to his accuser for answers."

"I went to prove that Duke was innocent."

"No, you went to have her confirm what you knew to be true in the pit of your stomach. Granted, I'm willing to concede that maybe he didn't try to rape her, but we both know something happened between the two of them in that hotel room. The only question is whether or not it stopped being consensual at some point. My goodness, how many times does Duke have to make a fool out of you for you to wake up?"

Angel fired back. "That's a great question for me to ask Charles, since apparently he has yet to meet his quota with you! How you can stand there and degrade Duke for cheating when, for the longest time, you didn't even know who the father of your child was!"

"Don't bring Charles and Charity into this! My marriage has nothing to do with Duke's wandering eyes and hands. Say what you want about me, but nobody has ever accused me of forcing myself on them."

Angel's temper flared. "You know, Sullivan, I've spent many years turning a blind eye to your indiscretions. Mostly because I love you, and also because I thought underneath all the scheming and lying and manipulation and lawlessness, there was a real person in there who had a heart. I've always been willing to give you another chance to prove that you were not the person everyone said you were. Do you know how many times I've had to defend you and our friendship to other people? Do you have any idea how many I've been asked, 'Why do you hang out with that whore? Don't you know what kind of person she is?'"

"Hold up. I've never asked you to defend me. There's never been an ounce of shame in my game! I don't need you or anyone else trying to explain Sullivan Raquel Webb. I do what I want, when I want it, and banish to hell whoever doesn't like it. I don't need you taking up for me. All the Charity I need is in that upstairs bedroom, asleep. I don't want yours."

"Remember that next time you call wanting somebody to keep one of your many dirty little secrets," threatened Angel.

Sullivan gave her the once-over. "I'm not the only one in this room with dirty little secrets, not by a long shot."

"Let me get out of here before I say something that I can't take back. I'm leaving." Angel snatched up her car keys and bottled water. "I'm not about to stand here and let you disrespect me and talk to me any kind of way."

"You're right. That's Duke's job."

Angel brushed past Sullivan on her way out.

"Fine. Why don't you go run to your good friend Lawson, and the two of you can congratulate each other on being better and more moral than anyone else!"

Angel turned around. "We may not be more moral than most, but we're certainly better and more moral than you! Honestly, I feel sorry for your daughter."

"I would feel sorry for yours, but I can't. You left her in a dead fetus pile at the abortion clinic."

Angel glared at Sullivan. "That was a low blow, Sullivan, even for you, who's no stranger to going below the belt, in every sense of the word."

Sullivan poured another glass of juice. "I thought you were leaving."

"I am. I'm also thinking that Lawson isn't the only one who needs a break from you."

Sullivan made a face, mocking her. "Take a break, Angel. Have a seat. In fact, you need to have several seats, preferably somewhere other than here!"

Angel marched out. At that moment, she knew they'd crossed a precipice. Outside, Angel was tempted to turn back and apologize but sided against it. Sullivan had finally gone too far. In truth, they both had.

# Chapter 38

"This circle shouldn't be a place where I have to worry about being judged or living up to a standard or keeping grown women from killing each other."

*—Angel King*

Lawson joined Angel for a cup of tea at Angel's house. It was one of the few places she still felt welcomed.

"How are you holding up these days?" she asked Angel.

"It depends on which minute you ask. Right now, I'm okay. Fifteen minutes ago, I was a mess. An hour from now, who knows? Duke's case is still pending, and it's stressing both of us out. He thinks I don't believe in him, and I can't say definitively that I do. I'm afraid this may be what finally ends our love story."

"Angel, I'm completely confident that you and Duke will find your way back to each other. You always do."

"Time will tell," said Angel. "You and Namon still on the outs?"

Lawson nodded.

"And Reggie?"

Lawson nodded again.

"What about you and Sully?"

Lawson sighed. "It's complicated with us."

"Dang, is there anyone you're still cool with?" joked Angel.

"I have you and Kina still ridin' for me."

"If it counts for anything, I did try to get Sully to reconcile with you. Of course, that was before she and I became fast frenemies."

Lawson was shocked to learn that Angel and Sullivan had fallen out too. "Et tu, Brute?'"

"Yeah, she started going in on Duke again, and I couldn't take it anymore. I said some things. She said some things. It got pretty nasty."

"I'm sad to hear that, but I know how hard it is when the people you love and count on don't support you."

"Ain't that the truth? I know everybody else has bailed, but you'll always have me," Angel assured her. "I've got your back. Despite what you have going on with Reggie and Sullivan, you've been great to me. You're an amazing friend, which is exactly what I've needed with everything going on with Duke. You have no idea what your support has meant to me."

"It's easy. I know Duke didn't do it."

"Thank you. Why can't anyone else see that?"

"Some people would rather believe the worst about everybody else. My mom used to always say that it's easier to believe than to think. Considering what Reggie and Sully have gone through with men, it's no surprise that they would side with Duke's accuser."

"I guess."

"It's kind of like my situation with Namon. Reggie and Sully don't agree with what I did regarding the abortion, but you understand why I did it, don't you?"

Angel leaned forward. "Actually, no, I don't."

Lawson was surprised by her answer. "Why not?"

"Lawson, you were so vehement with your disapproval a year ago, when I had an abortion. You droned on and on about how my baby deserved a chance at life and how selfish I was being for not telling the baby's father about the abortion. I was riddled with guilt because of it. That guilt was one of the reasons I started abusing painkillers."

"So it's my fault you started popping pills like they were candy?"

"No, but your condemnation didn't help! On top of that, you never even apologized for how you treated me. Then you turned around and tried to do the same thing to Namon that you shunned me for doing to Jordan. The same abortion that was such as sin for me to get was perfectly acceptable when you tried to force one on your son's girlfriend."

"Angel, the situation with Namon is completely different."

"How so?"

"Namon and Shari are in no position to raise a child."

"Yeah, but at the time, neither was I. I could barely afford to feed myself, much less anyone else. I was working three jobs just to make ends meet, and Jordan certainly wasn't the man I wanted to share a child with."

"True, but you were old enough to know better and established enough make it work. Shari and Namon aren't."

Angel shook her head. "That's amazing."

"What?"

"Your ability to commit the same sins you accuse everyone else of yet find a convenient way to rationalize it when you're at fault."

"I have principles, and at least I try to do the right thing. My heart and intentions are always in the right place."

"And ours aren't?"

"I don't know. Was your heart in the right place when Miley wound up in the hospital, getting stitches, because you were indulging in your porn obsession instead of watching her? Was Sully's heart in the right place when she was sleeping with Vaughn and Charles at the same time? What about Kina when she outed Reggie for TV ratings or Reggie when she was stripping for married men and dropping her drawers for tips?"

"Love doesn't keep a record of the wrong others do," said Angel, quoting. "Lawson, I could just as easily dredge up your past sins, like lying to your husband or the deplorable way you treated poor Simon in the beginning. Not to mention how you played Mark and Garrett against each other and tried to convince Reggie that Mark wanted her only for sex. But I guess your heart was in the right place all those times too, right?"

Lawson rolled her eyes.

"You're self-righteous and judgmental. You can dish it, but you sure as heck can't take it. This is the way you eventually drive all the people you love away from you."

"Angel, if I didn't set a standard, there wouldn't be one in this group."

"I don't think anybody has a problem with you having a standard. The issue is that you set one that not even you yourself can maintain, but you judge us when we fall short."

"Regardless of what I've done right or wrong, I've always been a friend and been there for all of you. I've been the one praying, holding your hand, letting you know it's going to be okay. Is it too much to ask for my friends to do the same?"

"No, but you make us not want to support you when you get all 'moral majority' on us."

Lawson pursed her lips together and set down her cup. "I think coming here was a mistake."

Angel paused before speaking. "Maybe it was."

"You have a pleasant day," declared Lawson in the nastiest tone possible. She stomped toward the door but stopped when she placed her hand on the doorknob. "What are we doing?"

"You were seeing yourself out," retorted Angel.

Lawson came back into the room with Angel. "Don't you see what's happening to us? Everybody is all splintered off and mad."

"It's not the first time that's happened," said Angel.

"It's never been this bad and for this long. We all know that Sullivan is a hothead and Reggie has a smart mouth, and both are usually the source of problems in our friendship. But you and I, Angel, are always the rational ones, the two who diffuse the drama and keep everyone together."

Angel stood up. "I think that's the problem, Lawson. Friendship shouldn't be this much work! My friends should be my refuge from the craziness out in the rest of the world. This circle shouldn't be a place where I have to worry about being judged or living up to a standard or keeping grown women from killing each other."

"But that's what we do! We argue, we get mad, we cuss each other out, but we always get it together. That's what friends do."

"No, that's what *we* do and it's exhausting! I don't even have this much drama in my relationships with men. It's like we're trapped in a bad marriage."

"And now you sound like you want out, is that it?"

Angel exhaled. "Why are you making it sound like I'm a defector for wanting a little break? Do you know how much I have going on in my life, Lawson? My own personal drama is enough without everybody else's."

"I get that. I'm just afraid that if we don't put a stop to all the infighting, we're going to end up losing our friendship."

Angel mulled it over. "Would that be so terrible?" She paused. "In fact, I think it might be exactly what we need."

# Chapter 39

"How could you toy with my emotions like that?"

*–Kina Battle*

Kina learned very quickly what could happen when a person shows up unannounced when she turned up at Desdemona's downtown loft without calling first.

"Des, I'm concerned about the latest notes you e-mailed me about the book," said Kina, barging in once Desdemona answered the door. "I think you're making me come off as a self-centered, confused, needy thirst trap! Is that how you see me?"

"Of course not, but we can talk about it later. Right now you have to go." Desdemona redirected Kina toward the door.

"Wait. I brought some notes. I wanted to go over a few details with you."

"Kina, this isn't a good time to talk shop. Let's table this until tomorrow."

Kina became suspicious. "What's going on? Why are you trying to get rid of me?"

"I'm busy. Look, I don't want to be rude, but—"

Kina heard what sounded like water running and spotted a pair of men's loafers on Desdemona's living room floor and grinned. "Des, do you have a man up in here?"

"Yes, so you understand why I'm not up for company today. I already have some."

Kina was intrigued. "Well, who is he? Where did you meet him?"

Desdemona started physically shuffling Kina toward the door. "I'll tell you about it later."

"Hey, D. Where did you put my razor? I don't see it where I left it," called a male voice from another room.

Kina stood in place, listening. The voice sounded familiar.

Elvin emerged, clad only in a towel. "Why do you keep moving my stuff? I put it one place and find it in another." He froze when he looked up and saw Kina.

Kina's blood ran cold. "Elvin, what are you doing here? Des, what the heck is going on?"

Elvin reached his hand out. "Kina, I can explain."

Kina moved toward him, still in shock. "So the two of you are sleeping together?"

Desdemona appeared unfazed. "This is why you should've called before dropping by."

"I don't . . . I don't understand any of this," stammered Kina, unable to process what she was seeing with her own eyes. "How did this happen? You asked me to let you move in, and I find out that you're sleeping with my ghostwriter. What is this?"

"Relax," said Desdemona. "Elvin isn't sleeping with me. He works for me."

The revelation did nothing to ease Kina's confusion and anger. "Works for you how? As a male prostitute?"

"No, he's more of an informant. Isn't that right, Elvin?"

Elvin stood cemented in place, exposed both literally and figuratively. "Kina, it's a long story."

Kina took a defiant stance. "Oh, I have time. I want to hear this."

Elvin tightened the towel around his waist. "Can I run and put some clothes on first?"

"No!" retorted Kina. "I wanna know what's going on, and I want to know now!"

Desdemona sighed. "Elvin here is what many people would call an opportunist, but he's not a very good one."

Kina shook her head. "I don't understand . . ."

"Well, Kina, I had to spice up your story, and your dull church life wasn't giving me what I needed. When you dropped the little nugget about your in-laws hating your guts, I figured it would make for an interesting story line for you."

"What?" asked Kina, astounded. "So you went and dug up this joker to give me a love interest?"

"Not entirely," replied Desdemona. "I wanted to test those Christian values that you like to tout so much and see if you'd give them up for the right man. The fact that the man happened to be your late husband's father was gravy."

Kina glared at Desdemona. "How could you toy with my emotions like that? I thought we were friends!"

"Kina, I'm not one of your messy little girlfriends. This is a business for me. Writing is how I earn a living. Terrilyn wanted me to find your story, and I did. You should be thanking me."

"Thanking you?" repeated Kina with disdain. "It's all I can do not to kill you!"

"Murder, Kina?" Desdemona shook her head, mocking Kina. "I swear, you Christians are about the most hypocritical people I've ever seen in my life."

Kina focused her attention back on Elvin. "It's clear Desdemona has no scruples and will do anything for money, but why did you do it, Elvin? What was in it for you? Are you that greedy that you'd use the memory of your son and your own grandson for a few measly bucks?"

"It didn't do it just for the money," Elvin tried to explain.

"I told you he is a very bad opportunist," remarked Desdemona. "When I tracked him down, he was living in a homeless shelter after squandering his dead wife's insurance money and losing his house. He needed somewhere to stay, so I offered him a roof in exchange for his services."

Kina was heartbroken. "Is it true? Did you cut a deal with this woman?"

Elvin adjusted his towel again. "Kina, if you let me explain . . ."

"It's a yes or no question, Elvin. Did she send you to me? Were you working on her behalf to destroy me?"

"It wasn't like that. She said—"

Kina interrupted him. "I really don't care what she said or what she promised you. I want to hear out of your own mouth whether or not you were a part of some scheme of hers."

"Kina, you gotta understand. When she came to me, I ain't have nothing! When you ain't got nothing, there's nothing you won't do, because you don't have nothing to lose. She said all I had to do was get close to you for a few weeks and that you'd be coming into a lot of money soon. She said I'd be set for life if I played my cards right."

"And how much did it cost to play with my heart, huh? How much did you charge to get closer to your grandson?"

"If it makes you feel better, he didn't come cheap," Desdemona said, chiming in. "I had to clean him up, buy him new clothes, provide date money, and let him sleep on my sofa. Plus, I gave a thousand dollars seed money."

Kina squinted her eyes in disbelief. "You sold your family out for a grand and a few suits?"

"I was desperate, Kina."

"He still is. He knows it's back to the homeless shelter once I return to Atlanta," said Desdemona.

Kina's eyes started to burn with tears. "It's all making sense now. I see why you were so adamant about us moving in together. You didn't want to build a life with me. You just needed someone else to mooch off of."

"Kina, it may have started out that way, but the love I have for you and Kenny, that's real," professed Elvin. "You've got to believe me."

Kina shook her head. "I will never make the mistake of believing anything you have to say ever again!"

"You know what we mean to each other," said Elvin.

Kina looked at him with disdain. "You mean nothing to me."

"As much as I'd love to see this soap opera play out, I have work to do," interjected Desdemona. "Kina, I'm sure you can find your way home. Elvin, now that you've gotten caught with your pants down, metaphorically speaking, I have no further use for you. You're dismissed as well."

Elvin's mouth gaped open. "I don't have nowhere else to go."

Desdemona scooped up his shoes and handed them to him. "You know what they say. You don't have to go home, but you've got to get outta here!"

Elvin had no choice but to accept his fate. He took the shoes and disappeared into the bedroom to get dressed.

"I'm not going anywhere, not yet," insisted Kina. "I want my friends to know what you did."

Desdemona shrugged. "Then tell them."

"Lawson said she had her suspicions about you. I see she was right."

"There's no crime in being very good at my job, Kina. This wouldn't have even been necessary if you were good at yours."

"What job is that, Des? As a master manipulator?"

"As a person who knows how to get a story and make things happen." Desdemona thought it over. "Matter of fact, call your friends. Tell them to meet at your place to-morrow. This should be interesting and definitely some-thing worth writing about!"

# Chapter 40

"Despite my best efforts, how did I manage to become just as screwed up as you?"

*–Sullivan Webb*

Later that night, Sullivan found herself at a seedy bar downtown with an even seedier companion.

"Can you believe I'm sitting here having a drink with you? Now I know I've hit rock bottom!" Sullivan looked down into her empty wineglass and signaled the bartender for a refill.

Her mother concurred. "That makes two of us. Another blackberry margarita for me too."

"You've sat across from worse than me, Vera."

"As have you," noted Vera, running her finger across the salt-rimmed glass.

Sullivan raised her glass. "Touché. Don't worry. I don't expect you to know what it means."

"Sullivan, you know we can sit here and exchange insults all night, but I'm sure that's not why you wanted me to meet you here, so what gives? And make it quick, because I have things to do."

Sullivan watched as the bartender refilled her glass. "Despite my best efforts, how did I manage to become just as screwed up as you?"

Vera rolled her eyes. "Maybe we need to stick to exchanging insults."

"I'm serious."

"Sullivan, I didn't screw you up. Even if I did when you were younger, you're a grown woman now. Any screwing up you did after you left my house is all on you."

"Why don't you understand that I'm screwed up as a grown woman *because* of what you did when I was younger?" Sullivan looked up at her mother and asked the one question that had weighed on her practically her whole life. "How could you let those men do that to me?"

Vera sucked her teeth. "Do what to you, Sullivan? Give you money? Buy you designer clothes and expensive gifts?"

"Don't sit there acting like they were doing it out of the goodness of their hearts!" raged Sullivan. "It's insulting! Those were guilt gifts for me and 'Hush your mouth and pretend you didn't see nothing' tokens for you."

"Nobody did anything to you that you weren't asking for," ranted Vera. "I'm not to blame for you being hot in the pants!"

"What?" Sullivan asked incredulously. "I was a child, and you allowed grown men to take advantage of me and didn't lift a manicured finger to help! You didn't protect me. You let pedophiles disguised as boyfriends do all kinds of horrible, vile things to me! I was your child, Vera. Why didn't you protect me?"

"Sullivan, with so many of those nasty li'l boys in the neighborhood you used to run around playing doctor with, how was I supposed to know you didn't like it or that you didn't encourage it?"

It took every ounce of her strength for Sullivan not to toss her drink in Vera's face. "Don't shovel that BS excuse at me. You knew better, and don't you dare try to deny it!"

Vera wanted to say something crushing to Sullivan, as that was her usual defense mechanism. Instead, she yielded to honesty. Vera's eyes veered over to Sullivan.

She gulped down her margarita, needing whatever liquid courage it would provide. "I thought it was normal," stated Vera.

Sullivan released a low scream. "On what planet is a grown man being with a naive young girl normal?"

"My mama always had men in the house, and they did the same thing to me. When I went to her, crying about it, she told me there was nothing wrong with it and that her uncles and cousins had done the same thing to her. She said she liked it because afterward they always gave her money and presents. She said that sex and money is what being a woman was all about and that if I acted right and kept my mouth shut, I could get money and pretty new things too. She made it seem okay, like it wasn't that bad, since they weren't beating me or trying to hurt me. My grandma's husband beat my grandma to death when my mama was thirteen. To her way of thinking, if a man wasn't trying to kill you, he wasn't all that bad."

"So you went along with it," stated Sullivan. "You shut your mouth and did what you were told, just like I did."

Vera nodded. "I did. That's what I thought you were supposed to do, but that doesn't mean I wasn't angry about it," she said, recalling the past. "I hated it. When I saw it happening to you, I don't know. I just . . . I guess a part of me wanted you to suffer the way I did. I wanted everybody to suffer, especially after your sister died and your daddy treated me so badly. Something burned out and died inside of me. I didn't care about nothing or nobody, including myself."

"But I was your daughter, your own flesh and blood. Didn't that mean anything to you?"

Vera shook her head. "Not when you're in the kind of pain I was in."

Sullivan wasn't moved. "I don't care how much pain I'm in. I could never do anything that heinous to Charity."

"I didn't know better then, but I do better now. Sullivan, I . . . I was wrong. You're right. I didn't look after you like I should have." Vera avoided eye contact with Sullivan. "I wasn't a good mother to you."

Sullivan folded her arms across her chest. "I hope you're not waiting for me to disagree."

"I'm not. A good mother wouldn't have allowed you to go through that." Vera waited before going on. "I'm sorry. I couldn't help you, because I was so messed up myself. I guess in a way I even tried to break you because you had something, a light and a fearless spirit, that I never had. A part of me was jealous of that."

"Jealous?" Sullivan's eyes widened. "Vera, all I ever wanted was for you to love me, for you to be proud of me."

"Sullivan, you didn't need nobody like me to be proud of you. I was a mess!"

"But you were my mother. What child doesn't want approval from her mom?"

Vera's eyes welled with emotion for her daughter. She affectionately reached out for Sullivan's hand. "Of course, I'm proud of you. You're a good woman . . . most of the time. You have a big heart, and you're good to your friends. You love your husband, and you're one hundred times the mother to sweet Charity that I ever was to you. And I'm sorry. I'm sorry I was a bad mama to you. You deserved better. I hope you can forgive me."

Sullivan broke into a half smile. "Why did it take you thirty-four years to tell me that?"

"I've been busy. Better late than never, right?" Vera grinned.

"That's what they say." Sullivan thought about Charles. "But that's not always true."

"Depends on what you're talking about."

"My marriage. It may already be too late to salvage it."

"Sullivan, I was dead wrong for letting those men hurt you, but I have a second chance to get it right with Charity. I'd never let anybody hurt her, not even you, by being fool enough to leave her daddy. I grew up without a daddy, and so did my mama and her mama and so did you. It doesn't have to be like that for this child. She can grow up knowing what it's like to have a man's protection. She can know what it's like for a man to touch her with love, not with lust. She can know what it's like to be a daddy's little girl, instead of some grown man's woman. Don't take that away from her. Go to your husband, Sullivan, before it's too late. That man loves you! He may be tired of you and your shenanigans, but he loves you. The fact that he didn't leave you years ago—shoot, the fact that he even *married* you—proves that he loves you."

"What if I can't make him happy?" Sullivan asked in a small voice. "What if I'm not enough? Maybe losing Charles is my ultimate punishment."

"Punishment for what? Being an idiot?"

"For all the people I've hurt in the past."

Vera rolled her eyes. "I don't know how this God of yours works, but I don't think He's sitting up in heaven, worrying about what you did and people you hurt years ago. He's more concerned about what you're doing now. That's what matters, ain't it?"

Sullivan nodded and laughed to herself. Who would've thought someone as worldly as Vera could sum up the grace of God in such a succinct way while sitting in the middle of a dusty bar?

"I must say," mused Sullivan, "this might be the most meaningful conversation we've ever had."

"And now it's coming to a close," said Vera, hopping down off the bar stool. "Cliff is coming home tonight, and I want to be there when he gets there."

"Cliff is coming home? Go quick, fast, and in a hurry!" directed Sullivan. "Who knows when that might happen again?"

Vera stared at Sullivan for a moment.

Sullivan frowned. "What?"

Vera didn't say anything. She simply kissed her daughter on the cheek and hurried out.

Sullivan was stunned. Any sign of affection from Vera was almost as unsettling as her making sense while waxing on about the grace of God.

Sullivan figured that if by some miracle, she could make her relationship with Vera work, there was hope for everything else in her life, including her marriage to Charles, assuming he'd still have her.

# Chapter 41

"I don't know if I'm ready . . . if I can be a good mother."

*—Reginell Vinson*

"Do you have any idea what this is about?" Reginell asked Mark as she dusted off the coffee table.

"No, all Namon said is that he and Shari were coming by to see us."

Reginell panicked. "You don't think there's something wrong with the baby, do you? It's not like Namon to come home in the middle of the week."

"Namon said her last doctor's visit went fine."

Reginell gasped. "They probably found out the sex of the baby and want to tell us in person! This is so exciting!"

Mark smiled. "I appreciate that."

"Appreciate what?"

"You being excited about this baby coming. Everyone else sees him or her as a burden. You're the only one who has seen this baby as a blessing right from the start."

"I can't help it. I love kids. Not being able to have one of my own makes this one that much more precious to me."

There was a knock at the front door.

"Don't tell me that boy has lost his key again," groaned Mark. "If he can't keep up with his keys, how's he supposed to take care of a child?"

Reginell laughed. "You stay here. I'll let him in."

Mark greeted Namon with a hug. "Glad you made it down safely."

"Thank you," said Shari.

"What are you? Five months along now?" Reginell ogled her blossoming belly. "You're getting so big, no thanks to the baby's grandmother."

"Reggie, don't go there." Mark offered them a seat. "So what's this all about, Nay? What's going on?"

Namon rubbed his hands together nervously. "Shari and I have an announcement."

Mark closed his eyes. "You ran off and got married, didn't you?"

"No, quite the opposite," replied Namon. "We broke up."

"Why?" asked Reginell, concerned. "Namon, you can't just leave the girl knocked up and alone!"

"It wasn't his idea," said Shari. "It was mine."

Namon turned to his father. "You and Mom are right. We aren't ready to handle this kind of relationship. We're too young."

"While I commend you for recognizing that I'm right, it's a little late for that now," retorted Mark. "The baby will be here in a couple of months. He or she deserves to be raised by both parents. You accepted the responsibility to keep the baby. Now accept the responsibility of taking care of it together."

Shari and Namon looked at each other, and then Namon addressed Reginell and Mark. "We don't think we're ready for the responsibility of raising a child, either."

"Namon, that's a moot point now," affirmed Mark. "This baby is coming whether you're ready or not."

"We already love these babies," said Shari. "But we know that our babies need more than just our love to make it in the world."

"*Babies?*" repeated Mark. "Did you say *babies?*"

Shari nodded. "The doctor said I'm having twins. A boy and a girl."

Reginell was floored. "Two babies? No wonder you're feeling overwhelmed!"

Namon nodded. "It was going to be hard enough taking care of one baby, but two?"

Reginell looked at Mark. "They're definitely going to need our help now."

"We were hoping for a little more than your help, Aunt Reggie." Namon took a deep breath. "Shari and I were hoping that you and my dad would consider raising the babies."

Reginell felt like the wind had been knocked out of her. "What?"

Mark was equally astounded. "Namon, have you thought this through carefully?"

"We want our babies to have a good home and two loving parents, like you said," expounded Shari. "It's become more obvious every day that we can't do it. We can't even take care of ourselves, much less two kids."

Reginell remembered Lawson suggesting the same thing. "Namon, did your mama put you up to this?"

Namon shook his head. "She has no idea I was even thinking about it."

"Okay, you know I never thought you having a kid was a great idea, but do you know what you're asking of us?" questioned Mark.

Namon nodded. "We do. We thought about it." He reached for Shari's hand. "We even prayed about it. We know we're not what's best for these kids, but we think you and Aunt Reggie are. Plus, Aunt Reggie can't have children. We thought it would be kind of like a gift."

Reginell spoke softly to her nephew. "I'm very honored that you'd think enough of me to ask me to take care of your children while you finish school, but I don't think I can do that. I know me. I'd fall in love with those babies, and it would devastate me to give them back."

"We're not loaning them to you, Aunt Reggie. We want you to adopt them," said Namon, clarifying the matter. "We want you to be their parents."

Reginell looked at her husband. "Mark and I need some time to think about this, okay?"

"Regardless of what we decide, I think that the two of you made a very mature decision today, and you made it on your own, without any interference from your mother or anyone else. I'm proud of you." Mark hugged Namon. He also hugged Shari.

"Thank you," said Shari.

Mark slapped his hands on his thighs. "Well, I'm in!"

Reginell's eyes grew twice their normal size. "Huh?"

"Baby, if you're with it, I'm with it," he told her. "You know I want nothing more than to share a child with you."

"Don't you need time to think it over?" asked Reginell.

Mark cupped her face. "You're my wife. Whether or not to have a baby with you is nothing I even have to think about."

"But they would be your grandchildren!" argued Reginell. "Wouldn't you think that's weird?"

Mark shrugged. "Children are raised by their grandparents all the time. Personally, I think it's a splendid idea. Shari and Namon could go on with their lives, and, Reggie, you and I will have the children that we want."

Reginell looked into the eager faces surrounding her. "I guess I'm the holdout, huh?"

"Baby, there's no pressure," Mark assured her. "You don't have to do anything that you don't want to do, especially something as huge as deciding whether or not to take on the responsibility of two kids."

Reginell's insecurities reared their heads. "I don't know if I'm ready . . . if I can be a good mother."

"Reggie, you'll be an excellent mother," Mark told her.

"Can we pray about it first?" asked Reginell. "I know that's more Lawson's territory, but I want to give it a shot."

"Yeah, of course," said Mark, linking hands with Reginell and Namon.

Shari and Reginell linked hands. "Lord," began Reginell, "we thank you for today and for the awesome blessing that you've bestowed on us in the form of these babies. Even if the rest of the world can't see the beauty in their lives, we can. We thank you for Namon and Shari loving their children enough to want the best for them, even if it means letting someone else raise them. Lord, if it's your will for Mark and me to raise these babies as our own, please give us the wisdom and the heart to do so. Let us be loving examples of your love for us. Let our home always be filled with you so that it'll always be filled with love. In Jesus's name I pray. Amen."

By the end of the day, Mark and Reginell were unofficially the proud parents of a future baby boy and baby girl.

# Chapter 42

"I hate to say it, but maybe this friendship or sisterhood, or whatever you want to call it, has run its course."

*—Angel King*

At Kina's town house later that afternoon, all Lawson, Sullivan, and Angel could say was, "*What?*" upon hearing about Elvin's link to Desdemona.

Angel faced Desdemona. "How could you do that?" she demanded. "Kina trusted you. We all did."

"I never asked any of you to do that," replied Desdemona. "My mission was pure and simple—to find Kina's story—and I did that."

Sullivan shook her head. "You don't even have any remorse, do you?"

"It makes no sense yet perfect sense at the same time," Lawson declared and directed her anger toward Desdemona. "I started figuring you out weeks ago. We didn't have all these problems till you came along with all your instigating and stirring the pot. You've been manipulating everybody this whole time."

"I think *manipulation* is a strong word," protested Desdemona. "Though I do admit I may have fanned a few flames."

"You did more than that! You took advantage of our insecurities and fears and pitted us against each other for your own entertainment. That's cruel, and it's sick," said Angel.

"I don't care what Terrilyn says. I want you gone," roared Kina. "The way I see it, we get rid of you and we get rid of the problem."

Desdemona laughed. "I'm the least of your problems. What did I do, other than make suggestions?"

Lawson sucked her teeth. "That's exactly how the devil operates! I should've known not to trust you. If you take off the first three letters and the last letter of your name, you get *demon,* which is exactly what you are!"

"Be that as it may, your friendships and your lives weren't nearly as together as you tried to make them out to be," said Desdemona, "especially if all it took was a few well-placed words from me to make it all crumble."

Angel narrowed her eyes at Desdemona. "How can you say that with a straight face, knowing that you orchestrated the whole thing?"

"The cracks in the foundation were there long before I was. Kina, I will see you at Terrilyn's office next week. Be sure to look over the book. It's a real page-turner." Desdemona seized her keys and purse. "It was most rewarding meeting all of you," she added, throwing them a wave before sauntering out.

The five of them were left standing there to try to pick up the pieces of their broken friendship. No one had a clue as to how to begin that process.

"See what happens when we let other people infiltrate the sister circle?" joked Lawson.

Kina tried to laugh, but the joke was met mostly with uncomfortable looks.

"I owe you all an apology," said Kina. "I'm the one who introduced her to everybody. I feel like this was all my fault."

Angel rested a hand on Kina's shoulder. "It wasn't you fault, Kina. All you did was bring her around. We took it upon ourselves to trust her."

Lawson was still heated. "I can't believe she manipulated us that way!"

Sullivan looked around at her friends. "I don't think she did, not really."

"Are you defending her?" asked Lawson.

Sullivan disputed the idea. "Of course not, but when it came down to it, what did she really *make* us do?"

"She made you question your marriage to Charles," noted Angel.

Sullivan shook her head. "I was already doing that. She only said out loud what I was thinking."

There was a long silence.

"Sully's right," conceded Angel. "Whether it was about our relationships or our friendship with each other, Desdemona just unearthed everything we were feeling beneath the surface. To be honest, I don't think she lied about or to any of us."

"Yeah, but we said some really hurtful things to each other because of Desdemona's mechanisms," Lawson pointed out.

Sullivan faced Lawson. "Maybe that's how we really feel and we have been afraid to admit it."

Tension wrapped around them like a thick blanket.

Angel sighed. "I hate to say it, but maybe this friendship or sisterhood, or whatever you want to call it, has run its course."

Kina squinted her eyes. "Are you serious?"

Angel nodded. "Can any of you honestly say that this friendship has made you better or helped you to grow as a person or a Christian?"

"Definitely!" affirmed Kina. "I wouldn't have made it without your support."

"You would've been fine," Angel assured her. "Look how you thrived out in California on your own. Frankly, I think being here with us has held you back. I think to a certain extent, we've all held each other back."

"How can you say that?" replied Lawson.

"How many times did we sit by idly while Sullivan cheated on Charles? Who came to Kina's rescue when she was being beaten by E'Bell?" Angel asked, rattling off their faults. "All of us have connections, but which of us stepped up to help Reggie find a decent job so she wouldn't have to keep stripping? Didn't we all help Lawson lie to Mark about Namon being his son?"

"That's what friends do," argued Kina.

Sullivan stepped forward. "A friend wouldn't have let you stay in that abusive marriage, Kina."

"What could you have done to stop me? I'm a grown woman!" returned Kina.

"We didn't even try, though. We may call each other out on our sins, but ultimately, we condone them," admitted Lawson.

"That's because real friends don't judge each other," asserted Kina. "They love and accept each other for who they are."

"Yeah, but at what point does that become counterproductive, destructive even?" asked Angel. "If we claim to be serious about our Christianity yet don't correct even those closest to us when they fall, what does that say about us as Christians?"

Lawson sighed. "As much as I'd like to, I can't argue with that logic."

"We've all been friends for so long that we have practically shut out the possibility of letting other people in our lives. Perhaps it's just time to move on and explore other friendships," suggested Angel. "Whether we want to admit it or not, I think it's pretty obvious that we're starting to outgrow this one."

Kina started tearing up. "Angel, I can't imagine not having all of you in my life."

"I didn't say we couldn't be civil and have the occasional lunch or conversation. I'm just saying maybe we don't need to be all up in each other's business. I think we need to set some boundaries and have some space, meet new people."

Lawson nodded. "If that's what you want, I guess we have to respect that."

"It's not necessarily what I want," said Angel. "It's what I think we need for a little while. There's nothing wrong with having friends outside of this group."

"Besides, most of us are married. I'm sure our husbands would probably be a lot happier if they got half the attention that we lavish on each other," added Sullivan.

Kina began to cry.

Angel hugged her. "This isn't the end, Kina. It's just re-arranging our priorities. We'll always have a role in each other's lives. Now it will be a smaller role, that's all."

Lawson patted Kina on the back. "We're family. You couldn't get rid of me if you tried."

"But it won't be the same," wailed Kina.

"Nothing ever stays the same," said Sullivan. "Things change. People evolve. That's life."

Kina looked around at everybody. "Is this really what you all want?"

Angel nodded. "I think it's what we need, for right now, anyway."

Kina wiped her eyes. "So this is it? This is good-bye?"

Sullivan squeezed Kina's hand. "It's . . . *see you later*."

Lawson put forth a brave front. "Well, then, I guess I'll see you all later."

"See you later." Angel smiled and reached out to hug her. "I do love you, Lawson, and I wish you all the best."

"Same here." Lawson let her go. "Good-bye, Angel."

"Aw, can't we at least have a group hug?" asked Kina.

They laughed and huddled together for a final group hug.

"I love you," whispered Sullivan. "You'll always be my sisters."

They all departed, leaving their most treasured friendships behind as each one went her separate way.

# Chapter 43

"Sometimes I don't know how to cope with pain."

*–Sullivan Webb*

Sullivan came home and found Charles already in bed, asleep. He stirred when he heard her come in the bedroom. She set her keys down on her dresser.

"Hey," she said.

Charles glanced over at the clock. "It's kind of late. Where were you?"

"I was with the girls. I didn't mean to wake you. I'm sorry."

"No need to apologize. I know you love spending time with your friends," said Charles.

"I think I've been showing them a little too much love." Sullivan gazed at Charles. "And not enough love to my husband."

That caught Charles's attention.

Sullivan sat at the foot of their bed. "And you're wrong, Charles. I do owe you an apology."

"For what?"

"I was talking to Vera yesterday. She reminded me what a good man you are and how blessed I am to have you."

Charles was surprised. "Vera said that?"

Sullivan nodded. "Anytime a falling-down, train wreck of a mother like Vera gives a compliment, it's worth taking note!"

They both laughed.

"Charles, I've been so caught up in my own grief and pain that I couldn't see what a completely selfless act you committed by saving my life. It was an impossible position for you to be in."

"Yes, it was," agreed Charles. "But I knew if Christian stayed inside of you, you both could die. If I let the doctor deliver him, there was a greater chance that both of you would survive. Maybe it was a little selfish on my part, but I couldn't risk losing you, Sullivan. I just couldn't."

Sullivan hugged him. "I know that now. It took an incredible amount of love and courage to do what you did, and I know that you grieved for our son just as much as I did."

"I really did, Sullivan. I had so many dreams and plans for that boy. I wanted to teach him how to fish and play ball, how to treat a lady, and how to be a man of God. It broke my heart when he didn't pull through. It broke again when you blamed me for killing him."

"I'm so sorry for that. I was hurt, and I needed someone to blame."

"It's okay, but, Sullivan, I can't be your whipping boy whenever you get ready to lash out at somebody, and you've got to find a way to handle your problems without turning to alcohol."

"What am I supposed to turn to?"

"It's not a *what*. It's a *who*. God."

"It's easy for you to say that. You're a pastor. You have an inside connection with Him."

Charles laughed. "I have the same inside connection you have, darling."

"Sometimes I don't know how to cope with pain. Unfortunately, when it comes to dealing with hurt and disappointment, I revert to acting like Vera. I become mean and destructive like her."

"I know you saw way more than you should have growing. Vera did and said things in front of you that no child should have to witness, but you're a grown woman now. You can't blame everything on Vera and your childhood. At some point, we've all got to grow up and realize who the problem really is."

Sullivan took a deep breath. "You're right. The issue is with me. I'm the one who hurt you, and I'm the one who's pushed you away time and time again."

"Well, I believe we've both been guilty on that end. I've let the church come between us, and I was wrong for that. Yes, God called me to preach, but he called me to minister to my wife and my family first. I'm sorry that I haven't always made you my priority."

Sullivan wouldn't let him blame himself. "Charles, I can't hold anything against you after all I've put you through."

"No, I still have to be held accountable just like you do. Sullivan, the only way this marriage is going to work is if we start taking responsibility for it and stop fighting each other and start fighting for our marriage."

"Do you still want to fight for it?"

Charles reached for Sullivan's hands. "I'm in it to win it, baby! You're my wife. I'm not going anywhere."

She smiled up at him. "Neither am I."

"It won't be easy, you know?" Charles warned her.

"I know, but you and Charity are worth fighting for."

Charles drew Sullivan in and kissed her.

They both knew that their marriage might always be mired with complications, but they also knew neither one of them wanted to walk away from it.

# Chapter 44

"You know, there are some things that are more important than notoriety and money, like being able to look at yourself in the mirror and not hate the person you see reflected back."

*−Kina Battle*

"This is brilliant!" declared Terrilyn after finishing the last of Desdemona's manuscript. "This is absolutely brilliant! I smell a bestseller. Heck, I smell a Pulitzer Prize! Excellent work, Kina."

"You can't be serious," cried Kina.

"I think *The Devil and Her Advocates* is Des's best work to date. It's dark. It draws you in right from the beginning. It's juicy. It's everything you want in a book."

"But she ripped everything right from our real lives," argued Kina. "She even goes into detail about how she played all of us."

"I know! Isn't it delicious?" gushed Terrilyn. "It's got it all—the slutty first lady who's a closet alcoholic, the self-righteous baby-killing choir director, the pill-popping nurse whose man can't keep it in his pants, the stripping whore-turned-housewife, and the reality starlet who's bedding her husband's father. Honestly, how much drama can exist in one group of friends? And it's all under the guise of Christianity! Honey, if the Christians are acting this way, I shudder to think what the rest of the world is doing!"

"Terrilyn, you can't print this book. My friends would kill me!" Kina flipped through the manuscript. "Look at the characters' names. Sally, Laura, Angela, Regina, and Tina. Any idiot could figure out that's Sully, Lawson, Angel, Reginell, and me."

"That's what makes it all the more salacious! Don't forget that we're marketing it as a work of fiction," explained Terrilyn. "Once we slap the sticker on it that says, 'This is a work of fiction. Any similarity in names, characters, places, and incidents is entirely coincidental,' we're good to go."

"Please don't do this," pleaded Kina. "These are real people with real lives. They didn't sign on for this. Everything they said to me or Desdemona was done in confidence. They thought the book was supposed to be about me. They had no idea she was going to be writing about them."

Terrilyn frowned. "That's their problem. Des never told them anything that was off the record."

"Desdemona also caused so much havoc in their lives. This would be adding insult to injury. They'd never forgive me for that."

"They may be true, but think of how good it'll feel to wipe those tears away with hundred-dollar bills!"

"What good is it for a man to gain the whole world, yet forfeit his soul?" asked Kina.

"Will you cut out the dramatics? We need to get down to business. I can't wait to get you out there on a media tour. We've got to start booking you on talk shows and blogs ASAP. You love attention, so I don't anticipate you having a problem with that. I want there to be a lot of buzz about this novel so people will be salivating for it by the time it comes out," Terrilyn said, plotting.

Kina vigorously shook her head. "I'm not comfortable with this at all. I don't want my name associated with this book."

"There's nothing to be ashamed of, Kina. It's a great book."

"Great for business maybe, but not for my friends. Sullivan's baby died and Lawson hurt her sister and Angel's boyfriend was falsely accused of rape, and that's all in there. I can't profit off the things that caused them the most hurt."

Terrilyn sighed and swung around in her chair. "Kina, we talked about this. You accepted the advance. You're under contract. The book will be published with or without you. The difference is you can either make thousands off of it or pay the thousands back that we advanced you. The choice is yours."

Kina thought it over. She didn't have anywhere near the five figures they'd advanced her, and she could definitely use the money and the exposure. Besides, she and her friends weren't even close anymore. What would it matter to her if they got upset? If she turned down the book, they wouldn't even know how great a sacrifice she made for them.

Kina opened her mouth to tell Terrilyn to move forward with the book, then remembered a televised interview Sullivan had done two years prior. It was the perfect opportunity for Sullivan to get revenge for Kina trying to seduce Charles and telling him about the question of Charity's paternity. Instead, she'd publicly praised Kina for being a true friend with principles and having the love of God in her heart.

"I can't do it. I'm sorry. I'll write another book if I have to or spend the rest of my life paying back that advance, but I can't let that book go out with my name on it."

"You're a fool, Kina. Only an idiot would pass up the kind of opportunity that's being presented to you. Do you have any idea what this book could do for your career? You could get that reality show you want out of the deal!

Endorsements, book sequels," said Terrilyn. "You'll get to travel and be relevant again. You're willing to walk away from all that for what? To keep some busybody women from being mad at you? That's ludicrous!"

"It's not just about that. I can't betray them this way. The Bible says anything you know in your heart to be wrong is a sin. What's the point of having all the money and success you mentioned if I'm not at peace with myself or my Father?"

"I'm sorry to hear that," Terrilyn said and faced her computer. "However, it's your decision and, essentially, your loss. Expect to hear from our legal team if the advance is not repaid within the next thirty days. You may go."

"Yeah, well, it feels good to know that I have a few scruples left." Kina stood up to leave. "There is just no way I can sell my soul to the devil in order to sell out the people I love. You know, there are some things that are more important than notoriety and money, like being able to look at yourself in the mirror and not hate the person you see reflected back."

"Well, Kina, I hope that mirror hangs up nice and pretty in the homeless shelter you'll probably find yourself in. Consider yourself dismissed."

Kina walked out with her pride and principles intact. They might not pay the bills, but they made for an excellent night's sleep. She would do what she could and trust God for the rest.

# Chapter 45

"It was way more comfortable for me to play the victim than to own up to the fact that I've been unfaithful to you and to us too."

*—Angel King*

"I didn't expect you to come," said Duke when Angel followed them home after Morgan's recital.

"As hard as Morgan has been working on that violin of hers, I wouldn't have missed it!" contended Angel.

"It was nice of you to come. I know it meant a lot to the girls. They keep asking why you haven't been around as much. I told them you've been working more hours lately. I can tell they miss you."

"I miss them. I miss you too." An awkward silence passed between them. "How is everything going with you?"

"Great . . . great. They, uh, dropped the charges a couple of days ago."

Angel's face lit up. "Really? Duke, that's wonderful!"

"It's definitely a relief. It turns out that Miss Mya has a history of pulling stunts like this and blackmailing men to make the charges go away."

"I knew you didn't attack her," declared Angel.

"Did you?" Duke's glower dimmed her enthusiasm.

"Duke, I've always said that."

"But you doubted that I was faithful to you."

Angel couldn't deny his claim. "You're an attractive man. She's a pretty girl. You were thousands of miles away, in a hotel, alone with her. Considering our history and the fact that she knew about the tattoo, it didn't seem like the possibility was out of the question."

"Angel, I love you enough to be faithful, and I respect you enough to be honest if I stray. You've got to trust in me enough to believe that. She knew about the tattoo because she saw me swimming in the hotel pool. Heck, everybody who was out there knows I have a tattoo on my chest."

She felt foolish. "Why didn't you just tell me that, Duke?"

"I didn't think I had to."

Angel breathed deeply. "I think it's pretty obvious that we have some major trust issues between us."

Duke nodded.

Angel sighed. "I'm not blaming you for all of it. I've done my part to screw up our relationship too."

"That's true, Angel. You've dished out as much hurt as I have."

She agreed. "I've had to face the truth about that. It was way more comfortable for me to play the victim than to own up to the fact that I've been unfaithful to you and to us too. I was wrong to put it all on your shoulders."

"Then again, most people would say you were right not to trust me. I've broken your heart more times than the law allows. You shouldn't put your trust in me any more than I should put mine in you. Whether or not we want to admit it, I think it's pretty obvious that if we go on like this, we're going to keep hurting each other, so I say we stop putting all this pressure on each other."

Angel acquiesced. It was another harsh reality she had to face, but this one was almost more than she could bear. Angel had already lost the closest thing she had to sisters. Now she was also losing the only man she'd ever loved.

Duke went on. "Let's stop putting our faith in this relationship and start putting our faith in God. If we keep
Him first, one of two things will happen. Either He will
help us to be sensitive to each other's needs and will show
us not to hurt one another. Or when we do screw up, He'll
make our hearts big enough to forgive. We're covered
either way."

Angel raised her head. "So what are you saying, Duke?"

"I'm . . . I'm staking my claiming, Angel!" asserted
Duke. "I won't let you go like this, not without a fight."

"But I thought—"

"Look, just hear me out, okay? I was upset that you
believed Mya over me. I was hurt. Now I see that nothing
would hurt me more than losing you again. Baby, we've
been through the fire together—to hell and back, like you
said. We can't just give up now. I love you. You and the
girls are my whole world. I can't do this thing called life
without you. I need you. The girls need you. I don't care
what it takes, but we've got to find a way to work this out."

Angel rushed into his arms. "There's nothing to figure
out. I'm yours now and forever. Always have been, always
will be."

Duke pulled her in for a kiss. "I love you, Angel. You're
the only woman for me. I don't want you to ever forget
that."

She shook her head. "I won't."

"Baby, will you put me out of my misery and just marry
me already?"

Angel's heart stopped. "What?"

"Wait! Don't answer that! I want to do this right."

He scampered up the stairs and returned a few minutes
later flanked by Miley and Morgan, a bouquet of plastic
flowers snatched from the bathroom, and a wrapped Ring
Pop from Morgan's candy stash.

Duke cleared his throat. "Okay, now I'm ready." He kneeled down in front of Angel and extended the flowers to her. "Angelique Renee Preston King, my beautiful angel and the love of my life, will you marry me?"

"And me!" added Morgan.

Miley giggled. "And me."

Angel beamed from the inside out. "Yes, yes, yes! Of course I'll marry you—*all of you!*" Angel kissed Duke, then hugged and kissed the girls.

Duke ripped the plastic wrapper off the candy ring and slipped it on Angel's finger. "You know this is temporary, right?"

"No, this time it's forever," said Angel, looking down at her edible ruby.

"When are you going to get married?" asked Miley.

"Tonight, if she wants to," answered Duke.

Angel started laughing. "I don't see why not!"

Duke was taken aback. "Are you serious?"

Angel nodded. "I don't want to wait. Shoot, it's been fifteen years! Let's go ahead and start happily ever after now."

"Sounds like a plan." Duke drew her in for another kiss.

Instinctively, Angel wanted to call her friends and share her good news, but she resisted the urge and reveled in the moment with her new family instead. Even though she'd lost one family, gaining a new one helped to lessen the pain considerably.

# Chapter 46

"Oh, you'll be surprised at how much can be accomplished over a bowl of ice cream and a bottle of wine!"

*–Sullivan Webb*

It took Vera's death to resurrect a friendship that had been buried for five years. Vera's funeral was the first time Lawson, Sullivan, Reginell, Kina, and Angel had all been in the same room together since parting ways at Kina's town house. The irony of the moment was that the person responsible for so much contention in her daughter's life was the catalyst for bringing them all together again.

Sullivan found her four long-lost friends waiting for her in the foyer of Mount Zion Ministries following Vera's burial and repast. She turned to Charles. "Baby, can you take Charity on to the car? I'd like to talk to the girls for a minute."

"Of course." Charles kissed Sullivan on the forehead before taking the time to hug each of the ladies. "It was so nice of you all to come out, and it's so good to see you again!"

Kina squeezed his hand. "Thank you for getting in touch with all of us."

"Yeah, it's been a long time," acknowledged Lawson.

"Too long," said Charles before leaving with his daughter. "Take your time, Sullivan. We'll be waiting."

They all stared at one another, as if trying to recognize the new women standing before them.

Angel was the first to step forward and speak. "How long has it been since we all occupied the same space at the same time?"

"Feels like forever," said Sullivan.

Lawson offered her sympathy. "I'm so sorry to hear about your mother's passing, Sully. It's never easy to lose a parent."

"It was a beautiful service," noted Kina. "It was very fitting for her."

Sullivan nodded. "Thank you. Vera was crass and loud and always inappropriate, but I'm going to miss her."

Angel agreed. "Vera was definitely in a league of her own."

"You wouldn't believe how much she changed in the last few years. She finally apologized and acknowledged the role she played in my being abused as a child, and she actually accepted Christ into her life two years ago. She and Charity got baptized at the same time. I feel so blessed that I was able to witness that. She really made an effort to be a better mother and grandmother. I was proud of her. She gave cancer a good fight too."

"She loved you, Sullivan," said Lawson. "I know she didn't always show it, but she did. She loved Charity too."

"I know." Sullivan smiled.

"Speaking of Charity, I can't believe how grown up she is!" exclaimed Kina. "She's a little lady. Where did the time go?"

"She's in third grade now. Can you believe it? And every bit the diva her mother is!" boasted Sullivan.

"You seem like a little less of a diva, though," said Angel, noting that Sullivan's over-the-top look had morphed into a softer, more sophisticated and subdued presence. "You cut your hair."

Sullivan laughed a little. "I didn't cut my hair. I just stopped buying it."

"Well, you look good!" Lawson said, praising her friend.

"I'm actually feeling good these days," bragged Sullivan. "Now that Charity is a little older, I'm finally putting that art degree to use. I teach painting classes to kids down at the children's museum. It's very rewarding. It makes me feel like I'm making a difference in a young person's life."

Angel was shocked. "Sully, you hate children!"

"Admittedly, I used to, but it's a new day. I found that the best way to honor Christian is to put a smile on as many kids' faces as possible."

"That's so beautiful," gushed Angel. "People really do change, I see."

"Hey, I'm living proof of that!" attested Reginell.

Sullivan turned to Reginell. "Yes, you are! Look at you. I never thought I'd see the day when you were a regular ole housewife. What happened to the sky-high heels and short skirts?"

"I had to put them out to pasture—unless, of course, it's Mark's birthday! It's kind of hard to chase after two kids wearing that," joked Reginell.

"I heard that Mark got a coaching job up at his old alma mater."

"Yeah, we're living in Virginia now. The kids love it up there."

Sullivan smiled with approval. "I'm glad you finally found a reason to settle down."

"And speaking of settling down, Duke and I finally did it—again!" revealed Angel, flashing her ring finger. "It'll be five years in the spring."

"I'm so happy for you!" Sullivan gave Angel a hug. "How are the girls?"

"Miley is graduating from high school this year, and Morgan is a freshman. We have a son now too!" Angel told them. She flashed pictures from her phone. "Donavan is three and has us completely wrapped around his finger, especially Duke. He's so proud of his mini me."

Kina gazed down at the picture of Donavan. "I bet he is! Your son is adorable, Angel. He's the perfect combination of you and your husband."

"How's Kenny?" asked Angel.

"Kenny is in the air force now. He is stationed in Texas and has been talking about getting married."

Sullivan laughed. "You ready to be a grandma?"

Kina wrinkled her brow. "I don't know about all that, but I'm one proud mama!"

"Not to mention a big-time reality star," Angel said, chiming in. "I love seeing you as one of the weight-loss coaches on *Lose Big*."

"Moving back out West proved to be the best thing I could've done," admitted Kina. "If I hadn't, I never would've met my fiancé, Karl, who helped me get the part on the show."

"Awww!" Lawson embraced her cousin. "I'm so proud of you!"

"So what's been going on with you, Lawson?" asked Sullivan.

"I'm an elementary school principal now!" Lawson revealed. "It's a small school in Crawford County, but I love it! Simon attends. He lives with us full-time now."

Angel was bowled over. "Really?"

"Yeah, Simone went to New York and fell in love, so she decided to stay up there. After a bit of a battle, she and Garrett both agreed that it was best that Simon stay down here with us. She gets him for the summer, but he lives with us."

Sullivan pressed for more details. "What about Namon? How's he?"

"He's wonderful. He's working on his MBA and working for a nonprofit up in Atlanta," said Lawson. "Things couldn't be better between us, probably because we're in two different cities! I can't run his life from Crawford County."

Sullivan laughed. "That's true! Wow . . . you don't know how much it warms my heart to see how well you are doing, especially today."

Kina looked glum. "It's weird. We all have new lives that none of us are a part of anymore."

"But I think we needed this time away from each other to fully become the people God intended us to be," mused Angel. "Kina, you never would've gone back to Cali or Reggie to Virginia if things had stayed the same. Our marriages might not be as strong or our careers as successful if we'd stayed in that comfort zone with each other."

"Plus, we don't have to see each other every day to be a part of each other's lives. I still pray for all of you every night," admitted Lawson.

"Same here," said Angel. "It makes me feel like we're still connected."

Sullivan smirked. "And I will admit, Kina, your weekly blog after each *Lose Big* episode is my guilty pleasure. I make a point to read it every time you post on it."

"Even though we're members of a different church now, Duke and I still stream Mount Zion Ministries online all the time," volunteered Angel.

"I do too," confessed Reginell. "It helps whenever I get homesick."

Lawson was touched. "We've been apart, but we've all discovered our own way to stay connected."

The former friends shared an awkward stare before falling into a hug.

"I wish we had more time together," wailed Kina. "I haven't seen all of y'all together in five years. I'm not ready for it to end."

"What time are you all flying back?" asked Sullivan.

"My flight doesn't leave until tomorrow," Reginell informed them.

"Mine either," said Kina.

"I drove, so time isn't an issue for me," reported Lawson.

Angel shook her head. "It isn't a factor for me, either."

"Why don't we all go back to my place and hang out, like we used to?" suggested Sullivan.

Lawson was hesitant. "Are you sure?"

"Of course," said Sullivan. "I think it's pretty safe to say that we've got a lot of catching up to do!"

"We don't have that long," pointed out Kina.

"Oh, you'll be surprised at how much can be accomplished over a bowl of ice cream and a bottle of wine!" proclaimed Sullivan.

"Dang, I've missed y'all!" exclaimed Angel at long last.

They all laughed and walked out to the parking lot, arm in arm, realizing that things between them would never be as they were but content in the knowledge that some things, like love and true friendship, never really change.

# Reader Discussion Questions

1. Do you think Desdemona was the source of problems for the group, or did her presence only bring the ladies' conflicts to the forefront?

2. Can Lawson's attempt to get Shari to terminate her pregnancy be considered an act of love? Why or why not?

3. Was Lawson out of line with her relationship with Mark? Why or why not?

4. If you were Charles, would you have chosen to save your wife or your child? Explain.

5. Do you think Sullivan's emotional problems stem from selfishness or from her tumultuous childhood?

6. Do you think anything inappropriate transpired between Duke and Mya? Why or why not?

7. If you were in Angel's position, would you have taken Duke back?

8. Is there anything wrong with Kina dating her late husband's father? Explain.

9. Did Reginell overreact in her treatment of Lawson with regard to Mark?

10. Should the ladies have remained in their tight friendship circle, or did they need to separate in order to grow? Explain.

# UC HIS GLORY BOOK CLUB!

## *www.uchisglorybookclub.net*

UC His Glory Book Club is the spirit-inspired brain-child of Joylynn Ross, an author and the acquisitions editor of Urban Christian, and Kendra Norman-Bellamy, an author for Urban Christian. It is an online book club that hosts authors of Urban Christian. We welcome as members all men and women who have a passion for reading Christian-based fiction.

UC His Glory Book Club pledges its commitment to provide support, positive feedback, encouragement, and a forum whereby members can openly discuss and review the literary works of Urban Christian authors.

There is no membership fee associated with UC His Glory Book Club; however, we do ask that you support the authors through purchasing their works, encouraging them, providing book reviews, and, of course, offering your prayers. We also ask that you respect our beliefs and follow the guidelines of the book club. We hope to receive your valuable input, opinions, and reviews that build up, rather than tear down, our authors.

# What We Believe:

—We believe that Jesus is the Christ, Son of the Living God.

—We believe that the Bible is the true, living Word of God.

—We believe that all Urban Christian authors should use their God-given writing ability to honor God and to share the message of the written word God has given to each of them uniquely.

—We believe in supporting Urban Christian authors in their literary endeavors by reading their titles, purchasing them, and sharing them with our online community.

—We believe that everything we do in our literary arena should be done in a manner that will lead to God being glorified and honored.

We look forward to online fellowship with you. Please visit us often at www.uchisglorybookclub.net

Many Blessings to You!

Shelia E. Lipsey,
President, UC His Glory Book Club

## ORDER FORM
## URBAN BOOKS, LLC
97 N18th Street
Wyandanch, NY 11798

Name (please print):_____

Address:          _____

City/State:       _____

Zip:              _____

| QTY | TITLES | PRICE |
|-----|--------|-------|
|     |        |       |
|     |        |       |
|     |        |       |
|     |        |       |
|     |        |       |
|     |        |       |
|     |        |       |
|     |        |       |
|     |        |       |
|     |        |       |
|     |        |       |
|     |        |       |

Shipping and handling: add $3.50 for 1$^{st}$ book, then $1.75 for each additional book.

Please send a check payable to:
   **Urban Books, LLC**
Please allow 4-6 weeks for delivery

# ORDER FORM
## URBAN BOOKS, LLC
97 N18th Street
Wyandanch, NY 11798

Name (please print):_____

Address:　　　_____

City/State:　　_____

Zip:　　　　_____

| QTY | TITLES | PRICE |
|---|---|---|
|  | California Connection 2 | $14.95 |
|  | Cheesecake And Teardrops | $14.95 |
|  | Congratulations | $14.95 |
|  | Crazy In Love | $14.95 |
|  | Cyber Case | $14.95 |
|  | Denim Diaries | $14.95 |
|  | Diary Of A Mad First Lady | $14.95 |
|  | Diary Of A Stalker | $14.95 |
|  | Diary Of A Street Diva | $14.95 |
|  | Diary Of A Young Girl | $14.95 |
|  | Dirty Money | $14.95 |
|  | Dirty To The Grave | $14.95 |

Shipping and handling: add $3.50 for 1$^{st}$ book, then $1.75 for each additional book.

Please send a check payable to:
**Urban Books, LLC**
Please allow 4-6 weeks for delivery

## ORDER FORM
## URBAN BOOKS, LLC
### 97 N18th Street
### Wyandanch, NY 11798

Name (please print):_____

Address:          _____

City/State:       _____

Zip:              _____

| QTY | TITLES | PRICE |
|---|---|---|
| | Gunz And Roses | $14.95 |
| | Happily Ever Now | $14.95 |
| | Hell Has No Fury | $14.95 |
| | Hush | $14.95 |
| | If It Isn't love | $14.95 |
| | Kiss Kiss Bang Bang | $14.95 |
| | Last Breath | $14.95 |
| | Little Black Girl Lost | $14.95 |
| | Little Black Girl Lost 2 | $14.95 |
| | Little Black Girl Lost 3 | $14.95 |
| | Little Black Girl Lost 4 | $14.95 |
| | Little Black Girl Lost 5 | $14.95 |

Shipping and handling: add $3.50 for 1st book, then $1.75 for each additional book.

Please send a check payable to:

**Urban Books, LLC**

Please allow 4-6 weeks for delivery

## ORDER FORM
## URBAN BOOKS, LLC
97 N18th Street
Wyandanch, NY 11798

Name (please print):_____

Address:         _____

City/State:      _____

Zip:             _____

| QTY | TITLES | PRICE |
|---|---|---|
|  | Loving Dasia | $14.95 |
|  | Material Girl | $14.95 |
|  | Moth To A Flame | $14.95 |
|  | Mr. High Maintenance | $14.95 |
|  | My Little Secret | $14.95 |
|  | Naughty | $14.95 |
|  | Naughty 2 | $14.95 |
|  | Naughty 3 | $14.95 |
|  | Queen Bee | $14.95 |
|  | Say It Ain't So | $14.95 |
|  | Snapped | $14.95 |
|  | Snow White | $14.95 |

Shipping and handling: add $3.50 for 1st book, then $1.75 for each additional book.

Please send a check payable to:

**Urban Books, LLC**

Please allow 4-6 weeks for delivery

Name (please print):_____

Address:            _____

City/State:         _____

Zip:                _____

| QTY | TITLES | PRICE |
|-----|--------|-------|
|     |        |       |
|     |        |       |
|     |        |       |
|     |        |       |
|     |        |       |
|     |        |       |
|     |        |       |
|     |        |       |
|     |        |       |

Shi...                                          5 for
eac...
Ple...

Ple...